DEBUT NOVEL

BRIAN O'SULLIVAN

This is a work of fiction. Names, characters, places, and incidents either are the product of the author's imagination or are used in a fictitious manner. Any resemblance to actual persons, living or dead, events, or locales is merely coincidental.

DEBUT NOVEL

Copyright @2025 **Brian O'Sullivan**

All rights reserved.

No parts of this publication may be reproduced, stored in a retrieval system, or transmitted in any form or by any means, electronic, mechanical, photocopying, recording, or otherwise, without the prior written permission to the copyright owner.

This book is sold subject to the condition that it shall not, by way of trade or otherwise, be lent, resold, hired out, or otherwise circulated without the publisher's prior consent in any form of binding or cover other than that in which it is published and without a similar condition including this condition being imposed on the subsequent purchaser.

This novel is dedicated to you!
Yeah, you!!
Thanks for reading my novels and allowing me to have a career.

I
BRYCE

LATE AUGUST:

There was nothing I could do now, and I resigned myself to my fate.
He was standing above me and had adjusted the gun, pointing it directly at my temple. In my last moments on earth, my thoughts turned to Elise, and I hoped she had managed to escape.
That was all that mattered to me now.
I closed my eyes and waited for the sound of the gun to go off.
And then I heard it.

2

BRYCE

A FEW MONTHS EARLIER

An old memory was making its way into my psyche lately. I was in the third grade, and eight neighborhood kids, including myself, were playing a game of tackle football on the lawn in front of my parents' house.

It was before the national hysteria about concussions, and it was just what children of my age did back then. We were young enough that a hard tackle wouldn't hurt us too bad, at least not physically. The shit-talking you would receive from your friends was a different matter entirely. Now, that could hurt.

Our team was down by a few points, and it was the last play of the game. Not by our choice, mind you. We would have played all night if we could have.

Unfortunately, the sun was starting to set, and all the parents had gathered to take their kids home.

Our quarterback was the local badass, Clint Wesson, who could already throw a football thirty yards in the air, which coincidentally was just about the length of my parents' lawn. Since we were next to our goal line, we needed everything Clint Wesson had.

As all the parents looked on, he hiked the ball to himself—standard protocol at the time —and the rushing defender started counting to seven alligators. Once he counted to seven alligators, he had free reign to rush the quarterback, so the other two wide receivers and I sprinted at full speed toward the opposing end zone. As the defender reached his seventh alligator, he ran full bore toward Clint, who lofted a beautiful, spiraling ball skyward.

I would eventually grow to be 6'2", but at the time, I was one of the shorter kids, and I knew I couldn't outjump everybody—but I could outthink them. Like the kid in youth soccer who stays away from the throng of players who conglomerate together only to find himself alone by the goal, I stayed away from the five players jumping for the ball, just waiting for it to be tipped my way.

The plan was working to perfection as the other two wide receivers and three defenders jumped in unison for the ball. No one was able to grasp it as all their hands reached for it together, and the ball got popped up farther in the air.

Unfortunately for me, the football had been tipped away from where I was standing and toward the back of the end zone. Sure, there were rocks at the back of the end zone, and we were repeatedly told not to go back that far, but this was the game's last play, and I had victory and bragging rights in my sight. I wasn't giving up because of a few rocks.

I took three steps toward the ball and realized how far away I still was, so I vaulted myself off the back of one of the players who had fallen to the ground during the initial midair collision. I rose farther in the air than I had ever been. For a brief moment, I imagined I was Michael Jordan, just flying through the air.

The football still looked like it was likely to evade me. It was falling end over end and appeared to be just out of my reach. As gravity took over and I plummeted toward earth, I extended my fingers toward the ball in what looked to be a frivolous attempt.

Then, I extended my fingers even farther. And farther once more. As the ball was about to hit the ground, I got my fingertips, or more specifically, my fingernails, just underneath the football and kept it from hitting the ground.

The ball popped up a few feet off my finger but angled away from me once again. This time, it was definitely going to land amongst the rocks, but at this point, I didn't care.

I lunged in the air one last time, using my arms to push off the ground. I extended my fingers again and felt like my body was stretched as far as humanly possible.

As I hit the ground, my shoulder landed on the corner of a rock, but I didn't even notice the pain as I took my fingers and cupped them under the ball right before it hit the ground. Against all odds, I was able to bring the cupped football into my body and complete the catch. Touchdown!

By this point, the parents were all running over, screaming, fearing I had hit my head on one of the rocks. I got up and told them that I was fine. The blood originating from my shoulder told a different story. All the parents shook their heads and wondered how I could be so careless, risking life and limb trying to catch a ball in a meaningless game.

All seven kids came over and congratulated me for the best catch they had ever seen. To them, I had just done what kids do, albeit spectacularly.

I had gone all out for something within my grasp. It's what any of us kids would have done.

You see, we hadn't become old enough to adopt the inevitable, undesirable trait of learning when to hold back and not give it your all.

IT DIDN'T TAKE A PSYCHOLOGIST TO REALIZE I HAD RECALLED THIS particular memory because I hadn't been giving it my all in life recently. I had not been diving all out. I had not been extending my fingers to make the catch.

I had adopted that undesirable trait of not giving it my all. My nine-year-old self couldn't have fathomed what I had turned into. At thirty-two, I had become complacent, mundane, listless, and apathetic—a murderer's row of SAT words that you didn't want to become.

Like most things in life, it was a combination of things. I was stuck in a dead-end job working at a cubicle for some nameless social media company. I hadn't had a girlfriend for going on two years now. Most importantly, I didn't have the "lust for life" that the younger Bryce Connor had in abundance. Yup, that's me. Bryce Augustus Connor, to be exact—no comments on the middle name.

So, I kept telling myself I needed something new in my life, and after weeks of deliberation, I decided to move to Europe for the summer to sow my wild oats. Yeah, I know I was thirty-two years old, and most people did this in their twenties, but I guess I'm just a late bloomer. It seems to be common to my generation.

MY EMPLOYER DIDN'T SEEM QUITE AS ENTHUSIASTIC ABOUT MY DECISION. Apparently, I hadn't accumulated three months of paid vacation in the six months I had worked there, but it was worth asking for the time off just to see the expression on my boss's face.

This asshole is asking for three months of paid vacation when he's only been here for six months total?

Needless to say, my request was not approved.

So, I did what every other responsible adult in my situation would have done.

Apologized and went back to work?

Hell no: I quit!

AND WHAT DID I WANT TO DO IN EUROPE?

In the pubs of Dublin and the cafes of Paris? I told myself I would renew my dream of writing the great American novel, but more likely, I would drink too much and try to get laid.

That doesn't mean I wasn't serious about writing while I was there; it's just that, like most men, the thought of beautiful women seemed to overshadow everything else. Still, I had this idea for a great novel rolling around in my brain. It was time to put it down on paper.

※

THE DAY AFTER I QUIT MY JOB, I STARTED TO SECOND-GUESS MY DECISION and consider everything that could go wrong there.

What if I ran out of money? What if I didn't meet any beautiful girls? What if I got writer's block?

That was when I thought back to the nine-year-old me going after that football, not caring about potential hindrances along the way and just giving everything I had. It was at that moment that I decided I was going to do this. I had to.

My soul needed it.

※

I STARTED TO PLAN MY TRIP.

I knew I wanted to visit some cities: Dublin, Paris, London, Prague, Amsterdam, and Warsaw. I wanted to see them all, but I was looking for a place to fly into, get an apartment, and set up a home base.

I initially planned to fly into Dublin but tossed that idea early on. The problem wasn't Dublin itself; in fact, I loved Dublin. Several distant relatives lived there.

The problem was that it was too familiar. I had spent time in Dublin, and if I got lonely, I could call one of my relatives. But I didn't want a safety net, a city I knew, or even a city where English was the first language.

Above all else, I WANTED SOMETHING DIFFERENT.

If I could put into words why I was going on this little shindig, the last sentence sums it up as well as any. I was tired of my lousy job, and I was tired of having no girlfriend. I was tired of all my friends getting married and having kids. I was tired of the questions of when I would get married—etc., etc., etc.

I needed a change, and since I had a little money saved up, I couldn't imagine anything better than sitting at a Parisian café like my idol Ernest Hemingway and spending a few months writing. All while keeping an eye on the girls who walked by.

That's when I decided that Paris would be my city of choice. I didn't know anyone. I had only been there once as a kid, and my French was limited to the little I learned in three years of high school, plus the occasional swear word. Putain being my favorite.

It would be like I was on an island, except the island was in the middle of one of the world's most robust cities. The fact that it had a reputation for beautiful women and was a great city to fall in love certainly didn't hurt the cause.

<hr />

Everything was going to be perfect, and it just may have been if I hadn't made the catastrophic decision to fly to New York first.

I had a few old college buddies living in Manhattan and figured I'd have a nice little send-off with my friends in New York since I was cutting myself off from friends and family for a while once I got to Paris.

And knowing these two friends, it would be quite the sendoff. It seemed like the perfect idea.

Boy, was I wrong.

3
BRYCE

THE NIGHT BEFORE NEW YORK

Before I left for New York and then to Paris, we had to have the Bryce Connor sendoff dinner.
 I wasn't against the idea per se, but I did have a feeling there would be a relative or two who didn't understand what a thirty-two-year-old guy was doing, quitting his job and moving to Europe to write the great American novel.
 My money was on Uncle Jake. Jake liked to speak his mind as it was. Give Jake a few glasses of wine and what little filter he had seemed to disappear.

※

My parents made reservations at an Italian restaurant in my hometown of San Francisco, Kuleto's.
 Approximately ten years ago, less than a block from Kuleto's, I had climbed a large streetlamp a few minutes after ringing in the New Year. This was in my wild and crazy, carefree days.
 As I started my ascent, the packed New Year's Eve crowd cheered for me. I'm sure they knew it wouldn't end well with all the cops around, but that was part of the fun. Several cops were already starting to wait at the bottom of the streetlamp when I arrived at the top, so I decided to milk it for a few minutes. I took off my nice dress shirt, twirled it around, and threw it into the crowd. It felt like the scene on the roof from *Almost Famous*.

And yes, when I scaffolded back to the bottom of the streetlamp, I was booked, shirtless, into jail. The police took pity on me because they only charged me with something minor and let me out two hours later. After being released, I met my friends and continued the party.

Oh, the good old days. It was ironic having the dinner here since this dinner was partly because I was once again trying to be that carefree kid of ten years ago.

But thirty-two-year-olds don't climb streetlamps on New Year's Eve or leave friends, jobs, and family to write novels in foreign countries.

I took one last long look at the streetlamp and walked into Kuleto's.

THE FIRST TWO PEOPLE I SAW WERE MY BUDDY RICH AND UNCLE JAKE, who was looking even heavier than usual, and that was saying something. I could already see that his face was flush when I heard him say to Rich, "Your generation is taking this whole 'Thirty is the new twenty' business way too literally," and he looked at me as he said it. This wasn't going to end well.

Luckily, my father saved me, hugging me as I walked in. "Hey everyone, they have our table ready, so let's follow the waiter. You can bring your drinks to the table."

Uncle Jake must have misheard because I saw him guzzle the last half of his red wine in one big gulp.

There were approximately twenty of us at the table: my parents, my two brothers, about ten relatives, and five friends.

As for the dinner, the first half hour was primarily small talk, with a few old, stale jokes about the French. Come on, America; aren't we better than that?

I was sitting at the head of the table—it was really like four or five tables put together—and I had a great view of the whole table. My parents, who had been as great as I could have expected with my decision, were sitting on my left and right, with my brothers immediately beside them.

I had my eye on Uncle Jake at the far end. The dinner had been easy up to this point, equal parts small talk and gentle ribbing of me.

"I'd like to make a toast to our dear friend and family member Bryce," another uncle, Uncle Gary, said.

He pushed his chair back and slowly, deliberately rose to his feet. Uncle Gary was 5'9" and the shortest Connor I knew, so it shouldn't have taken him ten seconds to do this. Depending on how his little toast went, I was willing to forgive him.

"First off, I just wanted to say that we all wish you the best. We hope you write another *Great Gatsby*, and when you find the right French girl, she will SURRENDER to you."

8

Uncle Gary looked around, but no one seemed overly impressed with the surrender comment.

He continued, "I still think forty-two is a bit old to go find yourself, but..."

"Thirty-two!" My always protective mother chimed in.

"But I respect you for following your dreams. Not enough people take a risk like this, and I'll at least give you credit for that. Give them hell over there. Cheers."

One bad anti-French joke and one bad age joke, but overall, I could live with it.

As we all yelled, "Cheers," I saw a figure rising at the end of the table. It was Uncle Jake. Might as well get it out of the way, I thought to myself.

"Hello, everyone. For those who don't know me, I'm Bryce's father's older and slightly less accepting brother, Jake. Most people simply know me as Uncle Jake. I know this is a celebration of sorts, but I feel like I should try to be the voice of reason. I think you've made a huge mistake here, Bryce."

He took a lengthy sip of his latest glass of wine. It was hard to tell if his face or the wine was a darker red.

He rambled on. "You don't just quit your job at your age and go travel around Europe. You should be settling down, getting married, and having kids. And what are you going to do when you burn through your money? Start bartending? What you should do is stay here and act your age. But instead, you're going to run around chasing tail in France and blow through whatever money you have saved."

The chasing tail line drew a few groans, and when he finished the line, my Dad looked at me as if to say, "Do you want me to stop this?'" but I shook my head.

I always felt that humor was the best antidote in instances like this. I couldn't tell if Uncle Jake was done, but when I stood up, he acquiesced and sat back down.

"Unfortunately, Uncle Jake, I think you just lost your invitation to appear at my first book signing."

No, it wasn't a great joke, but I heard a few laughs, which showed the table that I could laugh at his obnoxiousness.

"Honestly, I don't blame you for thinking the way you do. It's logical, and who knows, maybe I will regret this decision. But I don't think so. As a lot of you know, I haven't been happy with my job since, well, since I started it. And yeah, Uncle Jake, I could have probably toughed it out and slowly risen up the company, but that's not where my heart is. Ultimately, you have to go with your gut, and my gut was telling me that now is the time to go and try to do this. I don't think I'll be able to do this type of thing when I really am forty-two."

Uncle Gary smiled as I alluded to his previous joke.

"So I don't mean to belabor the point, but I am just going with my gut. It's a tough thing to ignore."

That's when I got an idea where I could give Uncle Jake and his ever-expanding waistline a verbal jab.

I stared at him. "Sometimes when your gut is growling at you, it's not growling for food; instead, it's growling for change."

There were a few muted laughs, and I saw some smiles, but I don't think anyone wanted to get Uncle Jake started again. He glared at me but didn't say anything and returned to eating. His stomach must have growled at him.

THE REST OF THE DINNER WENT BY EVENT-FREE. IT'S FUNNY, BUT I THINK no one was overly sad or dramatic (except for Jake) because no one believed I'd be gone that long. They probably figured I'd spend my money, get laid, have fun, and then return to the US earlier than expected.

ONCE THE RELATIVES DEPARTED, WE WERE LEFT WITH JUST MY BROTHERS and my friends, so we decided to go to the local pub for a few drinks.

MY FLIGHT WAS AT SEVEN A.M. THE FOLLOWING MORNING, SO IT WOULDN'T be an epic going-away bash. That would have to wait for New York.

My friends said the expected, "I'll come visit you in a few months," "Don't forget us when you're a famous writer," etc., etc., but I didn't quite feel the love.

Was I the only one who thought this was a good idea?

WHEN I RETURNED TO MY PARENTS' HOUSE, I SAW THE LIGHT ON AND knew what was coming. I had moved out of my apartment and into their house when I decided on my little European excursion, but I had been so busy the last few weeks that my parents hadn't had a chance to corner me and have "the talk."

When I opened the door and saw them sitting at the dining room table, I felt it was about to commence.

My mom spoke first, making it as simple as possible for me: "How was the bar? Did you guys have a good time?"

"It was nice, Mom. They knew I had an early flight, so they took it easy on me."

It was time for my Dad to chime in. "Well, we might not be that easy on you."

My parents met in San Francisco forty years ago. They had two mutual friends hosting a party, and my dad says he noticed this beautiful brunette immediately upon entering the party. My mom always counters by saying she didn't even notice him.

He says it took him a while to gather the courage, but when he did, the first words he uttered to her were, "I'm going to marry you someday."

The dichotomy of being afraid to approach a girl and then telling said girl that you would marry her never ceased to amaze me.

My mom's original thought was, "Who is this creep?"

Early on, the future marriage looked unlikely. Fortunately for them and me, their friends continued to have a lot of parties that summer and my Dad's persistence finally paid off when my Mom agreed to go on "one" date. The "one" date turned into two, three, and four; the rest is history.

My father became a successful architect, and my mother was about as great a housewife and mother as a son could hope for. Everyone always says their mom is the greatest; it just happens to be true in my case.

So yeah, they were great parents, but they could be tough when necessary. As I looked across at my father, I was afraid this would be one of those times.

"So Bryce, your mom and I feel you've avoided talking to us these last few weeks."

"Just been busy, Dad."

"I somehow doubt that's entirely true. Son, we realize you're a grown man now. We can't tell you what to do. And if we did, I would still hope you would do what you thought was right. That's what we raised: an independent-thinking young man."

"Thanks, Dad."

"I'm not done. That doesn't prevent us from offering some advice from time to time. We think that you've been too lackadaisical with your life. You've never committed to anything full bore. That's what I want from you this time."

My father stared at me with a fire in his eye. It didn't happen often, but you couldn't look away when he did.

"Here's what I want from you on this trip. I want you to write the best FUCKING novel ever, I want you to fall in love with the most beautiful FUCKING French girl in Paris, and I want you to have the best FUCKING trip a guy could possibly have. You may not get the chance again, son. There will be no "on a whim" jaunt to Europe when you have a child. You are the apple in the eye of your mother and me, but believe me, when we were raising you, we could never do something like you're about to do. Think about some of your friends raising children who could never have this opportunity. Make the most of this trip, son. Spend your last dollar, use your last pickup line, and write in your last binder, but whatever you do, I don't want you to have any regrets. You hear me, no regrets! If you come back in a month, homesick, we'll still love you, but we don't want that. We feel you've been in a bit of a malaise lately, and unlike most of our relatives and friends, we think this will be good for you. Now go to Paris and have the FUCKING trip of a lifetime."

I was floored. I was expecting a lecture on the litany of mistakes I was making. Instead, I got a "pump you up" speech straight out of a *Rocky* movie. I glanced at my mother, who looked like she was about to cry.

"And you feel the same, Mom?"

"I do, Bryce! Except I might have made the language a little less colorful than your father did."

All three of us got a good laugh out of that, and it was on that great note that I last saw my parents before embarking on my trip. It was important to me that we didn't leave on bad terms, but I couldn't have imagined this.

I went to bed soon after that.

My trip to New York was less than seven hours away.

4
BRYCE

NEW YORK

With my parents behind my decision and that potential burden behind me, I slept like someone with no worries. Unfortunately, that meant not hearing my iPhone's alarm and waking up only ninety minutes before my flight departed.

I had told my parents I would take a cab, and fortunately, the cabbie knew what I meant when I said I was in a rush. Despite two near accidents, we got there with enough time to spare.

Knowing that tipping is less prevalent in Europe, I gave the cabbie a twenty. I may have made his day with the gap-toothed smile he flashed me.

Except for oversleeping, the trip to New York was smooth. San Francisco International Airport (SFO) has always been hassle-free, and despite getting there a mere hour before my flight, I made it to the gate with time to spare.

Thirty minutes later, the wheels were up, and I was headed to the Big Apple.

※

THE TWO GUYS WHO CAME TO PICK ME UP HAD BEEN LONG-TIME FRIENDS.

Tim Sawyer and Chase Andrews met when they were only five. They grew up in Los Angeles and were so close in high school that they decided to go up the coast together and attend UC Santa Barbara.

They roomed together, and this is how a young, somewhat sheltered man from just outside San Francisco ended up in the room next to Tim and Chase. They looked at me as a project, and I guess I looked up to them slightly.

I wanted to get the girls, learn how to tap a keg, and experience what it was like to be "cool." I know this sounds superficial, but as an eighteen-year-old kid trying to get girls' attention, these were the things I needed to learn. I took some of their pointers, and my confidence improved. I also rejected a lot of their more tawdry advice.

As much as Tim and Chase tried to turn me into their little Casanova, I eventually realized I wasn't like them. The occasional one-night stand was okay, but I wanted to fall in love and date, and I didn't want to be labeled by girls as "that guy." And even though they were both "that guy" and I didn't play those games, we remained good friends through college.

We have remained relatively close in the years since, but our interactions have dwindled since they moved back east about three years ago. They both married in the last few years, and although I was invited, I didn't attend either.

I could blame the distance, but we'd always had a little friendly rivalry, and I was disappointed with my place in the world. Meanwhile, they were getting married and killing it financially, and I was probably a little jealous.

So yeah, it was my fault that we hadn't seen each other in a few years.

However, when they saw on Facebook that I was flying to New York first, they talked me into going out on the town. It was the least I could do, considering I hadn't exactly been the greatest lately.

One last night, for old-time's sake.

Tim and Chase pulled up next to me at the JFK airport in a brand new pitch-black Range Rover.

They were lucky my 2009 Toyota Camry wasn't around to show up his new Range Rover.

Unfortunately, that was the mindset I was still in. I feared this night would be one last ugly reminder of what I wasn't, what I didn't have, and what I hadn't accomplished.

They got out of the car, and I gave each one of them a bear hug.

As much as I gave them shit, they were still my friends, and it was good to see them—especially if it was only for one night.

They drove me to my hotel first.

I had another early flight the following morning, so I got a hotel despite their offer to let me stay at one of their houses.

The Fitzgerald Grand Central was an old Irish boutique hotel in Manhattan on East 44th Street, opposite Grand Central Station.

Since I had passed over Dublin in favor of Paris, I could give some Irish lads a few of my hard-earned dollars before the French took my money.

༺☙༻

After checking in, I changed clothes, and we drove straight from my hotel to Spark's, a steakhouse in midtown Manhattan.

It was a hangout of the infamous mafia boss John Gotti and had that cheesy Italian flair that even the nicer Italian restaurants sometimes have. Don't get me wrong, the food was great; it's just that every time someone hovered behind me for a bit too long, I half expected I was about to get whacked.

I ordered a sixteen-ounce filet mignon with roquefort sauce, creamed spinach, and a baked potato with the works. It was as filling as it sounded.

If I had known I would be running for my life later that evening, I might have just ordered the fish.

The guys ordered some expensive French wine for dinner after having Jaegar shots at the bar when we arrived. So I had yet to even get to Europe, and we were eating at an Italian restaurant while drinking German liquor and French wines. I guess my European vacation had unofficially begun a day early.

With a full belly and a slight buzz from the drinks, we set off to start the real fun of the night.

5

BRYCE

The 40/40 club, located at 6 West 25th Street in Manhattan, is owned by Jay Z. It opened in 2003 and has become one of NYC's most famous nightclubs.

They had branched out and created several 40/40s, but we were at the original.

As we walked through the club, I was surprised that I liked its look. It wasn't too swanky, and as a lifelong sports fan, I appreciated all the sports memorabilia on the walls.

After doing a quick walkthrough, we sat down at the main bar.

Tim ordered three shots of Fireball.

When we received them, Chase raised his shot glass, and we clinked them together.

"Cheers to a memorable last night in America, Bryce. To get American pussy one last time before you have to settle for that second-rate French shit."

Tim thought this was the greatest toast ever, "Hear, hear!"

This conversation couldn't get any less dignified, so I yelled, "Cheers." We hit our glasses together and pounded our shots of Fireball.

Why was I still friends with these guys? Had they gotten worse since college? It sure seemed that way. Back then, they were at least a bit charming. Now, they were just flat-out annoying.

"Bryce, you know those rooms on the second floor that you thought were straight out of the movie *Hostel*? Well, we got one reserved. I'm going to check and see when it will be ready."

Tim excused himself to talk to the host.

I turned to Chase and asked what I thought would be an innocuous question, "So, how are Tim and Gina doing?"

Chase shook his head, so I thought I must have gotten her name wrong. Even though I hadn't met her or been to their wedding, I was sure her name was Gina.

"Is it not Gina?" I asked.

"Oh, it's Gina. That's not why I was shaking my head. I was shaking it because they are not doing that well. In fact, they are taking a little trial separation."

I was shocked. "But their baby is only a year old."

"I know It's terrible. No one saw it coming."

"What happened?" I asked.

As Chase was about to speak again, we saw Tim walking back toward us.

"I talked to the host, and our room is ready," he said.

We got up to walk toward the room, and Chase looked at me as if to say, "I'll tell you later."

<hr>

THE ROOM WAS AS OPULENT AS A ROOM THAT SIZE COULD BE. AND I MEANT opulent in the best possible sense, not in the overpriced, smug way.

Four large chandeliers hung from the ceiling, and two three-piece black couches were made of what looked like the finest leather.

A huge glass table was between the couches, with a bottle each of Grey Goose, Jack Daniels, and Louis XIV Champagne.

I almost said it seemed like a lot of booze for the three of us, but I was pretty sure we weren't going to be alone.

I felt a knot beginning to form in my stomach.

I couldn't figure out why, but Chase's revelation about Tim and what I figured was the impending arrival of some girls didn't help my sense of uneasiness. I felt like some small talk might do me some good.

I went to a cheesy old line that was beneath me.

"So, how about those Yankees?"

Tim spoke first and judging by his answer, he didn't seem too concerned about the Yanks. "I could give a fuck about them right now. I'm just looking forward to the girls getting here."

I must have sounded like the biggest dunce ever when I responded, "Girls are coming?"

"No genius. We are going to spend your last night in the U.S. playing circle jerks with the three of us, all while drinking champagne." Tim shook his head, mad at himself. "I'm sorry, Bryce. I've just been a little stressed lately, and I'm trying to get everything perfect for tonight. Sorry for being an ass."

I was over this night and ready to get to Paris.

As Tim extended his fist to be bumped, I could see the door opening.

As the host opened the door, three of the most beautiful girls I had ever seen walked into the room. I was half expecting some worn-out, haggard-looking girls to join us, but that was not the case. They were gorgeous. There were two blondes and a redhead who would have made my knees buckle if I had been standing up.

Blonde #1 went directly to Chase and sat next to him, while Blonde #2 proceeded to sit beside Tim. As the blondes parted to the left and right, the redhead approached me. She was wearing a garter and white stockings with a low-cut top that revealed her large breasts.

She sat down on my thigh and whispered in my ear, "I bet those French girls don't look like this."

As she said this, she leaned in closer to me to give me a better look at her fantastic cleavage.

I felt something stirring inside me, or more precisely, on the outside of me. But while the thing on the outside was starting to grow, so was the gnawing feeling on my insides.

As beautiful as this girl was, this wasn't quite the sendoff I had in mind. It was, however, going to be near impossible to resist. Of that, I was certain.

As I looked to my left and right, I saw Tim starting to pour the champagne for the girls, and Chase was already making out with Blonde #1.

It was at this moment that I had an epiphany of sorts. I told myself never to be jealous of anyone again. Whenever I thought the grass was greener on the other side, there were weeds there, too.

I'd been scared I'd be jealous of Tim and Chase's success, but I had nothing to fear. One had a year-old son and was already separated from his wife, and the other one had a pregnant wife at home and yet was furiously going at it with a blond escort.

I was a better person than these guys, and for a second time, I asked myself, "Why was I still friends with them?"

As if they couldn't be any bigger douchebags, Chase pulled out a bag of cocaine. They knew I didn't touch the stuff, but that didn't prevent them from asking. I turned them down, but apparently, Blondie #1's breasts didn't have the same self-control I had because I saw Chase start doing a line off of them.

You may be asking why I didn't just leave at that point.

It certainly crossed my mind, and this may be hard to understand, but everything Tim or Chase did made me feel better about myself. It made me realize that while I was in a rut, it could have been worse. I could have been Tim or Chase.

After a few more drinks and a few more lines off Blonde #1's silicone (or was it saline?), Blonde #2 turned to Tim and said, "I know a room with a little more privacy if you'd like to go."

As if a room where a guy was doing cocaine off a girl's breasts wasn't private enough.

Tim waved goodbye to us and walked out with his blonde. About two minutes later, Blonde #1 offered Chase the same option. As he turned to leave, he yelled back at me, "We'll see you back at the main bar in about an hour."

As Chase shut the door behind him, the beautiful redhead slid her hand up my leg. As she slowly, deliberately moved her hand toward my groin, I needed to make a split-second decision. If I waited any longer, I knew myself, and there would be no turning back.

"I can't do this."

It was my voice, to be sure, but even I couldn't believe I was turning this girl down.

She looked at me with a one-of-a-kind expression, fitting since I was probably the first of any kind to turn this woman down. As I was about to explain my reason, she shot me a look and said, "This better be good."

I decided just to be honest.

"It's not that you aren't beautiful. The thing is, I'm moving to Europe, and I hope to fall in love there. And don't take this the wrong way, but when I dreamed about Europe, I hadn't planned on having sex with an escort, even a gorgeous one, before getting there. I'm looking for something a little more organic than sex on a couch with someone who is paid to seduce guys like me."

I was half expecting to get slapped, but she seemed to gather herself before she spoke.

"First off, we are not paid to have sex with our clients. If we find them attractive, we are encouraged to, but we are by no means required. I just thought you were kind of cute. Second, I hope you find love over there because if not, you'll regret not taking advantage of this opportunity for a long time."

"If I come back single, can I look you up?"

"Sorry honey, but this was a one-time offer."

With that, she scooted a few feet away on the couch, and I knew the time had passed.

I felt like John Belushi in *Animal House* with the devil on one shoulder saying, *"Look at that girl's body ... What the fuck is the matter with you?"* while on my other shoulder, an angel was saying, *"Good for you, Bryce. You can do better than sex with some random escort."*

We both were able to talk freely and easily after that. It was amazing how, once we realized we weren't going to have sex, she opened up to me.

Her real name was Crystal. Ironically, it sounded more like an escort's name than the fake name she used, Tiffany.

She had grown up here in Manhattan and started college at NYU. One night, a little broke, she had agreed to go out on one of these little escapades (or should I say sexcapades) with her friend. She ended up making $1000 and dropped out of school two months later. Obviously, no father would want this for his daughter, but if you were making $1000 a night as a poor college student, I understand how it might not be as easy to walk away from as one would hope.

We kept talking, and I explained my reasons for going to Europe. She seemed generally intrigued, and I appreciated her for listening. Before I knew it, we had been talking for almost an hour.

She sensed it might be time to part ways. "Is it time for you to go down and meet your friends?" she asked.

"Yeah, I'm afraid so."

"Well, I have to say that was one of the more interesting hours I've spent with a client. The others all seem to blend together, but this one will stand out. I wanted to tell you that you'll make some girl happy over there. You're not a jerk like your two friends, and there are still girls who will appreciate that."

"Thanks, but I probably will regret this decision for a while."

She laughed.

I knew I'd never see her again, so it was time for some brutal honesty.

"You can do anything you want in this world. You don't need this. You can do so much better."

I looked straight at her without blinking, and she seemed to consider my words.

"I'll try. I really will."

We hugged one last time as she walked out the door. I couldn't help but think that she was the proverbial "hooker with a heart of gold."

6

BRYCE

I walked downstairs, and Tim and Chase were already sitting at the bar, drinks in hand. I had decided on my walk down that I was going to lie and say I had sex with her.

It had nothing to do with trying to impress them (they weren't worth it), but I didn't want to spend fifteen minutes explaining why. It just seemed easier. Plus, I figured I could exaggerate and have a little fun with them.

"Look at Romeo," Chase said as I approached.

It was time to play my role. As I approached them, I raised my hands, "Guilty as charged."

"You were in there the whole hour? She must have rocked your world," Tim said.

"Sorry, my friend, but it was the other way around."

Tim looked skeptical. "Really?"

"She basically spent the last five minutes begging me to stay a little longer."

Tim and Chase looked at each other in awe. Chase spoke first, "You gave an escort such a good fucking that she was begging you for a second hour? In the annals of escorts, I think this might be a fucking first."

I had to hold in a smile to keep from giving away my little charade. "What can I say?"

"So why didn't you stay longer?"

"She was a wild one. I don't know if I could have handled another hour. Didn't want my dick falling off before I got to Paris."

They looked at each other and laughed out loud. I was generally a pretty honest person, but with these two, and at this time, I wasn't going to beat myself up about a few white lies.

The fun needed to end soon, though. It was already 12:30, and I didn't need another night without sleep. It was time to start heading back to my hotel.

"Guys, I have an early flight. I need to be heading back soon."

Surprisingly, Tim seemed to agree with me.

"I'll have the maitre d' call us a town car. There's a bar called O'Rourke's right by your hotel. We'll grab one last drink there and send you on your way. Sound good?"

It was easier than I expected. "That'll work."

THE WAIT FOR THE TOWN CAR WAS LESS THAN FIVE MINUTES. I HAD TO GIVE it to 40/40; they were very proficient—the host, the bouncers, and the bartenders. It was a first-class joint.

The town car driver was a black man from Uganda in his late thirties. He was effusively polite and went around to each door to open it for us. Tim sat shotgun while Chase and I shared a spacious backseat. I sat back and felt totally at ease for the first time in weeks.

I don't know if it was the impending departure, my realization that there was no reason to be jealous of my "friends," or the time with the "hooker with the heart of gold."

Regardless of what it was, I welcomed the feeling. There had been so much second-guessing about this trip—from myself and others—that I never had time to sit back, relax, and look forward to it.

So that's what I did in the back of that town car; I just sat back and let the realization soak in that in one day, I'd be sitting and writing in Paris. It was a wonderful feeling.

It sounded like Tim was telling the driver a back alley shortcut to get to the bar. I was too busy sitting back and enjoying the moment to be worried about the quickest way to get to O'Rourkes. Plus, it was just one drink, and then I was headed back to the hotel.

If I had been paying attention, I might have realized that the back alley wasn't lit and didn't look all that safe. If I'd had my wits about me, I would have just told Tim we could wait a few minutes and drive around the front.

If, if, if.

As we turned left down the alley, I heard Tim say, "It's about 200 yards up on the right, and I'm pretty sure they have a back entrance to O'Rourkes. If not, we can just walk around to the front ourselves."

After about fifty yards, the driver pulled up in front of a big garbage bin in the middle of the alley.

"Sorry guys, I can't get around that bin. You guys are going to have to get out here."

I finally decided that I didn't like the looks of this. "Tim, why don't we just have him drive around to the front?"

"It will take ten minutes to double back around and get on the main streets. It's about a hundred yards up. Get out. We're walking."

Begrudgingly, Chase and I got out of the town car. Tim took out a credit card to pay the guy.

"A credit card for a seven-minute drive?" I asked.

"Of course. I'm going to write tonight off as a business meeting."

"Even the blondes?" I asked.

"Even them, Bryce."

The driver processed Tim's card, and we started walking down the back alley. After about fifty yards, I realized something must be wrong.

Chase spoke up. "Tim, O'Rourkes is behind 26th, not 25th."

"Oh shit, you're right. Guess we're walking one more block, guys."

I was getting sick of Tim and was about to start an argument, but I figured, what was the point? I'd be done with these two in a half-hour or less.

As we crossed onto the back alley of 26th, it got even darker and more ominous. I looked over at Tim, and even his usual unflappable self looked on edge.

After walking twenty more feet, I started hearing voices. They were still quite a ways from us, but I thought I heard someone say, "We just want back what you stole."

Tim and Chase must not have heard it because they kept walking toward the voices. I forcibly grabbed both of their arms to slow them down and put a finger to my mouth to tell them not to make a sound. I guided us up against the fence where it was darker and we'd be more challenging to see.

As we sat there, the voices got closer. They were coming from one of the nooks in the alley, but it sounded like they were headed in our direction.

The voice I heard earlier spoke again. This time, I could hear him clearly.

"All we want is what belongs to our client. If you give that back, we will let you go and forget the whole thing."

This time, another voice spoke. It was the voice of someone scared. "I didn't take the money. You can threaten me all you want, but I still don't know where it is. Killing me isn't going to change that."

I held on to Tim and Chase as tight as I could and looked at them as if to say, "Don't move a fucking muscle."

I had led us to the fence and away from the light so we would be hard to see. Now, I just had to ensure we didn't make a noise that drew their attention.

The voices were only yards away now.

"Kill you? Now that's a novel concept."

"How's that going to help you find the money?"

"I think I might just have better luck with your wife. It's Tracy, isn't it?"

"Fuck you!"

"This is your last chance, Freddy."

As we heard this, three figures suddenly appeared from underneath one of the awnings in the alley.

The streetlights made them visible. There were two aggressors and one guy who was being held, an overweight guy in his fifties.

The man holding him was in his late forties and tall and skinny. The main aggressor was probably around forty-five, short, and extremely stocky. He wasn't overweight but thick and built like a wall. He was balding, with some hair on the sides but not much on top. You could tell he was menacing, even from where we stood. The butcher's knife dangling from his right arm only added to this.

"Freddy, did you not hear me? This is your last chance, or I'm going to kill you and try my luck with Tracy".

"Okay, I'll tell you where I hid it."

"You're finally talking some sense. Where the fuck is it, Freddy?"

Freddy took a long, deep breath as if it might be his last. It turned out that he was right about that.

He turned to the balding one, smiled, and said, "It's in your wife. I hid the money there, along with my dick."

With astonishing quickness for a man his size, the stocky guy raised the knife, and in a split second, he plunged it into Freddy four or five times. Freddy was being held by the taller one and never stood a chance.

Right then, Chase seemed to rustle a leaf underneath his foot. It was the slightest sound, but the stocky guy quickly glanced over, though I couldn't be sure.

He didn't look long because quickly his attention was back on the man he had just killed.

"That's why you don't screw with Mr. Solari," he said.

The dead man slid from the grip of the taller man and fell to the ground.

This was too much for Tim, who screamed and took off running. The killer and his partner looked up at us in shock. They made a move for us, and at this point, we didn't have a choice. Chase and I took off running as well.

TIM WAS FASTER THAN CHASE AND ME, AND WITH HIS TWO- OR THREE-second head start, he was gone. The killers were likely ten or fifteen years older than us, and with Tim's speed, there was no catching him. We saw him take a right up ahead, and he was home free.

That left the two of us, and as I heard them running behind us, I was just happy not to hear any gunshots being fired. I now assumed they only had the knife on them, which, as scary as it was, couldn't be used on me if I was able to keep a healthy distance from them.

As we approached the fork in the road, Chase said, "We need to split up. I'm going right. You go left."

The adrenaline (along with my heart) was pumping so hard that it was tough to get any words out, and I didn't argue. If I had time to consider it, I probably would have realized that the right had more dark alleys, which would have made it easier to ditch them. Unfortunately, my brain wouldn't allow me to think, and when Chase took the right, I took the left. I saw him disappear into the darkness, and that's when I realized I had made a mistake.

As I took the left, I noticed I was heading toward 25th Avenue, where many people were still walking around. I turned around quickly, and much to my disappointment, both guys had decided to follow me. They had reasoned, correctly, that there was no way they would catch Tim or Chase at this point.

They were right, but I was still fifty yards ahead and held the upper hand. Looking back on it, I probably should have just found a police officer, but I was so afraid of them catching up to me that I couldn't slow down and take the risk.

I planned to get to the Fitzgerald, which was only two blocks away. I had to make sure they didn't see me enter the hotel, and if they were close, I'd have to change plans.

I kept up a brisk pace as I crossed to 25th, but I was also trying to blend into the crowd rather than attract attention. That didn't seem to work because they were gaining on me slightly.

As I turned back to look at them, I tripped over a woman's heel and fell to the ground. They saw it as their chance and sprinted toward me, with the stocky one outpacing the skinny one.

As I began to get up, I saw the knife slightly hidden at the side of the killer. They were within twenty feet of me when I got to my feet. I bolted when I got up, and I was able to put a little more distance between us. Unfortunately, when I turned the next corner and saw the Fitzgerald, I wasn't far enough ahead of them to enter the hotel without being seen.

I made up another plan on the fly. I saw Grand Central across the street and sprinted as fast as possible toward it. I needed as much time as I could muster for this to work. My hotel was so close to Grand Central that I figured all I needed was a ten- or fifteen-second head start, and they wouldn't have time to see me run from Grand Central and enter the Fitzgerald Hotel.

Entering the turnstiles at Grand Central could take some time. If I could get to the other side and wait till they entered the turnstiles, it should give me enough time to get to the Fitzgerald without being seen.

After I made my way through the turnstiles, I ran to the other side, faced the turnstiles, and hid behind a wall where I could see people enter. They would not be able to see me, however.

Less than five seconds later, I saw the two men enter Grand Central and approach the turnstiles. As soon as they were surrounded by people in front and behind, effectively blocking them in, I took off sprinting toward the Fitzgerald.

I heard them yell, "There he fucking goes," "Let us fucking out of here," and "Move."

These were all good signs that they were being held up, but at this point, I was running faster than I had ever run and was concentrating on getting to Fitzgerald.

I ran across 25th again. I took one look back at Grand Central. They hadn't come out of the station yet, so I ran into the Fitzgerald and quickly turned the corner to get to the elevators, where they couldn't see me.

I took the elevator to my room, locked the deadbolt, turned off all the lights, and jumped into bed, fully clothed.

FOR THE NEXT HOUR, MY HEART FELT LIKE IT MIGHT EXPLODE WHENEVER someone walked by the room. Every little crack I heard made me believe they were waiting in the hall. I tried to set my mind at ease by telling myself there was no way they got out of Grand Central quickly enough to see me enter the hotel, but it didn't seem to help alleviate my anxiety.

I considered my options since sleep would be scarce. The obvious choice was to call 911, ask to speak to the police, and explain everything. Most anyone would do that, but my mind went in a different direction.

A few things gave me pause about turning myself over to the cops.

I didn't like the stocky guy saying, "That's why you don't screw with Mr. Solari."

It appeared they were doing this killing for someone else. If these were just two thugs who killed someone in an alley, then I'd have no problem going to the cops, but this was obviously at the behest of others.

And I didn't like hearing the last name Solari. It sounded pretty damn Italian to me. I may have watched too many mafia documentaries, but if you were testifying against them, that usually meant you were in witness protection.

I was thirty-two with my whole life ahead of me, and I wasn't ready to be looking over my shoulder for the rest of my life. You might think I was jumping to conclusions, but to me, it seemed pretty obvious that this murder was committed for a big shot, and this big shot sounded Italian. It didn't seem like a big leap to guess the mafia was involved.

I put every blanket over my head to keep the room dark and turned my laptop on beneath the blankets. Once it booted up, I went to Google and typed in "*Solari New York Mafia.*"

My suspicions were confirmed. There were multiple articles about Anthony Solari, a reputed NYC crime boss.

That's when I came across an article titled "*Two witnesses are slain before they can testify against Solari.*"

The article told the story of two German tourists who, similar to myself, saw something they weren't supposed to see. Even while having police protection, they were gunned down in their hotel the day before they were due to testify.

And that's when I knew I wasn't going to call 911.
I had to think of an alternative plan.
An hour later, the exhaustion finally caught up to me, and I was able to fall asleep.

※

When I woke up, I grabbed some stationery and started writing a note.

"Dear Police."

Wow, was I an idiot?!

Using stationary that said Fitzgerald Hotel right across the top wasn't too bright for someone trying to avoid being found. It wouldn't be too hard for the police to get a copy of all the people who had stayed at the Fitzgerald the previous night.

I tossed the Fitzgerald stationery, grabbed a piece of paper from my spiral notebook, and started writing.

I looked down at my hands and realized I was getting fingerprints all over the paper. I also tossed that piece of paper, threw on some gloves from my bag, and started my letter.

DEAR POLICE,

LAST NIGHT, AROUND ONE A.M., I WAS ON THE ALLEY BEHIND 25th STREET AND WITNESSED A MURDER. THE VICTIM'S NAME WAS FREDDY, AND THE TWO MEN BELIEVED HE HAD SOMETHING THAT BELONGED TO A MAN THEY REFERRED TO AS MR. SOLARI. WHEN HE DENIED HAVING IT, A SOLIDLY BUILT, BALDING MAN AROUND 5'9", MAYBE FORTY-FIVE YEARS OLD, STABBED HIM ABOUT FOUR OR FIVE TIMES WITH A KITCHEN KNIFE. HIS PARTNER, WHO HELD THE VICTIM DOWN, WAS AROUND FIFTY AND WAS TALL AND SKINNY WITH A LITTLE MORE HAIR THAN HIS PARTNER.

I DON'T WANT TO TESTIFY, AND I COULD GO THROUGH ALL THE REASONS WHY, BUT IF YOU KNOW WHO MR. SOLARI IS THEN I'M SURE YOU CAN GUESS MY REASONS. I CAN ASSURE YOU THIS IS ALL I SAW AND HEARD, AND I HOPE IT HELPS YOU IN YOUR INVESTIGATION. IF I CHANGE MY MIND AND DECIDE TO COME FORWARD, YOU WILL BE THE FIRST TO KNOW. THANK YOU.

I decided to leave out that I was with Tim and Chase. If they wanted to go to the police and testify while I was in Paris, then good for them, although I considered that a long shot. I also left out where they had chased me and how I had gotten away. I didn't feel like narrowing down where I had been staying for the police. I reread the letter, and when I was happy with it, I folded it up and put it in my pocket. I decided to keep the gloves on until I was finished with my little plan.

I'd be lying if I said I wasn't nervous as I exited my room, took the elevator down to the lobby, and headed out to the streets of NYC. I didn't take the time to check out of my room for obvious reasons. While I knew it was doubtful that the two killers were still around, it didn't stop me from being incredibly vigilant.

I walked about four blocks up and two blocks over from the Fitzgerald's location. I had decided to pay someone to deliver my letter to a police officer, and the farther away from the Fitzgerald, the better.

If the officer received the note near the Fitzgerald and asked a night watchman if someone came in last night in a hurry, well, you get the idea. Better to be safe than sorry, I reasoned.

When I believed I was far enough away and saw a police officer, I flagged down a cab. I asked the cab driver to give me thirty seconds and told him to go ahead and start the meter running.

◈

A YOUNG TEENAGER SAT ON THE CURB. IT WAS HARD TO TELL IF HE WAS homeless, but judging by his clothes, he could certainly use the money. I called him over and told him I would give him fifty bucks if he would just take my note over to the police officer that I pointed out.

Upon seeing the fifty, his eyes lit up, and I gave him the note to deliver. As he approached the officer, I got in the cab and told the driver to wait a little longer.

When I looked back, I saw the young kid giving the note to the police officer. I then told the cab driver to take me to the airport.

The police officer unfolded the note and started reading it. He raised his head and looked around, but by then, the cab driver had pulled out onto the street, and I was headed to the airport, unsure if I'd made the right decision.

I guess time would tell.

7
BRYCE

THE FLIGHT TO PARIS

As my flight from New York City to Paris progressed, I was unsure if my mind or the plane was moving faster.

So many emotions were running through my head that it was hard to track them all. Sadness, for I had seen a guy murdered right in front of me. I am angry at Tim for not listening to me and taking the town car to the front of the bar. Guilt, because I thought maybe I should have just gone to the police and let the chips fall where they may. Bitterness, since I should have been enjoying my impending trip to Paris. Instead, I was too busy thinking about this shit. Exhaustion, which was a result of little sleep and all that had happened. And most surprisingly, relief because I could have also easily been killed.

The more I thought about what happened, the more my mind went back to the two potential witnesses who had been killed. I realized that I really did not want to go back and have to potentially testify.

Despite all the people who would say, "It wasn't the Christian thing to do," my decision was better than the alternative.

And in my defense, I had given the police a lot of information. They had the name of the murdered man, the likely person who put out the hit, and a description of the killers. That should be enough to get them some arrests.

I tried to think of ways the NYPD could track me down. I didn't have a permanent place to stay in Paris (just a hostel for now), so that was good. And

I had left my old phone in the Bay Area, so they couldn't track me through that either.

The only two ways they could potentially locate me was through my email or Facebook account. I knew what I had to do, but that didn't make it any easier.

My mother was looking forward to weekly emails detailing my Parisian adventure, while I knew my friends would be expecting a few "Fish out of water" status updates on Facebook.

The risk was too significant, though. One status update or email could reveal where I had been and give the police the necessary information.

A sordid thought entered my mind: maybe the police weren't the people I should be worried about. I told myself I was just being paranoid and tried to push that idea out of my mind.

There was no way the killers could know who we were because I was positive they hadn't caught Tim or Chase, and neither of them was the type who would willingly join a police investigation.

If they did turn themselves in, Tim and Chase would have to admit where they were and what they had done on the night in question.

With two shaky marriages, they wouldn't want to bring their excursions into the light. Tales of cocaine, escorts, and infidelity generally didn't go over well with spouses.

I was confident the killers and the police had no idea who Tim and Chase were. And thus, didn't know who I was, either.

Still, there was always the chance I was overlooking something. I decided to delete my email address, which I had been using since 1998, and my Facebook account.

Before I deleted both, I wrote down the email addresses I might need and a few contact phone numbers from Facebook friends.

So, on June 27th, at 9:30 a.m. local Parisian time, about an hour outside of Paris and still at 28,000 feet, I deleted my Yahoo email and Facebook account.

Without a home address, phone, email address, or Facebook, I felt like I didn't exist, and that's how I wanted it.

8
BRYCE

PARIS

When I finally touched down in Paris and went through customs, I half expected my bags to be lost. I was pleasantly surprised when I saw them approaching on the conveyor belt.

I had been in Paris for ten minutes and already preferred it to New York.

My plan for the next week were one, try and put the events of New York behind me and two, find a place to live.

I had pre-booked a hostel for one week, which gave me enough time to find a place without being too rushed. I realized I might have to set up a new email account to contact landlords, but that didn't worry me. Setting up a new email was easy; no one would know it was me.

I hoped to find an apartment relatively cheap, but knowing this was Paris, anything that didn't cost me an arm and a leg would have to do.

As I grabbed my bags and headed toward the taxi stand, I tried to listen in on as many conversations as I could as I walked through the airport.

I had been listening to Rosetta Stone for a few hours a day over the last month and had my three years of high school French to fall back on, but I knew listening to actual French people speaking French was the only way I would truthfully learn.

Reading a textbook or listening to a CD doesn't prepare you to speak a language; just a heads-up to all you high schoolers out there.

I'd pick up words and phrases as they talked, but it was often hard to understand a whole sentence. One thing that I did hear more than a few times at the airport was the phrase "Je t'aime." I love you. Maybe it really was the city of love.

After all, an anagram of "Paris" was "Pairs." Okay, I was reaching.

<hr />

Charles De Gaulle Airport was the second busiest airport in Europe, behind only London's Heathrow. Unfortunately, it was a good fifteen miles from the center of Paris.

I had considered taking the train (RER) from the airport into the city, but with three bags to carry and not wanting to get lost on my first day, I had decided to take a cab. I was planning on living on the cheap after this, but I figured I could shell out a little extra money for a taxi into the city.

After all that had occurred, I just wanted to get to my hostel without the hassle of public transportation, losing a bag, getting on the wrong train, etc.

Also, I had read that if you entered the city from the west, you could see the Champs Elysees and the Arc De Triomphe on your drive in. That sounded like an excellent introduction to Paris.

As my taxi driver loaded my bags into the trunk, I practiced what I would say.

I had even typed it into my Google translator and repeated several times what I wanted to say: "Je voudrais aller à l'Auberge du stade sur Center Street dans le 6e arrondissement," which meant "I'd like to go to the Stadium Hostel on Center Street in the 6th arrondissement."

But as the taxi driver looked at me, I feared butchering the sentence, so I took the easy route. "6th arrondissement" was all I could muster.

Luckily, the cab driver spoke English reasonably well, and I informed him that I needed a ride to the Stadium Hostel. He got a good laugh when I told him that I had planned on saying a complete sentence and then couldn't pull the trigger.

"You'll get the hang of it before long."

Well, at least one of us believed that to be true. After what seemed like five minutes, he was finally able to pull out from the curb, and we started on our taxi ride into Paris.

<hr />

The city of Paris is divided into twenty arrondissements, which are basically administrative districts. They begin in the center of the city, along the Seine (the river that runs through Paris), and they increase in number as they spiral away from the center.

This isn't to say that #2 is better than #19, but there seems to be more going on in the lower-numbered arrondissements along the Seine.

Before coming to Paris, I had asked friends about the best place to live.

Everyone seemed to have a different opinion without any consensus, so I researched myself.

The 8th was an early consideration for me as it had the Champs Elysees and the Arc de Triomphe, both of which I would be seeing on my drive from the airport.

I also considered the 7th arrondissement. It's where the Eiffel Tower and several of the city's most famous museums are located. But since I was more of a writing at a café type of guy than a museum guy, I decided to find something more my style.

I wanted bustling streets, the ability to people-watch, and cafes where writers of the past could sit down and write.

Around this time, I came across an article on Ernest Hemingway and his time in Paris. The article stated that his favorite place to sit and write in Paris was at a place called Les Deux Magots.

I immediately googled it, and sure enough, Les Deux Magots was still thriving in the 6th arrondissement. It was something that simple that led me to live in the 6th arrondissement.

I'm not usually one who believes in things like destiny, but God smiled down upon me when I decided where to stay in Paris.

The more I read about the 6th arrondissement, the more I felt like it was where I was meant to be. It had long been known as the literary and intellectual capital of Paris, had great architecture, and was located on the left bank of the Seine.

And at 11:58 in the morning, about forty-two minutes after leaving Charles De Gaulle Airport, I finally arrived there.

I exchanged pleasantries with the cab driver, and he wished me a great trip.

※

THE STADIUM HOSTEL LOOKED NICE ENOUGH FROM THE OUTSIDE, BUT I knew I wasn't staying at the Ritz. That became abundantly clear as I walked through the front door.

Seeing a room the size of a basketball court with forty-five beds packed like sardines beside each other drove the point home. It looked clean, though, and that's all that mattered.

I checked in, and they said I could upgrade to a room for only twenty dollars more a night if I wanted. I looked at the close quarters of the beds, and for the second time since landing, I went over budget. Having a room to myself seemed well worth it.

Now, I'm pretty sure at this point that 99.84% of human beings would have laid on that bed and fallen asleep for as many hours as they could muster. But as you may have already figured out, I'm unlike everyone else.

There was a little tradition that I had started when I was a nineteen-year-old visiting Chicago for the first time. And even though there was some unwanted baggage that I brought with me to Paris, I wasn't going to bail on my tradition that easily.

My tradition was to take the double-decker bus tour whenever I arrived in a new city. It doesn't sound too exciting, huh? Well, the wrinkle I added was that after every museum/monument on the tour, I would go to the closest pub and have a pint with the locals. It didn't matter if the bus tour had five or fourteen stops. I was having a pint at each one, regardless.

During my freshman year in college, I visited a buddy of mine at Northwestern, and that's when it all started. The Chicago trip only had seven stops, but that was enough when you're nineteen years old with a fake ID.

I had vouched then that this would continue for however long I continued to travel. So far, I have done my pub crawl/bus tour in Chicago, New York, Atlanta, Miami, Los Angeles, Melbourne, Sydney, Dublin, London, and Barcelona.

I even did it once in San Francisco, even though I had seen all the sights multiple times. That one may have been done more in the name of partying than in the name of sightseeing.

⚜

I HAD AMASSED SOME PRETTY GOOD STORIES ALONG THE WAY.

On my first trip to Dublin, when I had just turned twenty-one, I managed to get myself kicked out of the Gravity Bar, which is on the top floor of the Guinness Storehouse and has a 360-degree view of Dublin.

My good friend Smitty and I were traveling Ireland, and since we were both of Irish heritage, we decided that at each stop, we would have a Guinness and a shot of Jameson's.

It was basically like having an Irish Car Bomb at each bar, but you would never call it that in Ireland for fear of getting your ass kicked.

The Guinness Storehouse was the last stop of a nine-stop tour, so you don't have to be Charles Bukowski to realize we were pretty drunk when we arrived. It probably didn't help that when I approached the bar, I asked for two Guinness and two shots of Jameson.

Usually, this wouldn't be a problem, but the Gravity Bar served Guinness and Guinness only.

"Here are the two Guinness, sir," the bartender said, hoping I would realize that we were at the Guinness Storehouse and this wasn't some bar with a full liquor license.

"You're cutting me off from hard booze already," I uttered, or to be fair, I stuttered. "This is bullshit!"

I think he had given me my one chance, and I had just crossed the line.

"Hey asshole," he said with a thick Dublin Brogue. "This is the bar at the

Guinness Storehouse. We serve Guinness, and we serve Guinness only. Look around. Do you see a bunch of liquor bottles? Yeah, I didn't think so."

If I had shut up and taken my beers, I think we could have stayed, but I could be a little troublesome when I was drunk, so I wasn't done. "So you're saying you guys don't have any Jameson?"

"That's what I'm saying."

"Okay, then we'd like two shots of Bushmills, please."

Before I had even finished my smart-ass comment, the guy had taken me and Smitty's beers and had called security over to escort us out. Irish Whiskey was not my friend on that day.

The pub crawl/bus tour in Dublin was just child's play compared to what happened a few years later in Barcelona. Four college buddies and I (no Tim and no Chase) had just graduated, and we decided to spend two weeks in Barcelona to celebrate.

As usual, I told them of my tradition the first day we arrived, and they all agreed to accompany me. We were twenty-three years old, just out of college, and ready to party.

It took them all of a split second to say yes. Garrett, the craziest of our little group, decided to put his own spin on my tradition.

His idea, which we all agreed on pretty quickly, was that the first person to have to take a piss had to buy drinks for the other four guys for the rest of the bus trip.

As we waited for the first bus to pick us up, we were taking turns going to the bathroom and finishing that one last piss before we had to get on the bus.

When the bus arrived, I can safely say that we were all on a level playing field, considering we had all taken a piss within the last few minutes.

The first two stops were easy. Dylan tried to convince us at the second stop that he had to pee, but we knew he was full of shit.

One of the only rules was that we all had to drink a 16 oz. beer. A shot or a drink wasn't allowed. After all, that wouldn't put as much liquid in you as a big glass of beer would.

It started to get interesting before the third stop, the beautiful Sagrada Familia Museum. Five Australian girls around our age walked to the top of the double-decker bus (I always chose to be in the open air) and toward the back, where we were all sitting.

Within seconds, Garrett was telling them about our bets and asked if they wanted to join us in the bar hopping.

"The way I look at it, you're only going to have to pay for a couple of drinks before we have a loser, and from there on in, you will be drinking for free," was Garrett's selling point.

They could tell this was going to be a wild time and accepted. Garrett had a pretty good rapport with the ladies; you could tell they thought he was charming. I think I was secretly hoping he would lose.

A couple of the guys looked at Garrett as if to say, "At every stop, that's going to be ten drinks the loser's going to have to buy."

The problem was, with the addition of all these attractive girls, no one wanted to look like the guy breaking up all the fun.

We all paired up with one of the girls and had a fantastic time riding on the top of a double-decker bus in the Barcelona sun.

We didn't seem to stay at the third, fourth, and fifth monuments very long. I don't know if it was the addition of the girls, getting a little buzz from the beers, or starting to feel a little pressure on our bladder, but we got out of each monument quickly.

As we began to speak louder, we were also told "Shhhh" and "Shush it" a few times, which may have led to our quick departures.

At the bar for our fourth beer, Steve, one of our friends, tried to take the girl he had paired up with outside. We knew it was to make out with her.

We told him if he walked past the bathrooms, he was eliminated because we couldn't know what he was doing back there. Could be taking a piss, for all we knew. He came back and stayed with the group, and the game continued.

You have to keep in mind that this wasn't just pounding beers at your house. That was easy to wait out. Here, we were getting out every ten minutes and walking around museums or monuments while riding a double-decker bus in between.

Since our first beer, it had already been almost three hours. And let me tell you when that bus hit a pothole, it wasn't doing your bladder any favors, and yes, it was a bumpy ride.

As we exited another fabulous museum, La Pedrera, and entered the closest bar, we could tell that this wouldn't last much longer. A few guys were stomping their feet and crossing their legs as we drank our sixth 16-oz beer— 96 ounces of beer.

That's six pounds of beer circling your insides, looking for a way out. I was feeling okay, and since my bladder wasn't under enormous pressure, I could smile at the other's agony.

The girls were enjoying the hell out of this. Considering that girls often had to stand in lines at bars or restaurants, waiting for the bathroom, while guys were done in a minute, they would enjoy this.

Jayne, the girl I was hanging with, loudly stated, "I'm going to the bathroom. This is going to feel great!" And the girls would all giggle. Yeah, it's safe to say they were having a blast.

As we waited in line for the next bus, I looked at Garrett, and he didn't appear to be doing too well. He was putting his hand down every few seconds to grab his groin.

Garrett, the guy who had come up with the idea for the game, was struggling the most. You have to love karma sometimes.

When we took our spot near the back of the open-air bus, we all realized it would be over very soon. The girls' theatrics alerted other people on the bus, including some parents with young kids, to what was happening. We all knew this wasn't going to end well.

I can't speak for Garrett, but I imagine he was just trying to get to the next stop, where he would quickly run off, find a bathroom, and admit defeat. Unfortunately for him, but fortunately for us, he didn't make it that long.

As we approached the Maritime Museum, we hit a huge pothole, and while it certainly affected all of us, it affected Garrett the most. He let out a girlish shriek. He was wearing jeans, and as we all looked over, we saw the beginnings of a wet spot, which quickly grew.

After a few seconds, it was taking up most of his upper groin. Before you knew it, it had spread down to his knees. Next, we saw liquid slowly seep from the bottom of his jeans. I guess when you've drank that much liquid and waited that long, once you start going, there's just no stopping.

I heard a couple of screams from the adults behind us, and a little girl said, "Mommy, is that man peeing himself?" However, we were cracking up too hard to be worried about anyone else.

This was the time when the rest of us had to watch ourselves. Laughing that hard on a full bladder is not recommended. When Garrett finished, a puddle had formed below his pants as we finally pulled into the Maritime Museum.

The girls were laughing uncontrollably and taking pictures at breakneck speed. It was glorious.

As everyone got off the bus and Garrett stood up, you could see how drenched his jeans were. I couldn't have imagined trying to walk in them.

Apparently, neither could Garrett because he ripped his pants off and was left with just a soaked pair of boxers. He saw one of the Australian girls had a towel in her bag.

"How much did you pay for that towel," he asked.

"Probably twenty Australian dollars," she said.

Garrett grabbed it out of her bag. "I'll give you forty American dollars in a minute."

In full view of everyone on the top of the bus, he dropped his boxers to the ground before quickly wrapping the towel around his waist.

He even threw his shirt off. The other patrons on the bus were not impressed, and a few people yelled at Garrett.

He ignored them, looked at us, and said, "I'll meet you outside the bus in five minutes."

With that, he ran off the bus, presumably searching for somewhere selling clothes. We all thought it was the funniest thing ever. The other patrons, not so much.

We didn't make it into the Maritime Museum that day, but after taking the longest piss of my entire life, I met our group at the bar.

Once there, a certain friend wearing pink sweatpants that only reached his calves and a yellow I Love Barcelona shirt that only made it to his belly button had to buy ten beers.

Considering the circumstances and the attire that Garrett wore, it might have been the best-tasting beer I've ever had.

9
BRYCE

As for the Paris tour, I was by myself, and it was one p.m. on a Sunday, so I didn't expect my tradition to be as story-inducing as previous ones.

That was fine by me. Hopefully, a drama-free day was on the docket.

As I sat on the top of the bus and took in the city, I was struck by the sheer beauty of Paris. I'm not an architectural buff, but I found myself interested in how and when these buildings were built.

As an American, I find it fascinating to see buildings and museums older than our country. The fact that these buildings were often located near the beautiful Seine, which intersected the city, made them all the more alluring.

I'm not breaking new ground here, but whether it be a river running through it or a city on the coast, a body of water always adds a certain charisma.

When people say that Paris is full of café's, this isn't an exaggeration. Every block seemed to have at least one, often with a big canopy extending to the outdoor seating area.

Several times in just the first few minutes, I wanted to jump off and write at one of the Café's I had seen. My writing juices were starting to flow.

<hr />

I decided to get off on a few stops, but this wouldn't be a seven or eight-pint trip. Instead, I just sat back, enjoyed the beautiful day, and sat atop *Les Car Rouges*—The Red Cars—even though they were technically buses.

They had audio in several languages, so I turned mine to English and started to learn the history of the city I was about to call home.

I rode the bus for an hour, getting off at the Eiffel Tower and having a pint at a bar called L'Alibi. The Eiffel Tower was fantastic, but for some reason, the word "Alibi" brought my mind back to New York, and I decided to end my trip a little abruptly.

I made a mental note that I'd have to do this tour again correctly. I left L'Alibi and got back on the bus. Even though I passed some world-famous monuments, I didn't get off the bus again until I arrived back in the 6th arrondissement.

When I returned to the hostel, it was probably only around five p.m., but it felt like midnight to me. I couldn't sleep at five, so I walked outside my hostel for an hour or so just to get a feel of where I would stay for the next week.

I passed a few tiny little grocery stores. I had been told it's cheaper just to buy a baguette and some ham instead of eating at a café. I knew where I was grabbing lunch tomorrow.

As I was walking the streets, I saw a pay phone on the side of the road. It reminded me that I hadn't called my parents yet. I'd blame it on laziness, but I was trying to prolong making the call after all that had happened in New York. I decided that I would call them tomorrow.

I didn't know what I would tell them about New York if anything, and I wasn't currently in the mood to lie to my parents. Not yet, at least.

When I returned to my tiny room, everything caught up to me. It was time to sleep. I threw on one of the French-speaking lessons on my iPod and listened to it as I crawled into bed. I don't think I made it through the first minute of chapter one before I fell fast asleep.

The next morning, I woke up feeling like a new man. I probably hadn't gone to sleep at seven o'clock since I was ten years old, but if anyone ever needed sleep, it was me.

Plus, having slept so much and woken up early, it felt like I was back on normal time. One day in, the jet lag was already a thing of the past.

After a relaxing early morning of grabbing a baguette at the local grocery store, I walked along the Seine. I thought a great deal and realized this wasn't what I needed. I had to start doing something that would occupy my mind, or I would keep reliving the events of New York.

I decided that it was time to start writing. After all, that's one of the main reasons I had come to Paris, and I didn't see anything preventing me from starting now. Before I left the hostel, I knew I would write at Les Deux Magots, where the great Ernest Hemingway had written ninety years ago.

The walk was a little farther than I had anticipated, but walking in a town like Paris was a pleasure. You can feel the culture and the history engulf you as you walk along Paris's streets.

As I entered the Saint-Germain-Des-Pres area, I knew I was getting close, and a minute later, I saw the green awning I had known to look for.

The café itself wasn't that different from most of the Parisian café's. It had an indoor seating area that was a bit dressier than the outdoor seating, which was pretty casual.

The awning extended out over all of the patio seating, which, as a writer, was nice since it would eliminate the potential of too much sun. The chairs were tan and extremely comfortable, but they did sit a little higher than I was used to.

I felt like I was constantly leaning over as I wrote. I guess it's one of the few times I didn't enjoy being 6'2".

I didn't get much writing done over the course of the first few hours. It was too easy to fall into a daze and start people-watching. Les Deux Magots was on a busy street, and beautiful women constantly walked by.

At one point, I adjusted my chair and had my back to the people walking by, but I was afraid I might miss something and turned back around.

A few waitresses had been cute, but I hadn't struck up any conversations. With a backpack next to me and a spiral notebook and pen on my table, they had probably pegged me as a writer, and I wondered if they resented a guy sitting there for hours and only ordering a few coffees. Since tips weren't essential to their wage, I decided it probably didn't bother them.

I had accomplished so little that I had resorted to writing potential names for my female lead in my notebook. I got a tap on my shoulder while deciding if Lily Flowers was too flower-centric of a name.

"Vous voulez quelque chose à manger?"

I'm pretty sure she had just asked me if I would like anything to eat. Her nametag read ELISE. It was short, to the point, and a lovely name.

I had already planned on my lead female character being French. So there was that.

I suddenly realized I had been staring at her nametag too long. I became flustered and, in English, said, "Sorry, just give me a second."

"I've had guys look at my chest for too long, but I have to say that having someone stare at my nametag for ten seconds is a first." She had spoken this in English. She had a beautiful French accent, but her English was quite good.

I finally raised my eyes, and they glimpsed a striking young woman. She had light brown hair that she wore in a bun, and it showed off her gorgeous skin.

I had always loved it when a woman with a pretty face wore her hair up, and to call her face beautiful would be an understatement. She was also wearing very little makeup, if any.

I realized that she might think I was staring again if I didn't say something quickly.

"I'm sorry. I've been considering different girl's names for my novel. When I saw the name Elise, I just got distracted. It's a beautiful name."

She stared at me intently with sexy, pale blue eyes. "I don't know what's more stereotypical ... a guy telling a girl she has a beautiful name or an American writing a novel at a Parisian café."

It may have sounded like a rude comment, but she said it in a very playful way. She even gave me a little smile at the end of it.

"You get both a lot?" I asked.

"What is that American phrase you guys have? If I had a nickel for every time..."

She was beautiful, quick-witted, and had a good sense of humor. It's safe to say that I was immediately smitten.

"Well, if I'm not already a caricature, this should complete it. I'd like a latte, please," I said.

"I've got three nickels now. Maybe I'll pitch them in toward your latte."

She walked away, and as she did, she looked back and gave me a big smile. She could have melted my heart.

To me, ever since I was a little kid, a beautiful smile on a girl was my favorite addendum. More than butt or boobs. A girl with a great smile, and even better, one who smiled often, was always a threat to steal my heart.

SHE RETURNED A FEW MINUTES LATER WITH ANOTHER SMILE AND A LATTE. The former heated my insides a lot quicker than the latter. Or was it latte-r.

I didn't want her to leave, but I couldn't come up with anything to say.

Screw it, just say something. Don't let her leave and forget about the little flirting you guys had going.

Not knowing what I was saying, I asked, "So what would be the one thing that would solidify me as being no different than anyone else? What would the stereotypical American ordering a latte while writing a novel do next?"

She pondered the question for a moment. She wasn't just humoring me; she was genuinely thinking about it. "See that bill I just gave you? He would write some cheesy line about wanting to take me out and then leave a phone number, an email address, or even worse, a Facebook URL."

I couldn't help but laugh, which she noticed.

"Well, I don't have a phone, and I just deleted my email and Facebook accounts yesterday."

I could hear someone trying to call her over to their table. She smiled at me and said, "That's too bad."

And with that, she walked to the other table.

I STARTED TO DEBATE WITH MYSELF. SHOULD I ASK HER OUT? AFTER ALL, she had just said, 'That's too bad' when I said I had no contact info.

With girls over the years, I had probably let them know too early that I liked them, so I didn't want to come on too strong. Should I play it cool and wait till I see her again? I knew where she worked; it's not like I'd never see her again.

And I knew I'd be writing at Les Deux Magots quite a bit. I decided to try to play it cool and not ask her out so quickly. I did, however, grab the bill and left a little note:

"No Phone, No Email, and No Facebook. Guess I can't be that typical."

I liked it. I didn't come on too strong and kept it in the playful banter. I left a few dollars (I hadn't gotten used to not tipping yet), slid the bill back into the sleeve, and set it on the edge of the table.

I returned to my writing but knew I wouldn't get much done. My mind was racing again, but this time with good thoughts. And after all, now I had a name for my female lead.

After about five minutes, I looked around, but there was no sign of Elise. I figured maybe she was just busy on the inside of the café. When five minutes turned to ten, I was considering getting up to go when I felt a shadow behind me and someone leaning to grab the check.

I turned around, expecting to see Elise's exceptional pale blue eyes, but instead, I saw a middle-aged, heavy-set woman with a nametag letting me know she was Dolores. I pathetically tried to say, "Where's Elise?" in French.

Before I finished, Dolores cut me off, "Elise rentre a la maison." *Elise went home.*

And after letting me in on that knowledge, Dolores grabbed the check and shuffled off.

Bummed out, I left the café and headed toward the hostel, knowing it was time to give my parents a call.

10

TIM AND CHASE

Tim had always thought running track would be the last thing that would benefit him.

He had run the 100-yard dash in high school but never saw any white guys in the sprinting events when he watched the Olympics. Sure, his speed helped him as the starting wide receiver on the high school varsity football team, but he didn't put much stock in it outside of that.

That changed when he saw the menacing, stocky, forty-something man plunge that butcher knife deep into the restrained, defenseless man. He realized that his speed was now his ultimate weapon, and while it didn't get him to the Olympics, it might just save his life.

He didn't consider, for even a second, waiting for Chase or Bryce. It could have been a matter of life and death, so wasting time worrying about others was of no use. It was survival of the fittest.

Tim knew when he started running that he was safe if they didn't have a gun. There was no way they were going to catch him.

When he didn't hear a gunshot in the first few seconds, he figured he was home free, and by the time he took a right at the fork in the road, he knew his speed had finally benefitted him.

He sprinted for another minute until he reached a main street and flagged down a cab. He told the driver his address and drove him straight home. It was only then that he allowed himself to consider what had happened to Chase and Bryce.

He contemplated calling Chase's or Bryce's cell phone but thought better of it. If the murderers had caught them, and then they saw an incoming call from someone named Tim, you can be sure they would find out who Tim was. He decided against calling tonight and figured he'd try to contact them tomorrow.

Usually a sound sleeper, Tim was awakened several times with violent dreams in which he saw the butcher knife being plunged into the man's sternum.

༺✦༻

CHASE HADN'T BEEN A TRACK STAR LIKE TIM, BUT HE HAD BEEN AN athletic kid growing up, and no man in his forties was going to outrun him. He wasn't ready to run, however, when Tim took off.

He thought the darkness shielded them, and if they had just shut up and not moved, they would not have been seen. That became moot when Tim took off, and there was no other option than to run as fast as he could.

He wasn't sure why he told Bryce to go left while he went right. It must have been an instinct that they would be easier to follow as a team. Within seconds of taking the right, Chase realized his route would be much easier than Bryce's.

Chase's route was dark and shadowy, and he'd be tough to see. He turned around once and saw that they had both followed Bryce, and he knew he would be safe.

Like Tim, he kept sprinting till he reached a main street and then flagged down a cab. When he got home, he snuck into bed beside his pregnant wife and didn't say a word.

༺✦༻

THE FOLLOWING DAY, AROUND 11:00 A.M., TIM DECIDED TO CALL CHASE'S wife, Victoria. She answered, and when Tim asked for Chase, she acted normal.

Tim's heart rate slowed down just a little bit. Chase came to the phone, but his wife stayed close to him after handing over the phone.

"Hey, Tim".

"Is your wife still in the room with you?"

"Yeah."

"Okay, let's meet at Infinity's for lunch in an hour." "I'll be there."

༺✦༻

TIM NEEDED TO FIND OUT IF BRYCE HAD BOARDED HIS FLIGHT. IT CHANGED everything.

If he had departed on the flight, he hadn't gone to the police. They wouldn't allow a witness to a murder to fly to Europe the following day. If Bryce was not on the flight, there were two likely possibilities. One, he had turned himself in to the police, or much worse, two, that the murderers had gotten to him.

Tim had a friend who worked for the airlines, and he gave him a call.

He had first considered calling the airline directly but felt no need to leave a trace of his calling to ask for a Bryce Connor.

Tim called his friend Dan Hilliard and made up a story that he had partied with a friend most of the night and wanted to ensure he got on his flight.

Like a lot of fiction, Tim's story contained several elements of truth. Dan said he'd call Tim back in ten minutes. Nine and a half minutes later, Dan Hilliard called Tim and told him that Bryce had made his flight.

First and foremost, Tim was glad that Bryce was safe. Yeah, he had felt it was survival of the fittest, and he ran when he had the chance, but Bryce was still a friend, and he was relieved to hear he had boarded his flight.

Tim was also happy because this confirmed that Bryce had not gone to the police. It meant that if he could talk Chase into it, they might avoid going to the police altogether.

This had been Tim's hope all along.

※

INFINITY'S WAS A CAFÉ IN MIDTOWN THAT TIM AND CHASE HAD OFTEN eaten at. They had discussed girls they wanted to screw and marital problems they were having, but never the fact that those two might somehow be related.

On this day, Tim had beaten Chase there and asked the maitre d', whom he knew well, for a secluded table. They put Tim in a corner where the closest table was a good twenty-five feet away.

Chase arrived about ten minutes after Tim, and the maitre d' showed him to the table. When he was beyond earshot, Tim said to Chase, "Bryce is alive. He got on his flight a few hours ago."

Chase relaxed a bit. "Thank God. He had a pretty good head start on them, but you never really know. It's been eating me up all morning just thinking about it."

Tim was not a sentimental man by nature and wouldn't start being one now. He got right to the point. "I don't think we should go to the police. He didn't go to them if he boarded that flight, so we don't have to either."

Chase had expected this. He wasn't necessarily against doing nothing, but he felt they should at least talk about it.

"Jeez, Tim, we saw a guy get murdered. Do you really want to do nothing?"

Tim looked at Chase with disdain. "Let's say we go to the cops. They are going to check out everything we did that night. You can be sure that they will find out about the cocaine and the hookers."

"Couldn't we just leave that part out?" Chase asked, realizing he sounded naïve.

"We will be the key witnesses to a murder in Manhattan. The DA's office would find out everything we did that night. And I do mean everything."

"Yeah, I guess you're right."

"I haven't even brought up Gina and Veronica. I'm trying to make up with Gina, and I'm pretty sure Veronica wouldn't take too kindly to you doing coke off a hooker's tits and god knows what else."

Chase looked up at Tim. He wanted to argue and say they should do the right thing, but he knew it would be useless. Plus, Tim was right. What they did would undoubtedly come out, and he didn't want to ruin his marriage with his pregnant wife.

Chase bowed his head in concession. "So what should we do?"

"Nothing. They didn't catch Bryce, so he couldn't tell them anything about us, and they've got nothing on you or me." Chase only nodded, so Tim continued, "And don't tell a fucking soul. Not Victoria, no one from work, not some chick you want to bang. No one! You got me?"

"I won't tell a soul, not even Victoria. When I returned last night, I didn't say a single word to her."

"Good. Also, I think we should lay low for a few weeks. I don't think they got much of a look at us, especially me, but why chance it by being out and about."

"I think you're being a little over-cautious, but all right, I'll lay low. I've got a pregnant wife at home anyway. I should be home, trying to be a better husband."

"That's the smartest thing you've said all day. And, need I remind you, the guy said the name Solari. Doesn't sound like someone I want to deal with."

So then and there, Tim and Chase decided they would not go to the police either. Not for the practical, realistic fears that Bryce had but for wholly selfish reasons. Sure, Tim had mentioned the name Solari, but the reason he didn't want to go to the police was to save his own ass.

Tim and Chase stayed and finished lunch, and as they left the restaurant, Chase swore a guy across the street was staring at him.

If he had to guess, he would have ventured the guy was of Italian descent.

11

BRYCE

PARIS

As I left Les Deux Magots, where the lovely Elise had gone home early, I realized I had some more pertinent worries to attend to.

It was time I finally called my parents. A day and a half was too long to leave them waiting, no matter what my circumstances were.

The question was whether I would tell them anything. I could say, "Something happened in New York" without being specific, but then I'd just get them worried for no reason. It's not like they could do anything about it, anyway.

I decided I wouldn't tell them anything. Assuming they had tried to email me, I'd have to explain why that was down. Luckily, they were too old school to have a Facebook account, so I didn't have to worry about those potential questions.

I realized I would be doing something extremely rare. I can hear you saying, "You must be a good son if you rarely lie to your parents," but no, I was alluding to the fact that I was about to use a pay phone.

I imagine the only people who use pay phones anymore are older people and tourists. Luckily, Paris was full of both, so I figured finding a pay phone wouldn't be too tough.

It turned out there was one just a few blocks up from Les Deux Magots, but a quick glance at my watch revealed it was only three p.m., which was six a.m. back in California. My parents usually woke up a little closer to seven, so I decided to give it more time.

I walked along the Seine and, at one point, found a nice little grassy area and sat down to write. The temperature was probably in the mid-sixties (I wasn't great at the whole Celsius thing yet), with a nice breeze blowing.

I could have sat there and written for hours, but needed to make the call.

I started heading back to the hostel, looking for a pay phone. Once again, I found one quicker than I expected.

Maybe payphones were more abundant than I realized; you just don't notice them when staring down at your cell phone all day, as my generation is prone to do.

It was now a little after eight a.m. back in California, which meant my parents were both up, and my Dad hadn't left for work yet. Perfect. I dialed the US international code and pressed my parents' number. After about four rings, I became a little worried, but then I heard my dad's gravelly voice pick up the phone.

"Hello?"

"Hi, Dad."

"Bryce!!" His octave rose sharply as his excitement was evident. "How are you doing, son?"

"Everything's great," I lied. "Listen, I'm sorry I didn't call you yesterday. I was just so tired with the flight, moving into the hostel, and everything else."

"Don't worry about it. I kind of figured that was the case. So tell me about it. It's a beautiful city, isn't it?"

"It's magnificent, Dad." I finally told the truth. "I've already seen some sights, walked along the Seine, and even found a café I enjoy writing at."

"How about the girls?"

"C'mon, Dad, I've been here less than two days."

"It's never too early to start."

"I guess. I will say I love the accents. So sexy."

"Indeed. So, how was New York? Have Tim and Chase mellowed at all since they got married?"

"New York was pretty mellow. Nothing spectacular happened, and yeah, Tim and Chase seem more under control these days."

Wow, three lies in five seconds—a new record.

"I'm glad to hear it. Never did fully trust those kids, but since they were your friends, I gave them the benefit of the doubt."

The phrase "the cat got your tongue" applied to me right there. I truthfully had no answer to that.

"Bryce?"

"Yeah, sorry, Dad. Reception cut out for a second."

"No problem. Hey, let me hand you off to your mother. I'm glad you're having a great time. Have a blast, son."

"Thanks, Dad."

I heard a rustling in the background as the phone was transferred.

This was a call from a pay phone received by a landline. You didn't get many of those anymore.

"Bryce, honey, can you hear me?"

"I sure can. Hi, Mom."

"Oh, you sound great, sweetie. I bet you are enjoying Paris."

She had called me honey and sweetie in back-to-back sentences. I am glad my mom wasn't diabetic because she loved her sugars.

"It's all I had hoped and more."

"Have you seen the Eiffel Tower yet?"

"Sure have. And my hostel is a stone's throw from the Seine."

"Any luck on a place yet?"

"No, but I will be looking over the next few days."

"Oh, I'm so happy for you, sweetie. One thing, though. What happened to your Yahoo email? I tried to send you something this morning, and it came back to me saying it wasn't an active email."

I had already planned what I was going to say next: "I just wanted some peace and quiet for my first few weeks here. I didn't want to have to answer emails from everyone when I should be out getting acquainted with the city. I'll set up a new email soon, and I promise you will be the first person I send one to."

"Oh, thanks, honey. You better send me a long email. I don't like not being able to get ahold of you. When will you get a phone?"

Damn, Mom was tough.

"I'll get a phone soon also."

"Okay, sorry. I'm being a worrier. I guess it comes with being a mother. It's in the job description."

"I know, Mom. You don't have to worry about me." I sure hoped I was right.

"I'll let you go, son. I'm sure you're busy. Give me a call or an email as soon as you can."

"I will. I love you, and tell Dad I love him as well."

"Will do. Take care, Bryce."

With that, she hung up, and I immediately felt guilty about the lies I had told my parents. I tried to tell myself that it was the practical and smart thing to do, but that rationale was starting to wear thin on me.

12

BRYCE

The next three days were a combination of frustrations and letdowns. I had found two potential places in the 6th arrondissement, both of which the landlord assured me were mine, only to have them rented to someone else at the last moment.

I only had two days left at the hostel. I could stay longer if I had to, but I had made this a self-imposed time to leave and wanted to stick to it.

I'd also hit a wall in my writing, and it appeared that my great American debut novel was stuck in neutral. I wasn't a very happy customer when I went to sleep that night.

I WOKE UP THE FOLLOWING DAY WITH RENEWED VIGOR AND FELT THINGS would go my way. I had two more places to check out, including one just a few blocks from the Seine near a beautiful rustic old house with its own separate entrance.

When I arrived at the house, the landlord, Lorraine, a woman in her fifties, greeted me. She had traveled several times to San Francisco and knew the area where my parents raised me. Our discussion was all in English, which greatly benefited me.

I told her my situation and that, in all likelihood, I would be here for six months but would prefer to sign only a three-month lease.

She seemed to want to stick to six months, but I came up with an idea that she found agreeable.

I suggested a four-month lease, in which I would pay for it all upfront.

Also, I told her I'd let her know at the end of the third month if I would stay all six.

This would give her plenty of time to find someone to rent it if need be. She agreed, saying it helped me that August was coming up, and that was Paris's downtime.

It was a house by definition, but my living spaces were separate from the actual house. My domicile was more like a guest house, or as Lorraine called it, a cottage. The main house was also mine to come and go as I pleased, but I almost preferred the anonymity of the cottage.

There was even a little garden between the cottage and the main house. Maybe I would take up gardening. Okay, maybe not

The tenants in the main house were two professionals from France. One man and one woman. Lorraine said they traveled a lot and were out of town more often than at the house.

A beautiful place where frequently I would be the only one around? This place couldn't get any better. Lorraine and I agreed to meet in a few days once I got a cashier's check, and she'd have the keys for me to move in.

This would have been a fantastic day if this had been the best thing that happened to me. Happily for me, it was a distant second.

I decided to celebrate by getting some writing done. Sure, I could have got a drink instead, but I had always been a more productive writer when I was happily sober.

Unlike many writers, especially the drunks, who wrote better when they wallowed in the gutter while looking up at the stars, I wrote better when I was on cloud nine and closer to the aforementioned stars.

13
BRYCE

I hadn't been to Les Deux Magots in four days, so I figured I'd give it another chance. With how great this day had gone thus far, I fancifully hoped Elise would be standing outside, eagerly awaiting my arrival. No such luck.

Instead, I saw my old friend Dolores and ordered a latte.

I STARTED WRITING AND WAS HAPPY WITH HOW IT WAS GOING. My writing was crisp and precise. I had probably written ten pages in my spiral notebook during my first hour there when I heard a voice behind me say, "Look, it's Mr. Atypical."

I turned around and saw Elise. She again wore her light brown hair in a bun and looked even more beautiful the second time. I would have doubted that was possible. As I was taking in her beauty, I didn't want to have a long pause again. "Atypical?" I quickly asked.

"Yeah, don't you remember? No Facebook, no phone, no email. Guess I'm not that typical."

"I remember, but you had left, so I figured you never got my note."

"Dolores found me the next day and said, 'Some handsome young man left this for you yesterday.'"

I knew I always liked Dolores. "What happened to you that day?" I asked.

"I didn't realize what time it was, and when I returned inside, my shift was over. Our manager doesn't like us to return and collect checks once our shift ends."

Elise must have sensed my disappointment. "Oh, I hope you didn't think I ditched you," she said.

I just lied to my parents, so I decided I wouldn't start by lying to Elise. "Well, yeah, I guess it did cross my mind."

"You don't have to worry about that today. I just got on at eleven and have to work a five-hour shift."

I looked at my watch, which read 11:15. "Wow, what a coincidence. I planned on writing here for the next four hours and forty-five minutes."

Elise put her hands behind her hair and let out a great laugh. I remember thinking at that exact moment that I could get used to that laugh. It was the kind of laugh that showed someone was in love with life. There's no other way you could describe that laugh. I think the French called it *Joie De Vivre*.

"I've got to check some of my other tables, Bryce. Don't worry, I'll be back."

Again, I was stunned. "Did I tell you my name last time?"

She grabbed something from her waistband. I could see the writing. It was the check stub with the note that I had left her. "You paid by credit card. Your name was on the love letter."

I laughed as she said, "Love Letter." It wasn't with the Joie de Vivre that her laugh exuded, but after the frustration of the last few days, it just felt great to laugh.

"Love letter is a bit much," I said.

Elise smiled and told me she had to check on some other tables.

※

I SAT OUTSIDE LES DEUX MAGOTS FOR SEVERAL HOURS, WRITING AWAY ON what I hoped was the next great American novel.

I didn't know if I had the next *Moby Dick* in front of me, but what I did know was that about every fifteen minutes, a beautiful French girl with light brown hair, a great figure, and small dimples would come to talk to me and that was enough for me.

Over the course of the day—often in just two-minute spurts—I learned a great deal about Elise.

She grew up in Chambery, in the southeast of France. When she was twelve, her dad was transferred to Paris for work, and he took his family (wife Camille, Elise, and younger sister Emilie) with him to Paris.

Elise finished high school in Paris and enrolled at the prestigious Sorbonne University. After two years, she realized she wanted to see more of the world and decided to study abroad.

※

SHE HAD APPLIED TO SCHOOLS IN MADRID, ROME, AND THE U.S. SHE GOT into Villanova, located in Philadelphia, Pennsylvania, and the schools in Madrid and Rome.

Elise decided the U.S. was the farthest away and the most different from home, so she decided to go there. Sound familiar?

She said her English consisted of what she had learned in school and nothing more. Sound familiar again? On her first day at school, she realized that she would need to improve her English if she wanted to keep up, so she enrolled in night classes.

<hr />

ELISE SEEMED LIKE A REAL GO-GETTER, AND AT THIS POINT, I ALMOST interrupted to ask her how she ended up working as a waitress. I held my tongue, figuring the answer would come eventually.

Elise did very well at Villanova and said her English improved dramatically. I told her there was no doubt about that; I understood everything she said perfectly.

She would have liked to stay longer in the U.S., but it was only a semester program, so she had to return to the Sorbonne.

During that time, she fell in love with the theater. Her then-boyfriend had taken her to a play for her birthday, and she was immediately hooked.

Subsequently, she enrolled in theater classes at Sorbonne and switched her emphasis to drama.

She joined a local theater group when she graduated and has acted in local plays ever since. Now twenty-six, she has recently been cast in some reasonably big parts.

Unfortunately, the pay isn't great, so she has to work at Les Deux Magots to cover the bills.

"I bet you were starting to wonder why a college graduate from the Sorbonne was working as a waitress at a café," Elise said.

Beautiful and insightful, I thought. I said the same thing, and she blushed.

"I guess the theater is to me what your writing is to you. I bet you sacrificed a great deal to write consistently."

"Not nearly enough. That's one of the big reasons I took this trip."

"What were the other reasons?"

I wanted to say, "To meet a girl like you," but I couldn't bring myself to say it. "To travel, live in a different country, and learn a new language—probably the same reasons you decided to go to Villanova."

She slapped her hand down on my spiral notebook. "So what's the novel about? I'm curious."

This was my chance.

"I'll tell you what. You come to dinner with me this week, and I'll tell you all about it."

My heart sat there for what felt like a minute when really, she answered quite quickly.

"I'd love to. But this time, I want to learn about you. I feel like I did all the talking today."

"I promise to do all the talking at dinner."

"Just not while you're eating," Elise said and smiled.

I told her we'd have to pick a place to meet since I didn't have a phone yet. I suggested her work, but she said she didn't need to have her coworkers see her leaving with some guy. I understood.

I told her I would be moving into my new place on the night of our dinner, so I suggested she come by there. It turned out to be close to where she lived so we agreed to meet at my place at eight p.m. in two days.

As I left the café, the phrase "grinning from ear to ear" wouldn't have done justice to the size of my smile.

14
BRYCE

The following day consisted mainly of saying goodbye to some of the friends I had made at the hostel.
A lot of people had come and gone over the last week, but there were still some people left with whom I had become friendly.

Plus, I had to come to know a few of the staff members, and they were invaluable when I needed directions, a cab called, etc.

I told them I wouldn't be a stranger and I'd drop by and say hello occasionally. That last night in the hostel, I went to sleep at about nine o'clock.

The next day, I would be moving into my new place and had my first date in Paris. I needed my beauty sleep.

The following day, I got up early, said goodbye to the woman at the front desk, and had her call me a cab. I had my three bags with me, and although my new place was close to the hostel, I didn't want to lug three bags for seven blocks.

As for public transportation, let's just say I didn't use the buses as often as I should have. I was still a bit of a lazy American who would rather call a cab than figure out when to transfer on/off buses.

LORRAINE WAS WAITING OUTSIDE WITH TWO KEYS WHEN I ARRIVED AT MY new place.

Obviously, I knew the place was mine, but just seeing the keys in her hand made it feel all the more real.

In my hand, I had a cashier's check for $6,000, which I had to give her in exchange for the key. It was $1500 a month for four months, but considering how nice the place was and that it was centrally located in Paris, I still felt like I was getting a good deal. Lorraine handed me the keys, and I played coy for a second.

"Does that mean I have to give you this?"

She smiled. "Oui."

I gave her the check and opened my new living area door. I quickly realized it was smaller than I had initially thought, but it was just me, and I could get by.

Plus, it had a small bathroom and a tiny kitchen, which was all I needed. It also came with a bed, a dresser, and a desk.

"Follow me. Let me show you the main house."

※

THE MAIN HOUSE WAS, UNLIKE MY COTTAGE, BIGGER THAN IT LOOKED. IT was two stories with both bedrooms upstairs, each with their own bathroom.

The downstairs consisted of a huge family room, a full-sized kitchen, and a washer and dryer. The downstairs also had a bathroom, but with one in my cottage, I wouldn't have any use for it. On the other hand, the washer and dryer would come in very handy.

Neither of the "roommates" were home, so that would have to wait for another time. The house was clean and spacious, and if the roommates were truly gone half the time, maybe I'd be using the main house more than I thought. After all, the family room was probably three times as big as my cottage.

Lorraine said she had to go and explained which keys were for the main house. "I'm not around very often. I like to give my tenants their space, but if you ever need anything, don't hesitate to call me."

She then gave me one of her business cards.

"Thanks for everything, Lorraine. You sure know how to make a foreigner feel at home."

"That's very nice, Bryce. You can give me some suggestions next time I visit San Francisco."

"Of course."

We shook hands, and she walked out the front door and onto the street.

I had the house to myself. I looked around and thought, "I did it!" I was in a foreign country, secured a nice new place, had been writing quite a bit, and had a date with a beautiful French girl tonight. Not bad for only having been there a week.

※

I NEEDED TO FIND A PLACE FOR DINNER. I HAD BEEN LAGGING, BUT THERE were so many restaurants along the Seine that I wasn't too worried.

As I was about to set out and find a restaurant for the night, I realized I had to make one change to the room.

The furnished desk was flush against a wall. Although I'd probably do most of my writing at cafés, I'd undoubtedly do some writing at home, and I didn't want to do it while facing a wall.

I moved the desk in front of the one window of my cottage. Now, when I wrote, I'd look at the little garden between my place and the main house. It's much better than staring at a wall.

I got ready to leave and looked back at my place. Yeah, it was small, but I had a bed, a dresser, and a desk. What more did a guy need?

Well, there was one more thing ... and she'd be here at eight.

※

I left the cottage and walked around Paris looking for a restaurant. I wanted something nice, but not too nice.

After all, we had only met twice; this was our first date. I didn't want to overwhelm her by taking her to some ritzy, expensive place. Nor did I want to damage my checking account any more than the $6,000 already had.

It was another lovely day in Paris, so I was looking for a place with outdoor seating. That didn't exactly narrow it down in Paris, but it was a must. I didn't want to venture too far from the apartment, so I was intrigued when I came upon a place called Fogon right along the Seine.

It was Spanish food, but I figured Elise was from France, and it might be a nice change of pace for her. Not all people would agree with this logic.

If I told my mother I was eating Spanish food while in Paris, she might disown me. But the place looked like a lot of fun and had outdoor seating, so I went with it.

"Vous avez toutes les ouvertures 8:30?"

"Oui."

"Je Vais prendre ce."

I spoke that entire three-line conversation—of which I said two— in French.

Was I becoming bilingual? Not exactly, but I was proud of myself.

15

BRYCE

I walked back to my place. I still had several hours until Elise was due to come over, so I laid down for a quick nap.

It must have been due to sleeping on a comfortable bed for the first time in over a week because my quick nap turned into a four-hour sleep.

I realized I had slept way longer than planned as soon as I woke up. I hadn't even looked at a clock, but it was just one of our innate abilities.

I looked at my watch, which read 7:45. I leaped out of bed, went into the bathroom, and started the shower. I just hoped she didn't arrive early.

I broke the record for the quickest shower ever. I looked in my closet and picked out a short-sleeved white dress shirt.

I matched this with my best jeans and some shiny brown dress shoes. I sprayed on a minimal amount of J.P. Gaultier cologne and looked in the mirror. I had to say, I didn't look half bad for getting ready in ten minutes.

It was 7:55, so I decided to wait for her outside. I told her I was in the smaller cottage, but since the main house kind of shielded it, it could get confusing, and I wouldn't be able to hear her knock if she went to the house.

I had to wait less than two minutes before I saw her approaching. I had told you how beautiful she had looked the first two times I had met her, but nothing could prepare me for this.

Although it should be a thing of the past, some guys still rank girls on a 1-10 scale. When I looked at Elise, I was reminded of the old line from *Spinal Tap*: "This one goes to eleven."

She was simply stunning. She wore a yellow sun dress that I used to see many girls wear while I was at UC Santa Barbara, but no girl ever wore it like this. The yellow ruffles ended at her lower thigh, but you could still make out her firm, fit legs.

She wore brown shoes, and I noticed her silver earrings.

And yes, this is the most precise I had ever been when describing what a girl was wearing.

I kissed her on the cheek. "You look stunning, Elise."

Then I saw her most beautiful addendum: her smile. "You look pretty handsome yourself," she said in that playful French accent.

I didn't even know if she was trying to be playful, but something about the French accents always seemed sensual.

"Thank you," I said.

We were a good-looking couple—a couple as in two people, not as in a dating couple—at least not yet.

"Would you like to see the house?" I asked.

"That would be great. It looks huge." She pointed at the big house, then motioned to my cottage, "That's cute too."

"Very funny."

I showed her the main house first. She, like I, was impressed with the size of the downstairs. I didn't know if the "roommates" were back, so I decided not to take her upstairs. As we walked the fifty feet to the cottage, I said, "And now, to the highlight of our tour."

"Best for last, huh?"

It could have taken twenty seconds, but I pretended each little crevice of the cottage was its own little entity.

When I finished the "tour," she asked, "Now, in which area do Dopey and Sneezy sleep?"

She was definitely in a playful mood tonight.

"The seven dwarves? Oh, that's low."

"I'm only kidding. I like it."

"Thanks."

※

I LOCKED UP MY PLACE, AND WE HEADED TOWARD FOGON. SINCE IT WAS located on the Seine, I led us over in that direction.

I could have waited till we got close and crossed over, but I selfishly wanted to walk with a beautiful girl along the Seine.

The host of Fogon asked if we'd like to eat inside or outside, and I said outside. Elise seemed happy with the decision.

He seated us, brought two glasses of water and two menus, and asked if we'd like anything to drink.

She ordered a vodka-grapefruit, also known as a greyhound, and I got a Kronenburg 1664. After we ordered our food and they brought us our drinks, I extended my beer to her greyhound, and we touched glasses.

"Cheers."

"Sante," she corrected. "You are in France ,after all."

We hit glasses, and both said, "Sante!"

Since she had done most of the talking the last time, it was my turn to divulge my childhood.

I told her I was born in San Francisco and spent my childhood in the Bay Area. We moved to the East Bay suburbs for one year, but my dad realized he preferred the city's vibrancy, so we moved back to San Francisco.

I had applied to several in-state schools as well as Vanderbilt and Virginia. I got into Virginia but decided to stay in California and attend UC Santa Barbara.

It was impossible to have more fun in college than I did at UCSB, but I always wished I had moved back east rather than played it safe and stayed on the West Coast.

After graduating, I was offered a position to manage a college-themed bar/restaurant I frequented often. I probably should have joined the "real workforce," but something about extending my college career appealed to me.

Elise said I was constantly trying to hold onto my youth. It was one of the more insightful things anyone had ever surmised about me.

I told her about my job working as a social media manager and how I'd quit.

"You quit your job before you came here?" Elise asked.

"Kind of. I asked for three months' vacation."

"After having worked there for six months total?"

I laughed at the absurdity of it. "I think it was my way of quitting. I knew there was no chance they'd give it to me."

"I've been at Les Deux Magots for three years, so by your logic, they owe me a year and a half of vacation."

We laughed.

"So what really brought you here, Bryce?"

It was a simple question but a complicated answer, and some of it wasn't very flattering to me. Nonetheless, I decided to be honest.

"I could easily make up some bullshit story here, but I figure I'll give you the truth."

She looked at me like she expected nothing less. It showed she expected honesty. Good.

"I was disappointed at where I was in my life. A lot of my friends were getting married or having kids, and it was always, 'When are you going to get married, Bryce?' I didn't want to be in the same cubicle at the same company in five years. I needed more out of my life. I was tired of waking up every day at 7:30, getting back at 6:00, working out, watching TV, going to sleep, and then doing the same thing the next day. I've always liked to travel the world and be spontaneous, but now I found myself in a rut. For the first time in my life, I was boring. I knew I needed a change."

"I like a guy with a thoughtful, emotional side," she said.

I grimaced.

"What, that's not a compliment?" she finished.

"Not when you put it like that," I said and started doing bicep curls with my beer.

She smiled. "That's not what I meant. I like it when a guy can open up and be honest."

"Then I guess I made the right choice."

"You did."

We sat there for about ten seconds, and neither of us said a word. On any other first date, this would probably have been an uncomfortable silence, but it didn't feel that way with Elise.

Ten turned to twenty, and we were enjoying looking at each other's eyes.

She finally broke the silence. "If we let this go any longer, it might get a little awkward."

"It's called an uncomfortable silence in the U.S."

"Didn't feel so uncomfortable to me."

"Me neither."

They brought us our entrees.

I ordered a flat iron steak, and Elise went with seafood soup. Both dishes looked delicious. Elise's bowl was steaming from the heat. They also brought over two glasses of a red cabernet I had ordered.

"Don't burn your tongue," I said.

"Oui. I think I'm going to give this a minute."

We sat there for most of the main course and said little. There was an occasional smile or compliment on how good the food was, but for the most part, we enjoyed the food and each other's company.

The waiter came and took away the entrees and gave us each a dessert menu.

Elise fanned herself off. "I think I'm still sweating from that soup."

"Yeah, you look hot."

She looked at me, trying to decipher what type of hot I was suggesting.

"And sweaty, too," I finished.

She winked. "You still haven't told me what your novel is about. That is, after all, how you convinced me to come on this date."

"It's not exactly great dinner talk."

"Is it that deep? I like talking about serious subjects, let's hear it."

"Okay, you asked for it. Well, it's partially a love story ... "

Elise jumped in at that point and interrupted. "Sorry to interrupt, but is Elise still the lead female's name?"

"It is for now. But if the real Elise keeps interrupting, I don't know."

Elise let out a quick laugh. "Okay. Sorry. Go ahead."

"So, it's partly a love story, but I'm trying to tackle a lot of issues that face our generation. Issues that I don't think have affected any other generations. These include how women are so independent these days and how that leads to people getting married later in life. How much more difficult it is to buy a home these days. How hard it is to stay in relationships, and all the added pressure that social media generates. Basically, the novel is going to be all over the place."

"Sounds interesting. I'd like to read it at some point. Most importantly, what does Elises's love interest look like?"

"Tall, dark, and handsome. Kind of like the guy sitting across from you."

"Are you sure this story is fictional?" Elise playfully asked.

"Yeah," I smiled. "With a little bit of real life thrown in."

"I think I know how it's going to end. I think Elise will end up solving all the world's crises."

"A woman saving the world? Now, that would truly be a work of fiction."

She grabbed some water with her spoon and flicked it at me, getting some on my shirt.

We both laughed.

"I deserved that," I said.

※

AFTER DINNER, WE WERE BOTH PRETTY FULL, SO WE SPLIT A DESSERT. IT was small enough that I didn't bust open a button as I got up from the table.

As we walked back along the Seine, I debated the proper move. Do I offer to walk her home? Do I invite her to my place? Do I try to kiss her? Do I just kiss her on the cheek because it's only a first date? All these things were going through my head as I tried to converse.

"You said you live pretty close to me?" I asked.

"Yeah, only about five blocks."

"Let me walk you home then."

"That would be great. Merci."

※

ABOUT TEN MINUTES LATER, WE ARRIVED AT HER APARTMENT COMPLEX. THE outside was all brick, with Ivy hanging off the brick. It reminded me of Wrigley Field. It looked like a great spot. I didn't expect to be seeing the inside, however.

"I had a great time tonight," I said.

"I enjoyed myself, Bryce. Thanks so much."

I leaned in and kissed her on the cheek.

"You missed," she said.

She then grabbed me and gave me a memorable five-second kiss on the lips. It was perfect.

She opened the front door of the apartment complex.

"That's all you're getting tonight," she said and smiled. "I work the next two days. Come by, and we'll make plans for this weekend."

"I'll be there," I said.

"Hey, there's one thing I never asked you."

"What is it?"

"How old are you?"

"Thirty-two," I said.

She seemed to contemplate this momentarily and did some pseudo-counting on her fingers.

"Wow, you're lucky," she said. "After my last immature boyfriend, I decided my next one should be at least five years older than me. Since I'm twenty-six, that means you just made the cut."

"Tally one up for the old guys," I said.

With that, we smiled and hugged goodbye.

She entered her apartment complex, and I headed back to my new place.

It had been a good night.

16

BRYCE

We went on two more dates over the next week. Once to the movies—we saw *Moonrise Kingdom*—and one more time to dinner. A proper French restaurant this time, so my mother wouldn't disown me.

While both dates went great, the ends of the night were becoming painfully redundant.

The second and third dates concluded exactly the way the first one had. I would walk her to her apartment, we would kiss one time on the lips, and she would enter her apartment alone.

There were many possible reasons why she didn't want to intensify the relationship, so I continued to respect her boundaries.

Maybe she liked me and didn't want to rush things. Maybe she just liked to wait longer than most.

But was I getting a little antsy? Yes.

We had agreed on another date, but for this date, we would not be sitting together. In fact, I would be sitting by myself in Row C, Seat 3. Elise had invited me to see her perform in her latest play.

The venue was a posh, medium-sized theater about a half mile north of where I lived. It looked to fit around 500 people. There was a beautiful balcony that gave a bird's-eye view of the stage.

When I arrived forty-five minutes before the play started, it was already 80-90% full, so I was sure a sell-out was in the cards.

The play was Les Liaisons Dangereuses, and while I didn't know the play, I

DEBUT NOVEL

knew Hollywood had made a movie out of it called *Dangerous Liaisons* starring John Malkovich, Glenn Close, and Michelle Pfeiffer.

I met Elise for a few minutes before the play, and I could tell she was nervous, so I didn't hang around long. I wished her luck and told her I'd see her after the play.

I can only imagine how nerve-wracking it must be to perform in front of several hundred people, and now she also had a date to worry about.

As I walked back and took my seat in the third row (I guess it paid to be dating one of the performers), I looked at the program for Les Liaisons Dangereuses.

Elise was playing Cecile de Volanges, and I imagine she was playing younger than her actual age because, in the paragraph about her character, she was called "eune fille," which meant young girl.

I'm glad I read the program because there wasn't much more that I picked up while watching the play. Watching a play spoken entirely in French made me realize how much work my French sorely needed.

Sure, I had become pretty adept at ordering food or drinks, asking for directions, and other such phrases, but those were small, quick phrases.

Listening to two hours straight of French (with no breaks for English) was a different animal. I would pick up words and phrases and have a general idea of what was going on, but if you asked me for specifics, I was screwed.

This didn't prevent me from enjoying the play immensely. Elise had a big part in it, and I was filled with pride every time she spoke.

The girl I was dating could hold an audience of 500 in the palm of her hand. I would look around when she spoke, and the audience members were on the edge of their seats with anticipation.

As I had guessed, Elise was playing a girl in her late teens, maybe younger. She was seduced by an older man and drawn into a game of sex and betrayal amongst the French aristocracy. That was about as much as I could surmise, and I figured I'd ask Elise about the rest.

❧

AFTER THE PLAY ENDED AND THE ACTORS AND ACTRESSES HAD DONE THEIR curtain call, I walked to the edge of the stage, where Elise had told me to meet her. She grabbed me, we kissed, and I told her how great she was.

She seemed so happy about how it went, and I was delighted to see her carefree after being so nervous only a few hours earlier.

She invited me backstage, where I was introduced to what seemed like the whole cast. I must have said "Enchante" fifty times.

After about a half hour, it started to wind down, so Elise and I decided to get a drink to celebrate. We walked to a local bar and ordered a drink. We found a corner booth and sat down.

I told her I couldn't follow as much as I wanted, and she filled me in on what I had missed.

"To be honest, all that doesn't even matter," I said. "I just loved seeing you up there. It's amazing how you can be nervous before it starts and then seem so calm and confident once you get up on stage to perform."

"I imagine it's like that in a lot of endeavors. I bet athletes get nervous before a game, but once they get on that field, they forget all about their nerves. It's like their safe haven."

"Yeah, you're probably right. Now, to the important question. How do we prevent you from being seduced by an older man."

It was an obvious joke, but I realized my mistake almost instantly.

"Let me rephrase. How do we prevent you from being seduced by a MUCH older man?"

She smiled. "You're lucky. I was going to use that line against you at a future date. I still might."

"How much longer does this play run for? Now that I know what's happening, I'd love to see it again."

We both took a sip of our drinks.

"We've got four more shows. Next Friday and Saturday and the following weekend's Friday and Saturday."

"And then what?"

"Then I have a few weeks off until I start auditioning for new roles in a new play."

"Well, you were fantastic. I'm not just saying that; you truly were great. I'd look at the audience, and they were mesmerized by you."

Elise slightly blushed. "Thanks, Bryce, that means a lot."

And then she grabbed me and kissed me. Maybe it was just positive thinking, but I felt we were getting even closer tonight. I was hoping this would be the night. We both finished our drinks, and I seized the opportunity.

"Want to get out of here?"

"Yeah, let's go."

As we walked along the Seine, I worried that the night would end like the previous three. I internally rebuffed myself and told myself to think positively.

It must have worked because two seconds later, Elise said, "I think we should go back to your house tonight."

And with that, I grabbed her hand and interlocked her wrist with mine. Tonight was the night.

WHEN WE ARRIVED BACK AT MY PLACE, THERE WERE NO LIGHTS ON IN THE main house, and it appeared Elise and I were alone on the premises. As I started to open the door, she swiveled me around.

"I just wanted to say that I really like you," Elise said.

"I like you, too."

And just like that, my nervousness was gone. I was with a beautiful woman, and I would enjoy this.

We both leaned in at the same time and started kissing each other.

We entered the cottage, our lips still locked.

I shut the door behind me and led us to the bed. We continued kissing as our hands explored the other's body.

After several more minutes of kissing/fondling, we started taking each other's clothes off. A minute later, Elise guided me into her, and we made love.

I don't know if the rumor that all French women are good in bed is true, but it certainly was the case with Elise.

I had never felt more elated or exhausted after being with a woman. It was a good exhaustion, and after holding each other for a short while, we fell asleep in each other's arms.

I wish I could tell you we had sex three more times that night, but that wasn't the case.

Maybe it was the play. Maybe it was the sex.

Whatever it was, we slept like two babies.

The next morning, I woke up first and used the restroom. When I got out and looked at the bed, Elise was awake.

"You were great," she said.

"Thanks," I said. "So were you."

We smiled at each other, and I returned and joined her in bed. Round two was about to commence.

An hour later, I walked Elise home.

She was working at noon and needed to get ready.

I started walking back to my place without a worry in the world.

I didn't realize it, but it had been days since I had thought about New York.

17

THE KILLERS

The man that Chase thought was staring at him outside the restaurant may have been Italian, but he was not affiliated with the two men they saw commit the murder.

Tim and Chase's lunch took place the day after the murder, and the murderers had no idea who Tim and Chase were. At least, not yet.

In fact, at the same time that Tim and Chase were having their lunch, the two murderers were fifteen blocks uptown, eating in their own little secluded corner of a restaurant. They were discussing their options as well.

The stocky guy who had plunged the knife into the deceased went by the name of Lou. The taller, slightly older one was known as Charles. Despite their difference in height, Lou and Charles Sessions were actually brothers.

Although Charles was the older brother, he was often intimidated by his younger brother, Lou, as Lou was undeniably the more menacing and street-smart of the two. Lou also did most of the talking when these two were together; this lunch would be no different.

Although no patrons were within fifty feet of them, Lou still looked around before talking.

"I don't know how the fuck you let Freddy get out of the fucking truck. You had one job, and that was to keep him from getting out. How the fuck do you let him overpower you and get out? We should have disposed of him professionally like we used to do in the old days with Solari. Instead, we committed a murder with a knife in a back alley and had to leave the body there. That body should be at the bottom of the ocean, or at least at the bottom of the Hudson, and don't even get me started on running through Manhattan chasing some kids. We look like fucking amateurs!"

Lou said this last part with such ferocity that Charles had to look away from his gaze.

"I don't know how he got out of the car, Boss." Although he was the younger brother, Charles had come to refer to Lou occasionally as Boss. "He must have grabbed the lock and pushed me out at the same time."

"You're fucking useless. If you weren't my brother ... well, I don't want to think about what I'd do."

"I'm sorry, Boss."

Lou put his arm on his brother Charles's shoulder. "Let's forget it. That part is over. What we have to worry about now is finding out who the fuck those kids are and hoping we find them before they go to the police. Or better yet, they don't go to the police at all."

"But if they do, at least what you said at the end about Solari may throw the cops off a bit."

Lou smiled, thinking about their history and everything that led up to him saying the word Solari. "That's what you call thinking on your feet, Charles."

The busboy walked over and started filling up their water glasses. Lou and Charles didn't say a word and waited for the busboy to leave.

Lou continued, "We need to find out who these fucking kids are. And I know they're not kids, but that's what I'm going to call them. They didn't see us for very long, but certainly long enough to be able to recognize us if they ever saw a mug shot or, even worse, a lineup. After all that has transpired, I won't allow that to happen."

"What do you plan on doing?" Charles asked.

"I don't think there's that much we can do right now. I will call our mole in the police department and see if he can get any information. If they did go to the police, it would be the biggest mistake they've ever made. Our guy will find out their addresses, their pets' names, and how many times a week they jerk off. And then we will dispose of them. As I said, I won't let this be our downfall." Charles nodded, and Lou continued, "If they didn't go to the cops, they would be almost impossible to find."

"But if they didn't go to the police, then they aren't a threat to us." Charles looked unsure of himself, "Are they?"

"For a smart guy, you sure have some stupid observations now and then. There is no statute of limitations on murder, Charles. We don't know that in two months, one of them will grow a conscience and go to the cops. Then they look at the right mug shot, and we're fucked. As long as they are out there breathing, they are still a threat to us. But as I said, I won't let them get me."

Lou grabbed his brother by the shoulder for the second time. "And I'm not going to let them get my older brother either."

"You just tell me what to do, Boss. I want to get those kids as well."

"And if we catch them, we won't let them get away like Freddy almost did, will we?"

Once again, Charles feared looking into his younger brother's eyes. "No, Boss."

※

Lou went home that night and tried to rack his brain about ways to find the three kids.

Three spoiled brats who were at a place they shouldn't have been, and now they were causing Lou trouble. And what did you do to kids who did something they shouldn't? You punished them.

Only this wasn't going to be just a grounding. Although Lou reasoned, they might just end up in the ground.

Lou chuckled at this.

I should have been a stand-up comedian, he thought.

※

A few days passed, and Lou still hadn't heard back from his mole.

Lou took it as good news because if the kids had gone to the cops, he would have gotten back to him by now. Lou was starting to think they didn't go to the police.

They had just seen a brutal murder and then heard the name "Solari" mentioned. Even if these kids hadn't heard of Joseph Solari, it had to have crossed their minds that they had just seen a mafia-style murder.

Who in their right mind would want to testify against the mafia these days? It was safe to say that Lou was starting to feel safer by the day. This was better for the kids, too, because he wouldn't have to murder them.

Everybody wins.

※

Finally, after a whole week had passed, their mole called. Lou had been thinking less and less about it, and it took him a second to realize who was calling.

"Do you know who this is?" the voice said.

After a few seconds, Lou responded. "Yes, I know."

Lou knew the mole's name. He had been a business partner until a few years back, but Lou understood the discretion the mole wanted to use.

"In the case of the murder of Freddy Macon, there have been no witnesses to the murder who have stepped foot in the police department."

Lou smiled, or at least what passed for one with him. It wouldn't light up any marquee. He paused momentarily and realized he didn't like how the mole phrased his sentence. "What do you mean, none have stepped foot in the police department?"

"I'm impressed you picked that up, Louis," the mole said.

If it were anyone else, Lou would be furious, but he figured he'd let the mole call him by his full given name.

"I said that no witness has stepped foot in the police department because I've heard a rumor that they received a letter."

"A letter? A rumor? What are you saying?"

"Our police lieutenant likes to be inconspicuous, unlike some we've had recently. He doesn't let much out, so when I say it's a rumor, I have no concrete evidence that it is true. I have, however, heard from a few sources that the day after the murder of Freddy Macon, the department received a letter giving a primitive description of the murderers."

"Do they know who sent the letter?"

"From what I've heard, no."

"And the letter didn't name any names?"

"No. It doesn't sound like whoever sent the letter knows who did this. Just a description of the killers."

"Okay. Keep your ears open and call me if anything new comes up."

"Of course, Louis."

He let it slide the first time, but Lou did not enjoy being called Louis a second time. "If we want to use each other's given names, two can play at that game."

The mole sounded apologetic on the other end of the phone. "I'm sorry, Lou. I'm just trying to be funny."

"Remember, if we go down, you will join us."

"I understand. I'll call you when I hear something new. I'm sorry."

With that, the mole quickly got off the untraceable phone that he had called from.

※

LOU DECIDED TO CALL CHARLES AGAIN TO UPDATE HIM ON THE SITUATION. There were other people he could go to, but since he and Charles were the only members of his small crew present at the murder, Lou had decided to keep it between them.

Even the mole didn't know the particulars; he was just asked to take an interest in a specific case.

Lou contacted his brother, who agreed to meet him at Lou's house the next day. Charles seemed almost giddy on the phone and told Lou he wanted to run an idea by him.

Although not the most intelligent guy on the street, Charles had the occasional good idea.

Aloof? Yeah. Cowardly? Sometimes.

But this wouldn't be the first time Charles had come up with an idea that Lou hadn't thought of first.

<hr />

Charles arrived ten minutes early. Lou surmised it had something to do with his excitement on the phone.

They sat on a couch in Lou's family room. No one else was in the house. Lou had lived there alone since getting divorced five years ago.

"I know you've got something you want to tell me, Charles, but just listen to me first."

Lou told him about the conversation with the mole, the rumor of the letter, and the fact that they had no information on any of the witnesses.

"Is that good news?" Charlie asked.

"It's hard to say. Obviously, it's good news that they haven't physically gone to the police, but it scares me that they've sent them a letter. First off, that means the cops now know something. Who knows how well they could have described us, but any information the cops can deduce from the note is bad news for us. What scares me more is that now that the cops have this letter, they will use all the experts at their discretion to find out who wrote this letter. Fingerprint experts, paper experts, ink experts, DNA experts, whatever the fuck kind of experts they have. And these guys are good, so I'm afraid they will catch these kids. And then ... "

"Then listen to my plan," Charles interrupted.

You could count on one hand the number of times Charles had interrupted Lou over the years. Usually, Charles would get a scolding from his brother, but Lou, realizing this could be significant, decided to play nice this one time.

"Let's hear it, Charles."

"Here's what I've been thinking. We figured it was just random that they were walking down that back alley, but I think I have a guess as to why they may have been there." Charles paused.

"I'm listening."

"Well, these guys were young. They looked to be dressed nice, and it was a Saturday night after midnight. So my guess is they were out partying. Now, if you know that area, you know that traffic can be a bitch with all the cabs around late at night. It's often easier to get to 26th by being dropped near those alleys where we ran into them."

Lou liked where his brother was headed with this and didn't interrupt.

Charles continued, "If they were drinking, which I'd say is pretty likely, then I doubt they were driving themselves. So I'm guessing they were dropped off in a cab, town car, or an Uber right next to that alley. It would help them avoid the commotion at the front of 26th. "

Lou just listened, so Charles kept talking. "Obviously, no one would give their destination as some alley behind 26th or 27th street, so I went down to that area.

"The only three bars in that immediate area are Slimey's, The Belly Flop, and O'Rourke's. Even if they ended up being dropped off in the alley, when they gave their cab driver their destination, they would have given one of these three bars."

Lou was impressed and finally spoke up. "That's great thinking, Charles. One problem, though. It's not like the old days when there were five cab companies, and we knew people who ran four of them. There are probably thirty cab companies in Manhattan today if you include cabs, limos, and town cars. And don't forget Uber. Plus, people are less likely to give out information these days. How do you plan on getting it?"

"It's been over a week, so they might be suspicious as to why I'm finally calling now, but I think I've come up with something."

Lou let loose his hideous smile. "I think I'm going to like this."

"I'm going to say I'm a bartender at one of the three joints I mentioned, and I'll say I had a week off, and when I came back to work, the lost and found had a gold-plated iPhone. I'll say I immediately recognized it from this group of three guys who had been in late Saturday night a week ago. They were great tippers and all-around good guys, so I feel I owe them to try to get their phone back. I'll also say that they were pretty drunk, so I asked them if they were driving, and they told me they got a cab here and would get a cab home. I'll tell them they were dropped off after midnight on Saturday the 18th at either Slimey's, The Belly Flop, or O'Rourkes."

"It's a great idea, Charles, but I'd change one thing," Lou said.

"What's that?"

"I wouldn't say it was an iPhone, and I certainly wouldn't say it had a gold casing. Some poorly paid cab dispatcher isn't going to go out of his way to help someone get back a gold-plated iPhone."

"I could make up a sob story. Maybe tell them he had a picture of his deceased parents on the back of the case."

"Not pathetic enough," Lou said.

"I've got it. I'll say his phone case was the Multiple Sclerosis hotline. He told me that his younger sister was dying of it, and that's how I remembered the case when I saw it."

"Perfect," Lou said. He grabbed his brother by the shoulder, but it was out of love this time. "If you tell that sob story to the cab dispatchers, they'll be eating out of your hand."

"I'm glad you like the idea, Lou. I'll start calling them right when I get home."

"You've done well, Charles."

18

THE KILLERS

Lou kept in constant touch with Charles over the next few days. At one point, Charlie snapped at Lou and said, "How the hell can I make all these phone calls if you keep calling me every ten minutes?" Lou was proud. Charlie was growing up, standing his ground, and being a man. In his late forties, no less.

FIVE DAYS AFTER THEIR INITIAL CONVERSATION, CHARLES CALLED LOU AND said they should meet. He had the same giddiness as before, which told Lou he was about to get some good news. They met again at Lou's, and for the second consecutive time, Charlie did most of the talking.

Charles told Lou everything that had happened. He had called every cab company, town car, and limo service in Manhattan and contacted Uber corporate.

He used the story of the dying sister with multiple sclerosis. Most of the dispatchers, upon hearing this, went out of their way to help.

Unfortunately, most of them couldn't do much. First off, most of the cab companies didn't write down how many people got in the cab, so that couldn't narrow it down.

Secondly, Charles discovered that approximately half of all cab fares are paid in cash. If they had paid in cash, this was a wild goose chase. Luckily, everyone who paid for Uber had their card on file, and that was easy to track.

Despite the limitations, Charles persevered and told Lou that he had come up with four solid leads. Lou sat up as Charles took out a piece of paper.

"The first lead was an Uber. They had a drop-off at Slimey's just after midnight. Remember, the kids saw us at one. They could have been loitering for a while, you never know. The credit card was under someone named Tommy McCallister."

Charles paused briefly and then continued, "The second lead was a Yellow cab. They don't know how many people were in it, but it was dropped off at the Belly Flop at 12:55 a.m. That cab was paid for by a joint credit card, Mark and Sophia Wilk. Probably a husband and wife, but I'm including it anyway. Third, a limo that dropped off five people at about ten minutes to one. I included them because three could have broken off from the others. A Jacob Atticus paid for that limo."

Charles took a deep breath and continued, "The last and most promising lead was from Saxon's Town Cars. By some stroke of luck, the dispatcher I talked to happened to be driving a town car the night in question. He remembered three guys in their early thirties wanting to be dropped off in the back of O'Rourkes. They didn't want to go the long way around, so he dropped them off in the back of 25th. I don't need to tell you that O'Rourke's is on 27th, and we were on 26th. It makes perfect sense that they'd walk through that alley."

Lou was ready to give Charles a rare compliment, but he could tell his brother had something to add, so he held his tongue.

"At first, the dispatcher resisted giving me a name. After a few guilt trips about the guy's dying sister, he caved. The town car was paid for with a credit card by someone named Timothy J. Sawyer. I did a little research, and there are eleven Timothy Sawyer's in New York City, but only two Timothy J. Sawyer."

"Thank god for middle names," Lou chimed in.

"One Timothy J. Sawyer is seventy-one years old, and the second one is a thirty-two-year-old named Timothy James Sawyer and lives on 345 East 26th Ave., Suite 2B."

Lou jumped out of his seat. Charles hadn't seen him this excited in years.

"Fantastic work, Charles. I think it's about time we learn more about Timothy James Sawyer and his friends." Lou released another one of his evil grins. "Maybe we'll even pay him a visit sometime soon."

19
BRYCE

PARIS

If Elise and I were in a movie, the two weeks that followed us making love would have been the montage scene.

It would have consisted of shots of Elise and me in bed, at the Louvre, in bed, me watching Les Liaisons Dangereuses again, in bed, me writing at the cafe, us constantly laughing and having a good time, and you guessed it; us in bed again.

All this would be done over a cheesy synthesizer like we were straight out of an eighties movie.

So yeah, you could say that things were going well. We were getting very close and were both close to muttering the L word. And I don't mean "like."

However, the events of New York had entered back into my psyche, creating an awkward moment.

I was writing at Les Deux Magots and decided to Google "Anthony Solari," "Mafia murder in New York," and a few other things to see if anything popped up. Nothing did, but Elise surprised me from behind as I looked at the search results, so I shrewdly—or so I thought—proceeded to lower my laptop screen.

Unfortunately, I wasn't as subtle as I had hoped, and she immediately noticed.

"Wow, you're a little jumpy! Shutting your laptop like that. You're not a spy, are you?"

"Caught me!" I tried to play it off as if it was nothing. "I was sent to France to seduce you and discover the secrets of French theater."

She smiled, and I exhaled. "And here I thought I had seduced you."

I smiled back, but inside, I felt guilty.

Here I was, telling myself I would never lie to Elise, but I had left out a giant secret. It was just as bad as lying. I decided if I really cared for her, which I did, I had to tell her about what happened in New York.

If she decided to be done with me, it would be because I had been honest with her.

Her final performance of the play was on Saturday, and I had been planning a little two-day getaway for us. I promised myself I would tell her everything when we got back—no need to scare her before leaving on our brief vacation.

Plus, nothing seemed to be going on in New York.

20

THE KILLERS

Finding Timothy J. Sawyer had buoyed Lou and Charles's spirits. They were no longer on the defensive.

They were about to play offense, which is what Lou enjoyed most. He wasn't a man who would kill someone just to kill, but if someone were a threat to him, he would most certainly stand up for his own interest. And Tim Sawyer was a threat to him.

So, it was time for Lou to plan his demise. He wouldn't like doing it, but he wouldn't lose any sleep over it either.

Charles had helped find Tim, and Lou would never forget that. However, planning a murder was a bit out of Charles's expertise, so Lou would do it alone.

After thinking it over for a few days, he devised what he believed to be a foolproof plan and invited Charles over to his house.

CHARLES ARRIVED AND TOOK BACK HIS ROLE AS THE PASSIVE BROTHER. LOU had appreciated all Charles had done, but from then on, it was all Lou.

"So I've given this a lot of thought, and I think killing the three of them is the path we must take," Lou said.

Charles nodded, not surprised that his brother had come to this conclusion.

Lou continued, "I considered confronting Mr. Sawyer and telling him that if he, or any of his friends, ever went to the police, we would be forced to kill them, but even then, we'd still be living in fear. They could go behind our backs and turn themselves in whenever they wanted. We'd never know. And if we scared the shit out of them by threatening them, that's likely what they would do. The other thing I considered was doing nothing and hoping they didn't go to the police. I wanted to like this option more. You see, Charles, I'm not a cold-blooded killer. You know that. If we could get out of this and spare their lives, I'd be fine with that. The problem with doing nothing is, just like threatening them, we would never know if they went to the cops and our day was up. As I said before, there is no statute of limitations on murder."

Lou grabbed a sip of water and continued. "The fact that the police got a letter from one of the three means I can't assume they will stay quiet. When a small domino like that falls, it almost always means the others will fall also, and those dominoes end with us going to jail. That's what I'm trying to prevent here, Charles. I'm just a man looking out for his own self-interest. And his brother's."

For the third time, Charles just nodded, so Lou kept going.

"Since I can tell you'd just prefer to listen tonight, I'll go ahead and tell you what my plan is. I had to consider all potential plans and do a little reconnaissance to ensure the plan I came up with would work. I tried to think of something to enable us to do this all in a night's work. If we kill one of the three, you can be sure that when one of the other two hears about it, he will go straight to the cops. So we need to do this in one night. And I've come up with the perfect plan ... "

Charles finally decided to chime in. "Stop beating around the bush. Let's hear it!"

Even with them alone in the house, Lou leaned in closer to describe his brilliant, barbaric plan.

21

TIM

Tim had been thinking less and less about the gruesome murder he had witnessed three weeks ago. He figured if anything were going to happen, it would have already.

Plus, he just didn't envision any way that the cops (or the killers) could find him.

Tim prioritized getting his marriage back on track. Seeing someone get killed had caused him to reconsider some of his previous actions, and he had been making headway in regaining Gina's trust. He promised to settle down and behave like an adult. She seemed close to giving him a second chance.

Tim would never outwardly admit that witnessing a murder was a blessing, but it might just help him get his wife back.

He worried now and then about Chase. Chase had sent him two separate messages complaining about being followed.

This may have worried Tim if not for a recent incident.

Chase and he were out at a restaurant getting some lunch. Chase went to the bathroom, and as he returned to his seat, he looked like he'd seen a ghost.

"There was a guy who came to take a piss next to me in the bathroom. He looked just like the stocky guy who committed the stabbing."

Tim put his finger up to tell Chase to keep quiet. Their table had a good look at the bathroom, and about thirty seconds later, a guy walked out.

"That's the guy," Chase said.

The guy left the bathroom and walked by Tim and Chase's table. The guy was maybe twenty-five years old and Hispanic.

Chase realized he was way off and briefly buried his head in his hands.

"I'm sorry," he said.

Tim leaned in to whisper to Chase. "They have no idea who we are, Chase. Stop being so emotional and unstable. You remind me of a damn woman."

"Okay, Tim," Chase said, but without much conviction.

THREE DAYS HAD PASSED SINCE THAT EVENT, AND TIM TOOK IT AS A positive sign that Chase had not tried to contact him again.

Maybe Chase was starting to realize they were safe, and nobody would find out who they were. They had fled from the scene of a crime and saved themselves many headaches in the process.

And it was not over a crime that they had committed. Tim kept telling himself that and was happy with his decision not to go to the cops.

TIM WOKE UP THE NEXT MORNING AT FIVE A.M. AND WENT TO WORK AN hour earlier than usual.

There were two days left in the pay period, and Tim was close to breaking his earnings record. He knew if he had a great day, he might just break that record today.

Timothy J. Sawyer would be correct about that.

Unfortunately for him, his most proud day at work would also be his last.

22

THE KILLERS

Lou had explained his final plan to Charles, but he'd left out the devilish details about how he had constructed it. These are what Lou was most proud of.

When Charles initially told Lou Tim's name, Lou searched the internet for information. Since there were only two Timothy J. Sawyers in New York City, he felt it would be easy to find some information on the young Timothy.

The first thing that popped up on Google was a LinkedIn page for a Timothy J. Sawyer, who worked in New York City. The pic wasn't great, but it was a white man and in the general age range that Lou was looking for.

Lou hadn't got a good look at the guy who took off running first, so he figured that this might be him. This Timothy J. Sawyer was the junior vice president of a company called AssetMark Financial.

From there, Lou googled AssetMark Financial and found their location. Next, he used Google Maps to set up his likely route.

He'd have to scope out Tim's apartment complex to ensure he didn't go to the gym first, etc. He needed to narrow down a time when Tim would arrive home after a day of work. This wouldn't be Lou's first stakeout.

Next, Lou googled *"Timothy J. Sawyer Facebook."* He had to click through a few before finding a picture that looked similar to the one he had previously seen on LinkedIn. He hit a minor roadblock when he saw that this user had set his Facebook profile to private.

No problem, Lou thought, opening a fake Facebook profile he was forced to use occasionally. The profile picture was of a gorgeous brunette girl with whom any hot-blooded male would love to be friends.

He had posted a few other pics of her, so the profile looked legitimate. He clicked on Timothy J. Sawyer's profile from the brunette's Facebook account and clicked "Add Friend."

"You're a young, good-looking guy with a job in finance in New York City. I hope you think with your dick," Lou said aloud.

While he waited for the friend request to be accepted, he researched a little about Tim's apartment complex. Judging by the astronomical rent they charged and the name of the complex (Tier One Towers), he gathered it was pretty high-end.

He called Tier One Towers pretending to be interested in a lease and found out that there was no parking garage on site but that people who owned a car used a private parking garage a block and a half down the street.

This was New York, so there was a good chance Tim used public transportation, but something about him made Lou think he owned a car.

As Lou considered the parking garage and the apartment complex, he began to form an inkling of a plan. It wasn't foolproof, but not many multiple murder plots were. However, it was contingent on Tim having a car.

The only problem Lou envisioned was that he'd have to use a third person. This was unavoidable since Tim and his friends had seen Lou and Charles.

He had considered hiring someone to shoot Timothy on his way to work or to stage a mugging, but then Timothy's friends would find out and go straight to the police.

His plan had to consist of getting all three of them at once. As he reviewed his plan's intricacies, he heard a little alert from his computer.

Tim had taken the bait and accepted the friend request from "Kimberly Cousins."

With Tim accepting "Kimberly's" friend request, Lou could now view Tim's pictures and status updates. Lou went to Tim's pictures and recognized the guy who ran away right after Tim, the guy they didn't follow.

I'll be damned, Lou thought! Charles had done it. Against all odds, they had found the guys who had witnessed them commit murder.

Lou had thought it would be like finding a needle in a haystack. It had turned out to be far easier.

The guy's name was Chase Andrews, and there were several pictures of him and Tim together. These two appeared to be pretty tight.

There was no mistaken that this was the guy. Lou had only seen him for a few seconds, but a face gets etched in your memory in a time like that.

He clicked on Chase's Facebook profile, but his was also private. He briefly considered using the "Kimberly Cousins" account to add him, but it was too big a risk.

If they talked or, even worse, were together right now, they might realize something was up. He decided it wasn't necessary.

He went back to Tim's profile and looked under photo albums. One was titled "My New Baby!" but the pictures were of a beautiful new Range Rover, not a newborn. He must have had thirty photos with the sleek, black truck.

This helped confirm one of Lou's suspicions. Tim did own a car!

Lou knew he'd be staking out the parking garage. Someone wouldn't buy a beautiful car like this and not drive it around town.

He was about to check Tim's status updates when he heard another alert. Tim had messaged "Kimberly."

Tim: *'I'd usually remember a girl as beautiful as you!!! Where did we meet?'*

Lou only needed a few more minutes on Tim's Facebook page before he ended their "friendship," but he figured he'd respond just to be safe.

"Kimberly": *'You don't remember? You were a bad boy.'*

As he let Tim stew over that, Lou went back and looked at status updates from around the time of the murder. Tim didn't post much, so this ended up being quite easy.

Two days before the murder, Tim had posted, "College Reunion in two days!" and tagged Chase Andrews and Bryce Connor in an old picture of the three of them.

Bryce Connor was undoubtedly the third man—the one they had chased through Manhattan.

"God, I am good," Lou muttered to himself.

He clicked on Bryce Connor's profile but received an alert saying, "This profile has been deleted."

It was a minor setback, Lou thought. Just as with Chase, he didn't need Bryce's Facebook info to make his plan work. But he did have Bryce's name now, and Lou knew what he looked like.

Before he logged out, Lou decided to needle Tim.

Kimberly: *'If you can't remember me, then I guess there is no point in being friends."* With that, Lou pressed send and deleted Timothy J. Sawyer as a friend.

<hr />

AFTER SCOPING OUT THE PARKING GARAGE AND THE APARTMENT COMPLEX for a few nights, Lou had finalized his plan.

He invited Charles and Paul, an occasional lackey of theirs, over for dinner at his house on Thursday.

Paul was a childhood friend from the neighborhood who always admired the Sessions brothers. Although he wasn't very smart, he followed orders and didn't cause any trouble.

He was precisely what Lou needed. He had helped them over the years when necessary, and Lou knew he would jump at the chance to help them.

Paul wasn't afraid of violence, and that was a prerequisite.

DEBUT NOVEL

On Thursday night, Charles and Paul arrived within a minute of each other. He'd ordered a pepperoni pizza and put paper plates, a pitcher of water, and the pizza on the table before them. They each grabbed a slice and took a bite, nodding their approval.

Over the next several minutes, Lou proceeded to tell Paul how the Freddy Macon murder had gone horribly wrong, and three young men had stumbled upon them committing a murder.

He explained that he had thought of other ways to diffuse the situation but felt that eliminating the three of them was the only way to ensure their safety.

Although the police were sent a letter, they had done nothing to contact Lou or Charles, so he knew they weren't suspects. At least not yet.

That meant their problems would disappear if the three witnesses were disposed of. He described all he had learned from Tim's Facebook account, how he knew Chase Andrews was the second guy who ran, and that Bryce Connor was the man they chased through the streets of Manhattan.

He had given Paul the backstory, and now Paul and Charles waited patiently for the plan.

Lou paused, stood up from his chair, and started talking. "First off, I've decided this will go down tomorrow night. There's no reason to go through this weekend, giving them more time to go to the police. So spend the night putting your game face on or whatever you have to do. Because this is a go tomorrow. Is there any problem with that?"

Lou looked at Paul, knowing his brother was already in.

Paul shrugged. "I didn't think I was coming here to play Tiddly Winks. I'm in."

Lou grabbed a sip of water and continued, "Good. Tim gets back from work at about six p.m. each night. I've staked out his place for a few days now, and there's no reason to think tomorrow will be any different. He parks a Range Rover at a garage a block and a half from his apartment and then walks from there. It's on a reasonably quiet street in Manhattan, which should help us with our plan. Paul, I need you to drive the Lincoln Continental. It looks like a cop car, and that's what you will pretend to be."

Paul looked on, uncertain what to make of Lou's words. "You think I can pass for a cop?"

"No question. You look like a fat old Irish cop. No offense."

If Paul was offended, he wasn't going to tell Lou.

"After what I said at the murder scene, Tim may be suspicious of an Italian guy. It helps that you're even less Italian than us. Plus, he has seen Charles and I. It has to be you. I have a few cops' uniforms courtesy of our friend in the police department. Once you are wearing that, he won't question you."

"So what am I supposed to do?"

"You're going to park the car in this little alley between the parking garage and his apartment complex. Charles and I will be in the back of the Lincoln. You will get out and show him the badge when he approaches your car. Tell him that you are a police officer and need a few minutes. Hopefully, he will willingly get in the car. If he puts up any sort of argument, you tell him that you think his life might be in danger. Mention that the police know what he saw. I'd even add that you aren't sure if his apartment is safe at the moment. He will be scared, and I can almost guarantee he will get in the car. When he does, you will immediately lock the doors, and Charles here will put a chloroform-laden cloth over his mouth. I will also have a Taser, just in case. Trust me, if you get him in the car, he will not get out!"

It was Charles's time to chime in. "What if he doesn't agree to get in the car?"

"He witnessed a murder. I'm sure he's considered the possibility the police might come for him at some point. And then he'll see a guy in uniform, a car that looks like a cop car, and be told that his apartment may not be safe. What do you think he's going to do?"

"I'll make sure he gets in that car," Paul said.

"That's the confidence I'm looking for," Lou said as he patted Paul on the back.

"And what about his friends? Chase and Bryce, right?" Paul asked.

"We are going to drive Tim down by the docks. There's an abandoned warehouse there. No one ever uses it. No cops. No civilians. Not even any bums. We will tie Tim up, get his cell phone, and text Chase and Bryce. We'll say, "Hey, we need to talk about what we saw. Something has come up. I'm with a few cops, and we have to meet away from the station; they have a mole at the downtown station, and they are afraid we'd be in danger there.""

"And we do have a mole," Charles joked.

Lou didn't like being interrupted, but even he had to chuckle. "That's right, Charles. We do."

Paul looked on, not as easily convinced.

"What if his friends don't buy it? Or what if they call Tim back instead of texting?"

Lou stared intently at Paul.

"It will work, Paul. Everyone texts these days. And if, by some chance, Tim has to talk on the phone, he will do whatever we say. After all, he'll have a gun pointed at his head."

Paul seemed to relax. "Okay, whatever you say, Lou. I trust you."

"My plan will work. I'm sure of it. And Charles, why not bring a few tools just in case Mr. Sawyer isn't as easy to convince as I hope."

Charles knew what his brother meant by "tools."

Lou went over a few more contingencies that might come up.

He was outwardly confident but couldn't shake the feeling that something very minor had been overlooked; he just couldn't identify it.

23

TIM

Tim got up early on the last Friday of his life. He shit, shaved, and showered, in that order, and then put on a good-looking suit. He stared at himself in the mirror and smiled. He looked sharp.

He got to AssetMark Financial and strutted through the halls. Although he was only a junior vice president, people within the company all knew he would continue to rise quickly.

The girls couldn't help but glance at him as he walked. He was tall, dark, handsome, and, most importantly, he walked around like he owned the place, which he hoped he would someday.

Tim noticed the stares from the fairer sex, but for one of the rare times in his life, he didn't acknowledge their glances. After all, he was trying to get Gina back. That was the most important thing in his life right now.

If he wanted to cheat in the future, that would always be available to him. While women grew old, men just grew more distinguished. He laughed at how lucky he was to be a good-looking white male. They caught all the breaks.

It ended up being quite a long day at work for Tim. He eventually secured the client he had been working on all week but had to work an hour longer than usual.

He almost became upset until he realized that the client had pushed him

89

over the edge. Tim had just completed his most profitable pay period yet, and he knew that senior vice president was just around the corner.

He left the office to a chorus of cheers. Someone told those remaining that Tim had just passed a personal milestone. He raised his hand in appreciation and glanced briefly at the females clapping.

I'm not a eunuch just yet, he thought.

He strode to his Range Rover with a big smile on his face.

This was a great day!

Now, it was time to go home, call Gina, and continue making progress in hopes of winning her back. It was going to happen soon; Tim just knew it.

AS USUAL, HE CAUGHT TRAFFIC DRIVING HOME.

He often wondered why he even owned a car in New York City. It would have been easier to pay for subways and cabbies, which would be way cheaper than the ridiculous monthly amount he paid for the parking garage.

He probably paid more in parking fees than most people paid in rent. Tim shrugged. He just had his biggest pay period ever. Who was he to complain?

Tim pulled up to the aforementioned garage and parked the Range Rover. He got out of the car and started taking his usual walk toward his high-rise building.

He grabbed his phone out of his pocket and was ready to call Gina when he looked up just ahead of him and saw a police officer standing next to an undercover cop car.

The officer stepped out of the car. He was about fifty and looked like your prototypical cop—probably Irish.

"Is your name Timothy J. Sawyer?" he asked.

Fuck! Tim swore to himself. How the hell did they find out?

"What do you need, Officer?" Tim asked.

"We think you may have witnessed a murder three weeks ago, and we'd like to ask you a few questions about it."

Tim had always been a stubborn, cocky guy, and that wouldn't stop just because there was a cop in front of him.

"And what if I said I don't want to go with you?"

"Mr. Sawyer, we're afraid your life may be in danger as we speak. We can't even be sure that your apartment is safe."

That gave Tim time to consider his options, but he didn't have many. The cops were better than the alternative.

"Okay. Okay."

Tim had a million things racing through his head, but what else was he supposed to do? Risk going to his apartment? Screw that!

If he went with the cops, he might get in a bit of trouble but it's not like

Chase, Bryce, and he did anything terribly wrong. A lot of people wouldn't want to be state's witness #1 in a murder case.

They would probably get off with a slap on the wrist from the courts. If the killers were truly staking out his apartment, he wouldn't be so lucky.

Begrudgingly, Tim moved to enter the car. As he was about to get in, he asked himself a different question. *Why would a uniformed police officer cop have an undercover car?*

"Get in," the cop said.

Tim grabbed the back door, but the officer motioned toward the front door. Tim looked at the officer and wondered why.

"We're not arresting you. If we were, then we throw you in the back."

Tim liked that answer. He was not being arrested and was confident that he would get out of this mess.

Tim went to the front door and opened it. As he sat down, the police officer immediately locked Tim's door, and someone from the back seat grabbed his head and put a towel over his face.

Tim tried to resist but got light-headed almost immediately from the smell of the towel. Before he passed out, he looked in the rearview mirror and recognized the face.

It wasn't the cops he was dealing with.

I've made a colossal mistake.

24

THE KILLERS

Lou had a few tense moments before they got Tim into the car.
Tim still hadn't appeared an hour after Lou had expected him. Lou was afraid maybe he had gone to the gym or, even worse, left on vacation. It was Friday, after all. Luckily, just as Lou started panicking, he saw the Range Rover pulling into the garage.

The other moment was when Paul told him to get in the car. Lou couldn't hear anything, but he saw Paul motion toward the car, so he knew what point of the conversation they were in.

Tim looked apprehensive, and for a moment, Lou was afraid he might just walk away.

As Lou expected, though, when Paul mentioned his apartment might be unsafe, Tim wasn't left with much of an option.

When they finally got him in the car, the chloroform only took a few seconds to knock him out. Before he went under, Lou saw the recognition in Tim's eyes. He knew who he was dealing with now.

He instructed Paul to follow every conceivable rule of the road. Getting pulled over with a guy knocked out in the passenger seat of a car driven by a fake police officer wouldn't end well. Paul did as he was told—almost too well. He slowed too far below the speed limit at one point, and Lou told him to pick it up a little.

When they arrived at the vacated docks, no one was around, just as Lou had predicted. They exited the car and pushed open the massive sliding warehouse door.

The warehouse Lou had selected was the last in the row, probably sixty feet wide and a few hundred feet deep. Lou had Paul drive the car inside, and they slid the door back to its closed position.

Charles knew what he was supposed to do: put Tim on a chair and thoroughly duct-tape his arms, legs, and mouth. He removed his wallet and, more importantly, his cell phone before he taped him to the chair.

Paul was supposed to hang out for now, but he had to stay in uniform for when the others arrived.

Charles had brought some pliers, a pen knife, a small blow torch, and a few other items in case they felt the need to torture. Charles hoped it wouldn't come to this but knew if Lou asked him to do it, he would.

Lou motioned to Charles to try to wake Tim up.

He was still out of it, but he was slowly coming around. Charles slapped him and threw water at him, and Tim woke up.

His eyes were full of pure terror as he looked down at his arms and feet taped to the chair.

He tried to move his arms but realized it would be useless. A dire thought entered his mind: He reminded himself of the police officer who is tied up in *Reservoir Dogs*. Even the inside of the abandoned warehouse looked similar.

Lou walked over to stand beside Tim, smiling his hideous smile.

"Hello, Timothy," Lou started. "You've been a hard man to track down. I could bore you with all the details of how we found you, but let me just thank you for paying for your town car with a credit card the night you happened upon us."

You've got to be fucking kidding me, Tim thought.

"But that's neither here nor there. What's important is that you are here now. And I will only say this once, so listen very carefully. If you are one-hundred percent honest with me, you will leave here alive."

Tim nodded. He would have breathed a sigh of relief if he could, but breathing was difficult with the tape around his mouth. He had always had trouble breathing through his nose but had no choice.

"Now, I'm going to take the tape from your mouth and ask you a few questions. There is no one near us, so screaming would be futile. It would also be fatal for you, so don't try it."

Tim nodded.

Just do what they want. If they wanted me dead, they would have done it already.

"Okay. I'm going to take it off. Remember not to say anything unless I ask you to."

Lou ripped off the tape, which stung like hell, but Tim didn't yell or complain. He had more important things on his mind.

"I'll get straight to the point, Timothy," Lou said. "What were the names of the other two people you were with that night?"

Tim paused for a moment.

Do I lie? They found me. They must have figured out who the other two were. But what if they hadn't? I'd be putting my friends in harm's way.

Lou looked at him intently. "Chase and Bryce are their names, I believe."

Lou was glad Tim didn't answer immediately. He was able to show him that he held all the cards. It might prevent Tim from lying later on.

"Yes, that's right," Tim quietly muttered.

"So my goal is to get the three of you here today and explain in person that if you guys ever say word one to the cops or send another letter to them, I will kill you all."

"I never sent a letter to the cops!" Tim said a bit too loudly.

"Don't make me put the tape back on."

Tim talked much quieter. "I'm sorry. I never sent a letter to the police."

"One of you did."

"Well, it wasn't me. Listen, I would never go to the police. I've forgotten that anything even happened. I'm sure the guy deserved whatever he got. I don't want to meddle in other people's business. I'm trying to get my marriage back together. Do you think I want to deal with cops and lawyers? You have nothing to fear from me."

"That's what I like to hear, Timothy. But I want to make sure your friends think similarly. So we're going to text them from your phone and get them down here. If they promise to keep their mouths shut like you, we will let you all go."

They're going to get us together and then kill us, Tim thought. *He has no plans on letting us go.*

Tim considered what he could do. With his text, he could subtly alert Chase that something was wrong, Chase could notify the police, and Tim could potentially be saved.

Also, once they understood that Bryce wasn't even in the country, they might abort their plan.

Tim had to hang on to those two possibilities. The alternative was too scary to consider.

"I'll text Chase for you, but good luck getting ahold of Bryce."

"What do you mean?" Lou asked. He looked pissed.

"Bryce was in town for one night. He flew to Paris the next day."

Tim regretted saying Paris almost immediately. He should have just said Europe.

And that's when Lou remembered why he had a nagging feeling that he was overlooking something. Tim's status update said, "College Reunion." You don't have a reunion if you all live in the same city. Someone was visiting.

Fuck! Lou cursed at himself. *How could I overlook something so obvious? They were never going to get all three of them tonight!*

Lou grabbed Tim's phone, scrolled through until he saw the name Bryce, and pressed dial. "The number you dialed is no longer in service," the automated voice said.

"I'm not lying," Tim said.

Maybe I'm gaining the upper hand here, Tim thought to himself. *Now, let them allow you to text Chase, and you can find a way to warn him. They will be watching what I text. What could I say? What would alert him? C'mon, think of something!*

And then Tim did think of something.

This guy has been calling me Timothy the whole time. They don't know I go by Tim. I'll start my text by saying, "Hey, it's Timothy." I'd never begin a text like that. Chase knows that. He has known me long enough to know something would be off. That's what I have to do. It's subtle, but it could work!

"Timothy, I do believe you are telling us the truth about Bryce."

"I am. I promise. If you'll let me text Chase, I can get him here, and I promise he'll swear never to say anything. And you don't have to worry about Bryce. He's out of the country after all."

Lou didn't like that Tim had twice asked to text Chase himself.

"We're going to get Chase, all right, but you won't be the one texting him."

Tim tried not to show his disappointment as his heart sank. "He'll listen to me. I can get him here."

"You're crazy if you think I'll give you the phone. But okay, I'll play along. What would you text him?"

This is your chance, Tim. Use it wisely.

"Hey, it's Timothy. The cops know what we saw. They took me down by the docks."

Tim saw Lou typing his words on the phone. He thought his plan just might work.

Tim continued, "They are afraid of the mafia and thought they might be staking out police headquarters, so they brought me down to the docks. Come here as soon as possible, and they'll explain everything."

Lou and Charles couldn't help but smile when they heard him say, "Solari." Tim misinterpreted this to mean they liked the message.

Lou read his own version aloud. "Hey, it's Timothy. The cops know what we saw. They brought me down by the docks because they thought the mafia might be staking out police headquarters. Come down here as soon as possible, and they'll explain everything." He paused. "I like it, except for one thing."

"What's that," Tim asked as his heart sank again.

"The 'This is Timothy' part sounds a little hokie. He knows who is texting him, so there is no need to include that."

Lou smiled directly at Tim as if he knew something. He then patted him on the shoulder. "The rest I will use, though."

Lou deleted the part saying Timothy, showed Tim the text, and then pressed send.

He leaned toward Tim and whispered, "I read the comments on your Facebook posts. No one ever called you Timothy. Only Tim. And by the way, Kimberly Cousins says hello."

For the third time in as many minutes, Tim's heart sank.

25

CHASE

Chase had been thinking lately of the quote, "Just because you're paranoid, doesn't mean they're not after you."

He remembered it from a Nirvana song but was pretty sure they stole it from someone else. He'd have to look that up.

To him, every Italian guy he passed on the street was after him, and every police officer knew he had done something wrong.

He had talked to Tim several times about it, but there was no convincing Tim they should go to the cops.

He had contemplated going to them himself, but every time he got the courage to do it, he felt he was stabbing his best friend in the back. He was considering it more every day, though. He couldn't keep dealing with this paranoia. Or, at least, he hoped it was only paranoia.

He was sitting next to his wife, Victoria, when Tim sent a text.

"The cops know what we saw. They brought me down by the docks because they thought the mafia might be staking out police headquarters. Come down here as soon as possible, and they'll explain everything."

His initial reaction was one of relief. It's not like he wanted to testify in a murder trial, but it was better than the alternative. At least it was for him.

He didn't really want to go down by the docks on a Friday night, but if the mafia was monitoring the police, he understood why they were being overly protective.

Chase realized there were several warehouses down by the docks, so he texted Tim back.

"*Where exactly? A lot of empty space down there.*"

Within a few seconds, he received a text back:

"*Just park at 3rd & Buck and walk down toward the water.*"

At this point, if Chase had been a bit more insightful, he would have realized that something was amiss. Lou, pretending to be Tim, had texted, "*Park at 3rd & Buck.*"

Chase, however, unlike Tim, did not have a car.

If Tim had really been the one texting Chase, he would have said, "*Have the cab drop you off at 3rd & Buck,*" or something to that effect.

It was something very small and would be tough to pick up on under normal circumstances. With all that was going through Chase's mind, it flew right over him.

"*Okay. I'll be there as soon as I can.*" Chase texted back.

Chase explained to Victoria that he wouldn't be long.

"What is it?" Victoria asked.

"Something came up with Tim."

"That boy just can't stay out of trouble, can he?"

"It's nothing. I'll be back before you know it."

❧

CHASE CALLED AN UBER AND DECIDED TO WAIT OUTSIDE FOR IT. THERE WAS no reason to stay inside and continue fighting with his pregnant wife.

As Chase waited, he started thinking of what penalties the three of them would suffer at the hands of the law. He couldn't imagine they would get much jail time, if any.

They were put in a shitty situation; any judge or jury would understand that. However, he had resigned himself to the fact that what happened at the 20/20 club would inevitably come out.

So he did a little cocaine off an escort's breasts? It wasn't the worst sin ever committed. He wouldn't admit to having sex with an escort. No one else was there when that occurred besides the woman in question, of course.

Wait, they wouldn't get the escorts to testify, would they?

Chase's thoughts were racing a mile a minute. He hated living like this and couldn't wait to get it over with.

He saw his Uber approaching, raised his hand, and got in the cab.

"Where to?" the Uber driver asked.

"To the docks down by the Hudson," Chase responded.

"Big party down there on a Friday night?" the Uber driver asked sarcastically.

Chase didn't have the time for this right now.

"Just drive."

After fifteen minutes of driving and exchanging no words, Chase finally told the Uber driver where to drop him off.

As he exited the car, Chase said to the Uber driver, "Here's a tip."

The Uber driver looked back, expecting a few dollars from Chase, but Chase continued talking instead. "Don't offend your customers. There's your tip for the day."

Chase slammed the door but didn't feel good about himself. All this stress was getting to him.

I'm not a jerk, but I'm certainly acting like one right now. What is that phrase about a person's real character coming out in the worst of times? If that's the case, I'm failing miserably.

As Chase beat himself up over his rudeness, he walked toward the water. After about twenty seconds, a police officer stood about a hundred yards away.

Chase walked closer and cautiously asked, "Where's Tim?"

"He's in here," the officer said, motioning Chase toward an open warehouse door. "Sorry, we had to have you guys come here. We fear there's a mole in the department downtown. And if we think we know who was behind the murder you witnessed, trust me, you don't want to deal with them."

Chase didn't know how to explain it but was almost giddy with anticipation. Giddy wasn't the right word, but he was looking forward to this no longer burdening him.

And he would find out who committed the murder he had witnessed. "It was the mafia, wasn't it?" he asked.

"You'll find out very soon," the officer said and gestured for Chase to walk with him through the warehouse door.

Chase did as instructed and walked in.

Upon entering, he looked to his left and saw Tim tied to a chair. The man who committed the murder was standing right next to him.

Chase knew this was a horrible situation but didn't know what to do. Chase looked at Tim and saw his eyes dart back and to his right. He realized he was trying to alert him to something.

The problem was that Chase had turned to his left when he saw Tim, so he couldn't see what was coming from behind him on the right.

Chase finally realized why Tim was darting his eyes to the right, alerting Chase to look in that direction.

As he did, Chase thought he saw someone raising a handgun out of the corner of his eye but then realized it was too long to be a handgun.

That's when Chase had the final thought of his life.

Unless that's a silencer attached to the end of it.

26

TIM

Tim decided he wasn't going to go out like a chump.

If they killed him, so be it, but he would at least go out fighting. Once the murderer sent Chase the text, Tim figured he had about twenty minutes until Chase got there.

Tim needed to devise a plan to alert Chase as the text had not worked. If he was fortunate, Chase might escape, and the murderers would have to abort their plans. It was a long shot, but it was Tim's only hope.

When Charles put the tape back over his mouth, Tim repeatedly tried to jab the duct tape with his tongue. Unfortunately, the tip of his tongue could barely reach the tape, and it would be nearly impossible to puncture it. He continued trying but to no avail.

A few minutes later, the three of them huddled together: Lou (who, to Tim, was just Killer #1), Charles (Killer #2), and The Fake Cop.

The Fake Cop went outside, and "Killer #2" hid behind the corner where the large door would shut. Tim realized their grotesque plan.

When Chase entered the warehouse, he'd naturally look over and see Tim and be blind to "Killer #2" behind him. He saw "Murderer #2" attaching a long silencer to a gun.

A shiver went up Tim's spine.

He continued trying to puncture the duct tape, but it was truly a lost cause. He had to think of a Plan B. He felt that maybe when he heard Chase approaching, he could thrash his chair in hopes of falling over, and if it made enough noise, maybe, just maybe, Chase would realize something was up, and he'd run before it was too late.

It would be his, and by extension, Tim's last chance.

❧

Ten more minutes passed.

"Killer #1" was standing right next to Tim when he heard people talking outside of the warehouse. He couldn't rush it. He had to ensure Chase was close enough to hear his chair tumble over.

The voices came closer. Thirty feet. Twenty-five feet. Twenty feet. Fifteen feet.

When they sounded like they were about ten feet away, Tim shook his shoulders and legs as violently as he could. His arms and legs were taped so tight to the chair that it was hard to gain much momentum.

Instead of falling over immediately, the chair first swayed from side to side. It was about to fall over when "Killer #1" noticed it, jumped toward the chair, and grabbed the back of it, stabilizing it.

Tim was a beaten man, but he thought of one last idea.

A few seconds later, Chase entered the warehouse and caught Tim's eye. Tim bobbed his head and darted his eyes as if to say to Chase, "Watch out behind you!"

Chase caught his eyes and realized that Tim was trying to warn him.

Unfortunately, "Killer #2" was already behind him, raising the gun, and even though Chase tried to swivel as fast as he possibly could, it was too late.

"Killer #2" shot Chase in the head, and Chase went down to the ground.

Within seconds, a pool of blood formed around Chase's dead body.

Tim dropped his head and started crying. In his mind, he said his goodbyes to his parents, wife, and infant child.

He asked himself how it had ever come to this. He wasn't a saint by a long shot, but he didn't deserve this. He just hoped they would make it quick.

Lou came over and removed the duct tape.

In a flat monotone, Tim said, "Let's just get this over with."

It wouldn't happen quite as soon as Tim had hoped.

27

THE KILLERS

Lou had a few questions for Tim before he was going to do away with him, so he removed the duct tape after killing Chase.

He didn't relish torture, but he had to ensure that Tim told the truth about Bryce. He kept the tools nearby to warn Tim of what would happen if he didn't cooperate.

It didn't take long for Lou to realize that Tim was telling the truth about everything. He hadn't written a letter to the police, and Chase likely hadn't, either.

Lou also became convinced that Bryce was in Paris and probably wrote the letter.

Tim's end came shortly after that.

As usual, when he was forced to kill, Lou thought that movies always got it wrong. There was never a late-inning comeback, a last-second three-pointer.

People didn't get out of handcuffs, and guns didn't lock up at opportune times.

There was never an unexpected last stand, and there wouldn't be one for Tim.

All things considered, Lou thought Tim went out like a man. Not that it mattered, but he didn't whine or beg like many others. A gunshot to the head ended it.

❦

Next up was the all-important cleanup. Many more criminals were caught by the police after the fact than during the commission of a crime. Plus, after the debacle with Freddy Macon, Lou was adamant they wouldn't fuck this up.

The first thing Lou did was throw Paul some gloves. He and his brother had been wearing them the whole time, but they thought a police officer with gloves might look suspicious, so they had Paul hold off.

With that part of the operation over, it was time for Paul to put them on. If the cops ever found the bodies or the crime scene, which Lou highly doubted, they might as well not leave any DNA behind.

He had Paul and Charles begin cleaning up the blood surrounding their bodies. He had brought a huge trunk in the Lincoln containing many cleaning supplies and gave them what they needed. The trunk was also brought for a different reason and would be used later.

Lou was in charge of dismantling the chair Tim had been taped to. This object may have contained some of their DNA, and Lou ensured it would be disposed of correctly. He started sawing the legs into smaller pieces.

"I hope these are the only legs we will have to saw tonight," he chuckled.

"What's so funny at a time like this?" Charles asked.

"Don't worry about it!" Lou said. "Just keep mopping up that blood."

"We're making progress," Paul chimed in.

❦

Twenty minutes later, they were done. Lou came over and looked. There were minute traces of blood on the cement, but that was inevitable.

It was barely noticeable, and the odds were so extreme that anyone would ever end up suspecting this warehouse that he was okay with it.

After all, it's not like he could just call in Winston Wolf to finish cleaning up the mess.

❦

The next part was a little tricky, but he knew from experience that it could work. He motioned for Paul and Tim to get the bodies and put them in the trunk. It might be a tight squeeze to fit both Tim and Chase in the trunk, but he didn't think they'd mind.

There I go again, Lou thought.

I really, really, really should have been a comedian. I kill myself. Actually, no I kill others. I'll call myself "The Killmedian." Hahaha. I should write this shit down.

"And be sure not to spill any more blood as you bring them over," Lou said.

He removed the clothes he had in the trunk and watched as Paul and Charles carried the bodies and put them in the massive trunk.

They had to contort some body parts in awkward positions, but eventually, they fit both bodies in the trunk. There would be no sawing legs tonight.

"Now what?" Charles asked.

"We wait."

"Why? There's no one around here," Paul interrupted.

Lou didn't like to be interrupted.

"Because I don't want to take any chances, Paul. We sit here for another hour or two, and then we will dispose of the bodies. And while we are waiting, I need you guys to go ahead and strip out of those clothes."

"What?" Paul asked.

"Are you fucking dense? You guys have blood stains all over your shirts. I brought clothes for you to change into."

Lou pointed to the clothes.

Lou locked both latches on the trunk as the other two changed out of their clothes. The trunk had been modified so that each side had a slight crack.

Thus, when they put it in the river it would absorb water and sink to the bottom. The last thing they wanted was a big trunk full of two bodies floating down the Hudson.

⁂

WHEN CHARLES AND LOU FINISHED CHANGING, LOU GRABBED THEIR OLD clothes and put them in the bag, which also held the remnants of the chair.

He had considered putting the bag in the trunk, but he thought they still wouldn't know who committed the crime if they somehow found the trunk.

No reason to leave the clothes with their DNA on them.

Instead, Lou would have a nice little bonfire when he got home tonight.

⁂

AFTER WAITING FOR TWO HOURS, LOU TOLD THEM IT WAS TIME. THE THREE of them carried the trunk down the little embankment to the edge of the Hudson River.

It was heavy as all hell, but what choice did they have? They stopped a few times to rest but eventually reached the river's edge.

Lou instructed Charles and Paul to hold the trunk in the water until it had gained a lot of weight and then push it out as far as they could.

"If that fucking thing doesn't sink and I see it floating away, I will shoot you guys dead right here," Lou said.

Paul had no doubt he meant what he said.

Charles and Paul walked to the edge of the Hudson. They held the trunk in the water and let it gradually fill up.

The Hudson River got deep quickly, so they weren't in danger of the trunk getting stuck and sticking above water for all to see.

They waited another minute until they could tell that the trunk had taken on enough water and would certainly sink.

Charles and Paul tried to give it a shove farther out, but it was a feeble attempt since it was so damn heavy at this point.

It did, however, immediately sink, and the three of them watched as the bottom went down, the top went up, and then the top slid down and disappeared underneath the water. Lou was reminded of the movie *Titanic*.

Charles and Paul walked up a few feet to meet Lou. He hugged both of them and said, "You guys did a great job."

This meant a lot to both of them. They returned to the warehouse, took the car out, shut the door behind them, and drove home.

As they drove, Lou went back over everything in his mind and was pretty sure they had committed the perfect murders.

And while they didn't realize it yet, they had made two tiny, yet crucial, mistakes.

Ironically, one of the mistakes was the same thing that led them to Tim and Chase in the first place.

WHEN LOU GOT HOME, HE LIT TWO MATCHES.

He threw the first one in his outdoor bonfire pit, which included all of their clothes and the chair's sawed-down legs. As soon as it hit the accelerant, the fire rose in a big flame.

With the second match, he lit a cigar. He leaned back, kicked his legs up, and enjoyed the bonfire. He was content.

The business of looking at flights to Paris could wait until the morning.

28
BRYCE

PARIS

The final showing of Les Liaisons Dangereuses was more of the same. And I meant that in a good way. Elise stole the show again, and when they came out for their curtain calls, she received the loudest ovation. Her role was for the third lead in the play, mind you.

As had become my custom, I went backstage to congratulate Elise and the other cast members I had come to know, including Laurent (who played Chevalier Dasceny) and Claire (who played Madame de Tourvel).

"Excellent travail comme d'habitude," I said.

Great job, as usual.

"Thank you!" Claire said.

"No. Repondre en Francais. Je vais mieux," I said.

No. Respond in French. I'm getting better.

"Oui, Monsieur," she said.

In broken French, I told them that I was taking Elise on a short vacation the following morning.

"Où êtes-vous deux allez?" Laurent asked.

Where are you two going?

"Quelque part par la Normandie , qui est tout ce que je sais," Elise stated.

Somewhere up by Normandy, that's all I know.

"Voilà tout ce que je lui dire . Le reste est une .... comment dites-vous la surprise?"

That's all I'm telling her. The rest is a ... how do you say surprise?

106

"Surprise is surprise."

"J'aurais dû savoir," I said.

I should have known.

All three of them laughed at this. Laurent and Claire seemed to enjoy our company. We said our goodbyes and headed home.

"Are Laurent and Claire dating?" I asked Elise a few minutes into our walk home.

As she pondered the question, I looked across at the beautiful Seine. This walk home from the play had become customary. I always remembered this was what led up to the first night we made love, so rehashing this scene twice a week was always nice.

"I would guess yes," Elise said. "The thing is, you don't ask. Imagine the drama if they broke up during the play's run. It could get ugly. I think it's better not to know. Nothing like a huge unscripted fight in the middle of the play."

"That's for sure. Although maybe the sexual tension is raised if they are banging in real life."

"Banging? Is that the proper nomenclature?" Elise didn't seem too happy with my choice of words.

"Having sex! Making love! Banging! I could name twenty more expressions, and banging would be low on the offensive meter."

"What's your favorite?" she asked sarcastically.

"As long as it's with you, people can call it whatever they want."

Elise leaned in and kissed me. I was out of the mini doghouse I had built for myself. I grabbed her hand, and we walked in silence along the Seine.

❧

WE DID END THE NIGHT "BANGING." BUT TO BE HONEST, WHAT WE DID was make love.

I've "banged" girls before, and this was different. This wasn't a wham bam, thank you, ma'am. Quite the opposite. I wanted to take my time and explore every part of her body. I even found myself spending a lot of time talking after sex. This was a new one. I was usually asleep ten minutes later.

What I'm trying to say is that it had been a long time since I had been in love, and I knew that's exactly what this was. Maybe we hadn't explicitly told each other yet, but I was convinced we both felt the same way.

❧

THE NEXT MORNING, WE WOKE, AND I STARTED PACKING. I COULD HAVE done it the night before, but was always a last-minute packer.

In this case, it truly was last minute, and we headed to Elise's as soon as I finished.

As she showered and got ready, my mind wandered to Tim and Chase. I had been so busy spending time with Elise that I hadn't thought back to New York very often.

I truly hoped that night scared them into becoming better people. If they could repair their marriages and change their lives around, at least the terrible thing we witnessed would have led to some good.

"The red or the white?"

Elise held up two beautiful dresses. What would usually be a question about wine was a preference for dresses.

She would have killed in either one, but the white one was slightly shorter. Why not go ahead and let my girlfriend show off?

"I'd go with the white," I said.

As usual, Elise read my mind. "You just want to see more leg."

"Or maybe I want other people to see how beautiful my girlfriend is."

"I'm fine with either reason." She smiled brightly. I could never get tired of that smile.

She finished packing and called a cab to pick us up. She had asked when I would get a mobile phone, and I said this still felt like a vacation, and I enjoyed living without one. I told her she was the only one I wanted to talk to.

She persisted. "I will soon," I had told her.

As soon as I tell you what happened in New York, I thought.

❦

WHEN THE CAB ARRIVED, I GRABBED MY ONE BAG AND HER TWO BAGS AND carried them to the car. I looked like an overworked bellman. I put them in the trunk and got into the back seat with Elise.

"Ou vas-tu?" the cab driver asked.

"Saint Lazare," Elise answered, and we headed toward the train station.

❦

PARIS SAINT-LAZARE, OR *GARE SAINT-LAZARE,* WAS PARIS'S SECOND BUSIEST train station. It was constructed in 1837 by the French architect Juste Lisch.

It was truly breathtaking—as beautiful as ninety-five percent of the structures I had seen in the U.S., and this was a train station, for Pete's sake.

It was located across the Seine in the 8th arrondissement, but we arrived there in minutes. I again grabbed all three large bags out of the trunk.

I didn't want to say anything, but I hoped this wouldn't be a recurring theme this trip. Just as I was thinking that, Elise also handed me her handbag to hold. I fell for the bait and grabbed it.

She looked at me and laughed. "I was wondering how long you'd go without saying something."

She grabbed the handbag back and took one of her bags off my shoulder as well.

"Two each. Are we good now?" she asked.

"We were never not good," I said, wondering why I had just used a double negative. "Did you hear me complain?"

"No, but then again, you were too busy trying to play aerial acrobatics with all the bags you were holding."

I couldn't help but laugh. "Must have been quite a sight."

"Sure was," she said.

❦

WE PROCEEDED TO THE TRAIN STATION, WHERE I PRESENTED ELISE WITH the two tickets to Normandy I had already purchased.

The fact that we were going to Normandy was the extent of what she knew about the trip. I hadn't planned anything crazy, but I thought it would be nice if she could just sit back and enjoy the trip without worrying about any of the planning.

I don't know if it was the relief of the play being over, the excitement of the upcoming trip, or the lovemaking session from the previous night, but Elise was asleep within five minutes. She slept the entire two-and-a-half-hour train ride to Normandy.

29

THE KILLERS

As Bryce and Elise stepped off the train platform in Normandy at one p.m., Lou Sessions logged into his computer at seven a.m. Eastern Standard Time.

Lou went on Orbitz and a few other sites to look at flights from JFK to Paris. They would need at least one day to plan a strategy, so he looked at flights leaving the next day. Sure enough, a red-eye left at eight p.m. the following night to Paris. That would work.

AFTER LOU BOOKED THE FLIGHTS TO PARIS, HE CAME UP WITH ANOTHER quick idea.

After several Google searches, Lou found Bryce's parents' phone number. It was easier than he anticipated.

It was still too early in California, so Lou waited till a proper hour to call Bryce's parents' house.

When he did, he concocted a bullshit story—and did so with a terrible French accent—of having found a wallet in France that belonged to Bryce. Bryce's mother fell for it hook, line, and sinker, and Lou got some much-needed information.

This is all coming together quite nicely, Lou thought.

30

BRYCE

NORMANDY

The train station had been the most beautiful thing I'd seen all day until we approached our hotel.

Le Bellevue is on a bluff overlooking the English Channel. I later learned that it was built in the 1870s as a villa for the director of Paris's Comic Opera and did not become a hotel until the 1920s.

It's not that the structure was so breathtaking on its own, but as I've mentioned before, I had always been a sucker for ocean views. Knowing what happened on the beach below us only added to the intrigue.

As we walked up to the hotel, Elise took in the view and covered her mouth in awe.

"Have you ever been to Normandy?" I asked.

"Came through once as a child, but I've never been to this spot. This I would have remembered."

"So I assume you're impressed."

"It's one of the most beautiful spots I've ever seen. This place must have cost an arm, a leg, and another leg."

"The Friday and Saturday rates were steep, but Sunday and Monday aren't so bad."

"How much is not so bad?" she asked.

I blushed. "Okay. It's still pretty bad."

We walked up the stairs to check in, not taking our eyes off the view to our left. I checked in, shielding Elise from the bill as I signed it.

BRIAN O'SULLIVAN

We were given our room keys and walked through the perfectly manicured grounds to our room. The room was near the bluff's edge with a perfect view of the English Channel.

We unpacked our clothes, and Elise jumped up and down on the bed like a child with too much sugar.

"You're frisky this afternoon," I said.

"That nap on the train has me wide awake and ready to do something. Let's walk around the city!"

※

SINCE I DIDN'T HAVE ANYTHING PLANNED UNTIL DINNER, THAT SOUNDED fine. The sun was out, and even though there might be a slight breeze from the Channel, we both wore shorts. It was mid-August, after all.

We asked someone where the city center was and headed in that direction.

"So, I was thinking," Elise said as we continued walking. "When you are done with this 'vacation' what do you think about us moving to the United States for a while?"

We were dating and beginning to fall in love, but this was the first time that one of us had brought up our future together.

"It sounds great, but I'm not ready to leave Paris yet. I've only been here a month. Plus, I have the house for three more."

"Not now, silly. You can finish your novel, and I can perform in another play. Maybe near the end of the year. Trust me, Paris is much nicer in the summer and fall than in January and February."

It seemed so far away to me, but if it meant we were still together, I was all for it. My parents would be delighted.

"Why the States?" I asked.

"I love acting in my local plays, but I'd love to see if I could make it in Hollywood. I don't need to be a star, but I'd love to be a character actor."

"Girls as pretty as you don't become character actors," I said.

It was Elise's turn to blush.

"Thanks! But I'm serious. Money doesn't do anything for me; I just want to do it for the craft."

"If money doesn't mean anything to you, then let's split the cost of the hotel room."

Elise got a chuckle out of that. "You know I've practiced my American accent in front of the mirror a million times over the years, always dreaming of playing different roles."

She looked skyward like she was remembering all those times. Her eyes made their way back to me.

"I'm going to test out my American accent today."

"Oh yeah? And what accent are you going to choose?"

"I'll give you a hint. It's the most outlandish, eccentric in all of America."

"The South," I guessed.

"You got it. When I was going to Villanova, we took a weekend trip down to Biloxi, Mississippi, and I've been fascinated with their accent ever since. I'll go with that."

"And where will I be from?"

"You can remain from California. Remember, you are the writer. I am the actress."

She said the last sentence with a thick southern drawl. I couldn't tell if it was spot-on or an over-the-top caricature. Honestly, I don't think the two options were all that different.

I played along. "Are you from Mississippi, darling?"

She stayed in character. "Yes, I am, Mr. Handsome Gentleman Caller. Biloxi, to be exact. You sound like you are from Cal-a-forn-I-A."

We both laughed out loud. Yes, people still laugh out loud instead of just writing the abbreviation.

We arrived in the city center, and I had no idea how Elise's accent would go over. It could be utterly memorable, or she could go down in flames.

We walked up to an outdoor cafe and sat down. A French girl about Elise's age came over and asked what we'd like. Half of me thought Elise was about to ditch the accent, but then I remembered how strong-willed she could be.

"We'd like two cups of your blackest coffee there, sweetheart," Elise said in the exaggerated/perfect southern accent I heard earlier.

She looked at the waitress's nametag. "Your name is Juliet, is it? Mine is Savannah. That's S-A-V-A-N-N-A-H: one V, two N's. I bet you are named after Juliet from Romeo & Juliet, aren't ya? When I was growing up in Biloxi, Mississippi, which is in the United States of America, we had to read Romeo and Juliet. I cried my eyes out for four days until my best friend, Dixie..."

Juliet couldn't take it anymore and interrupted Elise, "Sorry, but I'll be right back with your coffee."

Elise/S-A-V-A-N-N-A-H pretended she wasn't cut off and that Juliet was just in a rush to bring back our coffees.

"Everyone is so nice in this country. I ain't never been to France before, but I love y'all. I've been to Paris, Texas, but that's not the same. You see, Paris, Texas, is in the United States of America."

"You're crazy," I whispered to her, hoping I didn't have to hear that chalkboard-scratching voice again—no such luck.

"My mom and Auntie Bertha always said crazy runs in our family. Auntie Bertha was my favorite."

"Well, who doesn't love Aunt Bertha," I said.

Elise laughed and then caught herself. She was determined to stay in character.

"Who didn't love Aunt Bertha," she stated.

"What?"

"Past tense. Aunt Bertha died in a tragic sharecropping accident involving some big Caterpillar equipment. I always thought that was a weird name cause all their stuff is huge, and caterpillars are real little creatures. Somebody told me once that caterpillars become moths, but I wasn't falling for that nonsense."

Juliet brought back the coffee as Elise said her last sentence. She was utterly baffled by how to deal with this woman in front of her.

"Here's your two coffees."

"Thanks! Hey Juliet, did you used to live in Biloxi, Mississippi?"

"No, I didn't."

"You look like one of the Lester clan. They are on the farm next to us, and I coulda sworn you was one of them."

Elise's accent was so outlandish that I noticed the neighboring tables started listening in on our conversation.

"Not me. I've never even been to the United States."

"Are you sure about that, sweetie?"

Juliet tried to hold it together but showed signs of crumbling. I couldn't tell if she wanted to laugh or cry.

"Uh, yeah, I'm pretty sure."

"Oh well. I could have sworn you was one of those Lesters. Although you seem pretty nice, and they are the opposite. One Christmas Eve, they came and painted all of our horses orange. Those Lester's are a crazy bunch. And don't even get me started about some other things they've done to the animals on our farm."

Julie looked over to me as if to say, *'You're normal, what the fuck is wrong with your girlfriend.'*

I just smiled back at her.

"Do you guys want to pay with cash or a credit card?"

Elise/S-A-V-A-N-N-A-H seized the moment once again.

"Do you take American credit cards?" she asked.

Juliet was baffled again. "What do you mean exactly?"

"Like, do you take Visa or MasterCard? I know they are based in the U.S., but somebody once told me you can also use them overseas."

Juliet played nice. "Yeah, we take "American" credit cards. Every place in Europe will."

Elise feigned surprise. "Really? That's awesome! Sometimes, I can be a little batty, I guess. It's like they say: You can take the girl out of Southwest Biloxi, but you can't take the Biloxi out of the Southwest girl ... or something like that."

Juliet looked like she'd prefer walking a plank to having to listen to any more of Elise/S-A-V-A-N-N- A-H.

"When you come to pay, you can close out with anyone. You don't have to try finding me. No, seriously, you can go to anyone. Just bring the credit card inside."

With that, Juliet went on her way.

"The American credit card, you mean. U-S-A! U-S-A!"

I could hear several tables behind us laughing their asses off. With her beautiful, natural voice, Elise leaned into me and said, "Did I go over the top?"

"Yeah, just a little bit."

Elise face showed she had empathy for what she'd put Juliet through.

"I know what it's like to deal with pain in the ass customers. I'm going to go inside and pay her."

I watched as Elise walked inside and approached Juliet. A few seconds later, they were laughing and hugging each other. Elise walked back out with Juliet in tow and introduced herself in her normal voice.

"How can you handle her?" Juliet asked me.

I motioned toward Elise. "I can handle her just fine. As for Savannah from Biloxi, I think I just got a lifetime's fill of her."

Juliet smiled. "You guys are cute. Let me bring you one more coffee on the house for the performance."

It was my turn to smile. "Thank you!"

"Thank Savannah," she joked and walked away.

We turned around, and two different tables were clapping at us.

I heard "Bravo!" and "Hilarante", which is French for hilarious.

Elise was beaming from ear to ear.

"They loved the show."

"They sure did. I'm not so sure someone from the South would," I said.

"It was done from a place of love. The people in Biloxi were some of the nicest people I ever met. Just playing on people's stereotypes of your American South."

"Whatever you say, Savannah!"

Juliet brought us another coffee, and we just sat there and basked in the afternoon sun and our newfound celebrity status.

We must have walked five miles zigzagging the city over the next several hours.

We bought presents for each other at descending prices. She began by buying me a pendant, and as I had done at the hotel, she covered the price on the receipt, pretending it was costly. When I went to the section where she had bought it, I saw that it cost two euros.

"You shouldn't have." I joked.

"Broke the bank," she deadpanned.

I, in turn, bought her a $1 postcard at the next souvenir shop we passed by. Not to be outdone, she purchased a fifty-cent candy bracelet and put it on my wrist.

I picked a flower from a flower shrub and handed it to her. She grabbed a leaf off the ground and placed it in my hair.

Yes, this was all as silly as it sounds.

At some point, I looked at my watch and saw it was already seven p.m. Where had the last five hours gone?

"Let's head back. We've got dinner in an hour," I said.

"That should give me just enough time to throw on that red dress."

"Nice try. You mean the white one!"

"Just making sure you were paying attention."

"Always."

We flagged down a cab since we were running low on time. I listened to Elise and the cab driver talking in French, trying to soak it all in.

My French was improving every day.

31
BRYCE

We got back to the hotel and showered. She threw on the WHITE dress, we hopped in yet another cab, and showed up one minute before our reservation time.

Like our hotel, I wanted a restaurant on the water. After all, what is more romantic than a view of the water while drinking wine with a beautiful girl?

The restaurant I chose, *La Sapinier,* was twenty-five feet from Omaha Beach.

We were seated by what I believed to be our host. He was an old, jovial man of about sixty. He had probably had a few too many bottles of wine and butter and cream-based sauces over the years.

His stomach was a perfectly round semi-circle, but don't judge him by that. The old axiom that fat people enjoy their life more certainly seems to apply to him.

He had a permanent smile and made us feel like we were the most important people at the restaurant.

He sat us at the table and hugged us both—literally. Your move, American restaurants. We immediately felt better about ourselves.

You have to love people like that. He had taken so much pride in seating us that I wondered if he was more than just the host.

Our server soon followed, and I just had to know. I asked Elise to ask her.

"Était le gars qui nous a assis un hôte ou le propriétaire?"

Was the guy who sat us a host or the owner? "Bon œil . Il est le propriétaire."

Good eye. He is the owner.

"Seems like a great guy," Elise said in English.

The server responded in English, "Just as nice a guy behind the scenes as well. It's not just a front because he owns the restaurant. He's like that all the time."

I found it ironic that the American was trying to speak French while the two French girls were speaking English.

And I enjoyed hearing her kind words about the owner. I had seen the worst of people in New York. It was nice to see the best of people.

I hated to admit it, but I felt just a bit of jealousy. I wish I could always be happy and always look at the bright side of life, as Monty Python suggests in their great song.

The guy looked old and was terribly out of shape, yet he was smiling and having a great time. How nice must it be to walk around life with a permanent smile?

It was then that I realized I had been happy every day since I met Elise. Not some days. Not most days. Every day. And that's when I knew that I honestly did love her. It was something that simple.

"And the second special is," the waitress continued in English, "a blackened salmon served with a hollandaise sauce, asparagus, and rice pilaf with three different types of mushrooms."

The first special was escargot, and although I thoroughly enjoyed my time in France, I wasn't quite ready to accept all of what they considered fine dining. The snails would have to wait.

The salmon sounded good, but I ordered from the menu and chose a filet mignon with a roquefort sauce, a side of risotto, and assorted veggies. Elise chose the salmon.

I ordered a bottle of French Burgundy, despite Elise getting fish, and we toasted our glasses when our entrees arrived twenty minutes later.

"You know the one thing we haven't done together?" Elise asked.

The fact that we just toasted glasses gave it away.

"Gotten really drunk together," I guessed.

"Bingo!"

I was game. I called our waitress over and ordered two shots of Jameson, which I'd learned was quite popular in France. Maybe not at nice restaurants, but what the hell.

As we waited for our shots, we started to eat. We sampled each other's food and agreed they were both fantastic.

I was given an abundance of sauce, which I used to dip my potatoes in. Even the vegetables weren't immune to being coated with some roquefort sauce.

We looked over and saw the owner heading our way. For a split second, I thought we might be getting a reprimand for ordering shots at his nice restaurant. But then Elise and I noticed a third shot glass on his tray, and we knew what was coming. He walked up to our table.

"I'm never one to miss out on a party," he boasted.

We laughed, and he handed us each a shot and took one himself.

"Some people might think ordering shots during dinner is wrong, but if that's the case, I don't want to be right," he said in broken but understandable English.

We lifted our glasses, and despite the fact he had been speaking in English, we toasted in French. We all yelled Sante and clinked our shot glasses. After finishing his, he slammed it down on the table. Besides Elise, I had found my second favorite person in France.

"What's your name, sir?" I asked.

"My name is Hugo. And what are you two beautiful people's names?"

"I'm Bryce."

"I'm Elise."

"Ahhh, we've got a Yank and a filly from France."

"Hugo, you've got a great restaurant and an awesome outlook on life. I want to be just like you when I grow up."

"Then don't grow up," he said and meant it. "That's what has kept me young. Being young at heart!"

Don't grow up! Simple, yet profound.

"Beautiful advice," Elise said. I was happy she felt the same.

"I'm going to go out on a limb and guess that you guys are newlyweds," Hugo said.

Elise blushed, not knowing what to say.

I spoke for the both of us, "We're newly all, right. Newly dating."

Hugo got a big kick out of that. "Newly dating! I like that! I should have looked down to see if there were a couple of rings before I said that. In my defense, I was too busy thinking about our next shots."

"Now you're talking," I said.

"I'll tell you what. I'll let you guys finish your meal and give the people around you a break from me. When you're done, come to the bar, and we'll have another shot. Sound good?"

"Perfect. We'll see you there," Elise said.

Hugo started to walk away, but I caught him before he got too far.

"One more thing. As you can tell, we were thinking about having some drinks together tonight. Could we buy a bottle of champagne from the restaurant when we leave? Don't worry, we're not driving. I was going to take Elise for a walk along the ocean and thought the champagne would be a nice companion."

"Not a request I get every day, but the answer is yes. It will be waiting for you at the bar. See you two soon."

And with that, he walked away.

I looked over at Elise and grabbed her hand. "I don't know if we will grow old together, but if we do, I hope we end up just like that."

She smiled at me and held my hands even tighter. Then her look turned serious, and she stared straight into my eyes. I knew what was coming.

"I love you," she said.

I leaned over the table, avoiding the hollandaise and roquefort sauces, and kissed her for a solid ten seconds.

"I love you too," I said.

WE FINISHED OUR DINNERS, AND DUE TO THE RICHNESS OF THE MEAL AND the wine we had, we decided against getting a dessert. We paid for our meal and headed over to the bar. To no one's surprise, Hugo was there waiting for us.

"I saw that beautiful embrace after I left," he said.

"You don't miss a thing, do you?" I stated.

"If I didn't know better, I'd have guessed you just got engaged. Considering you are 'Newly Dating,' that's unlikely. Maybe the first "I love you?"

Elise echoed my sentiment, "Wow! You don't miss a thing."

"I've got a keen eye," Hugo said.

He motioned to the bar, where three shots of Jameson sat. Next to it sat a French Champagne (technically, all champagnes were French) that just screamed "I'm expensive." And next to that sat two plastic flute glasses which screamed, "We're cheap."

"Grab your shots," Hugo said, and we did as instructed. "Here's to young love."

We toasted glasses again and took down our shots.

"Although Bryce is thirty-two. Is that still young love?" Elise said and nudged me.

Hugo answered, whispering for the first time,

"It's not based on age, beautiful Elise. If two people in their seventies start falling for each other, I would still call that young love. I know people who have been happily married for fifty years. And they will tell you that the early part, when they originally fell in love, was truly the greatest part. And that's why I call it young love. Old love is great and something to aspire to, but it will never have the passion that young love brings."

Elise and I nodded in agreement.

Hugo continued, "Well, that's just me being the hopeless romantic I've been my whole life. I'll say one more thing, and then I will shut up. You two have something special about you, and I've always been a great judge of things like this. It's the keen eye! You guys are going to be happy together for a long, long time. Trust me on this."

Elise leaned in and hugged Hugo.

Hugo grabbed the champagne. "This bottle usually sells for about eight euros, but I'll only charge you fifty because that's what I pay wholesale."

"You've been way too generous, Hugo," I said. "We don't deserve all of this. Is there anything we can do for you?"

"There is one thing," he said.

Elise and I waited in anticipation.

"You can invite me to your wedding because if you don't, I'm going to crash it, anyway."

We laughed, smiled, and promised we would. And we meant it. In our short time with Hugo, he had made quite the impression.

I paid Hugo for the champagne and offered to pay for the last round of shots, but he refused to let me. I hugged him, and Elise kissed him on the cheek as we said our goodbyes.

"You two lovebirds take care of each other," he said as we walked away.

"We will," we said in unison.

I took Elise's hand as we walked off.

WE STROLLED FOR A FEW MINUTES ALONG THE OCEAN WITHOUT SAYING A word. We kind of just soaked in all that happened with Hugo while enjoying our surroundings.

Finally, Elise broke the silence. "Do you think he's right?"

"About what?"

"That we'll be together a long time."

I wasn't expecting that question. I gathered myself for a second. "I think Hugo is a very perceptive individual. If he says something, I would tend to believe it. So yes, I do think we will be together for a long time."

She held me tighter. "I hope so."

A SMALL PATH LED AWAY FROM THE BEACH TO ANOTHER BLUFF. WE WALKED up it and sat down, extending our legs off the bluff.

"I think it's time we opened this thing," I said.

"Finally."

I unhooked the cork and pointed it skyward. Just like that, a loud pop went off, and the cork shot up in the air. It must have caught a draft of wind because it redirected back toward us. It landed three feet behind Elise.

"It's God's way of saying don't litter," she said.

"Touche."

I grabbed the cheap plastic flute glasses, filled them, and raised them to each other for the fourth time that night. We each took a sip and marveled at the taste.

"Wow, this is good," I exclaimed.

"Definitely the best champagne ever served in a plastic flute glass."

We sat up on that bluff for two hours, slowly drinking champagne and talking about love, family, growing older, religion, and politics. Since we were looking out on Omaha Beach, we even talked about war and the unimaginable sacrifices that so many young men made on the beach below us. Nothing was off-limits when we spoke, especially when we were several drinks deep.

"Do you want to head back to the hotel soon?" I asked.

It was past midnight, and we hadn't seen anyone walk near us in over an hour. The main path was dimly lit and a good fifty feet from us. It was unlikely anyone would walk by and see us.

She not so subtly rubbed her breast up against my forearm and whispered in my ear, "What's the rush?"

Point taken. I leaned in and started softly kissing her neck. She did the same. A minute later, she grabbed my thigh and worked her way upward.

We slowly took each other's clothes off and gazed at the dark sea below us. We found a piece of nearby grass (or what passed for it), and Elise lay down on her back.

I lowered myself just above her, and we made love.

Our carnal sounds were the only noise emanating from the bluff.

Some people might think it's sacrilegious to make love above Omaha Beach, but it was an impulsive decision and not a reflection of what had taken place below us.

I was mindful of it, however, and after we finished and put on our clothes, I looked over the dark abyss below and said a prayer, thanking all those who had lost their lives.

32

BRYCE

I woke up the following day with a surprisingly clear head, considering I had two shots of Jameson and split a bottle of wine and a bottle of champagne.

I can't say the same thing for Elise. She rolled over and stuck her head firmly into the pillow.

"What time is it?" she mumbled.

"Almost ten," I said. It was by far the longest we had ever slept in together. "Are you hungry?"

She rolled over so I could see her. "I am, but I can't get out of bed. I'm hurting. I blame Hugo for the shots and you for the champagne."

I showed her a grass stain on my forearm. "Well then, I blame you for this."

She smiled seductively.

"Round two?" I asked.

She laughed and rolled over for the third time.

"No. My head hurts."

"Stay here. I'll bring you some breakfast in bed."

"You're the best boyfriend ever."

I'M A BIG GUY, BUT JUDGING BY THE PLATE I COMPILED AT THE continental breakfast, you would have thought it was meant for a 400-pound man.

On one plate, I managed to fit eight sausage links, twelve slices of bacon, a huge portion of scrambled eggs, six pieces of toast, and some assorted fruit to pretend there was something healthy on this beast of a plate.

When I got back to the room, Elise had fallen back asleep. I can't say I was surprised.

She wrestled back to life as I brought the food over.

"I was thinking," I said. "How about we make this a mellow day? I think after yesterday, we deserve it."

"This might be your best idea ever."

She finally sat up, and we ate the food. I finished three-quarters of it.

At one point, she got up and looked at herself in the mirror.

"Oh my god!"

Did she look like a hot mess who had drunk too much and whose hair and makeup were going every which way? Of course.

Did she still look like the most beautiful girl in the world to me? Of course, again.

"If we move to the U.S., you should go to your first audition looking like this," I said.

"It would be my last audition."

We laughed.

※

THE REST OF THE MORNING WAS MORE OF THE SAME. ELISE WOULD GET UP for a minute and then go back to bed. Rinse. Repeat. Finally, I'd had enough.

"Look, we're not going to do anything big today but get your lazy ass out of bed. We are on vacation, remember? We can't waste the whole day."

She looked up at me with bloodshot eyes. "You're right," she said, and I knew she felt guilty.

She was a trooper the rest of the day, even though she felt like shit. We did a little sightseeing, but it paled in comparison to the previous day.

Don't get me wrong, it was still enjoyable, but there was no fake Southern accent, great restaurant owner, or sex above Omaha Beach.

※

WE WOKE UP THE NEXT MORNING FEELING GREAT.

Let that be a lesson to you travelers out there. If you are going to party your ass off, do it on the first night, not the night before you leave. Trust me on this.

After we ate, we checked out, took another quick stroll through the city, and then took a cab to the train station. It was a Tuesday, so luckily, our train section was almost empty when we boarded it at three p.m.

On the train ride back, we discussed our immediate futures, and Elise said she was going to go on some auditions for a few upcoming plays.

DEBUT NOVEL

I told her my debut novel was progressing more quickly than I expected, and I planned to write several hours a day going forward.

We talked about potentially moving in together but decided to push that conversation back to a later date.

After all, I had my place for another three months, and as much as I liked my spot, it would be too cramped for the two of us.

About a half hour outside of Paris, something occurred to me. "Shit!" I said.

"What's the matter?" Elise asked.

"I forgot to call my parents yesterday. Considering they have no way to get ahold of me, they are probably a little worried."

"Use my phone."

"Isn't it costly to call the U.S.?"

"It's not too bad on my plan. Plus, you just paid for an awesome vacation for me. Of course, you can use it."

She handed me her phone.

"I have to go to the ladies' room anyway, so it's a good time to call them."

It was five p.m. in France, which was eight a.m. in San Francisco, so it was a perfect time to call them. I dialed o o and the U.S. country code, which was 1, and typed in their number. After only one ring, my mom picked up the phone.

"Hi, Mom, it's Bryce," I said.

"Bryce. Oh God, we were so scared when we didn't hear from you. Hold on a second."

I could hear my mom yelling for my dad. I knew something was wrong. My mom wouldn't be that worried about me calling one day late.

"Something happened, Bryce, but I'd rather have your father tell you. Here he comes."

My heart was beginning to sink. My dad got on the phone. "Bryce."

"What's going on, Dad? Mom's got me scared."

I could hear my father clear his throat. He sounded nervous as well.

"Your friends Tim and Chase are missing."

My head started to spin.

I had a million questions I wanted to ask and, in turn, a million questions I needed to answer. This had to be related to what happened in New York.

Although with Tim and Chase, you never knew. Maybe they flew to Tijuana for a few days. Maybe they were in a drug-induced haze and forgot to call their wives.

I tried to settle myself down. Don't jump to conclusions, I told myself.

"Did you hear me, Bryce?"

"Yeah, Dad, I heard you." My voice was barely above a whisper. "What do you know?"

"Apparently, they haven't been heard from since Friday night. Their wives talked to each other on Saturday morning, and once they hadn't shown up by

Saturday afternoon, they went to the police and reported them missing. I didn't find out until yesterday when Tim's wife, Gina, called me. She knew you were in New York with them five weeks ago and hoped maybe you had heard from them. I think she was grasping at straws."

How in the hell could the killers have located Tim and Chase?

It certainly wasn't my letter, and I was sure they wouldn't have turned themselves in.

For the second time, my dad had to get my attention. "Son, did you hear me? Have you heard from either of them?"

"No, Dad. I haven't talked to them since the night I spent with them in New York."

"There's something else, Bryce."

I figured this couldn't get any worse. I was wrong.

"Someone called the house on Saturday morning and spoke to your mother. He claimed you had left your wallet at a restaurant in Paris and he wanted to return it. Mom told him we didn't know your address, and you didn't have a cell phone."

I breathed a quick sigh of relief.

My father continued, "But she remembered that cafe you told us about. Les Deux something. Anyway, she told the guy to check there."

Les Deux Magots. Fuck!

I had never felt more worried or ashamed in my life. Although it was accidental, I had gotten Elise involved.

There was no other explanation for the call my parents received. I hadn't lost my wallet. It had to be either the killers or the cops, and with Tim and Chase missing, my money was on the bad guys.

Now, Elise and her workplace were involved. I was starting to feel lightheaded, so I sat back in my seat and tried to gather my thoughts.

"Was it a man who called Mom?" I asked.

"Yeah. Your mother guessed he was around fifty. The funny thing was even though he was calling from a Paris restaurant, she thought he sounded American. Like an east coaster, maybe."

I couldn't take much more of this. I wanted to scream.

After witnessing the murder, I was resolute in not going to the cops. Now I had no idea what the fuck to do.

The only thing I knew was I needed some time to think.

"Dad, stay by the phone. I'll call you in ten minutes."

"What's going on, Bryce? Are you in danger? Is this phone call related to their disappearances?"

"I'll call you back in ten."

I hung up before he could ask any more questions. I needed to clear my mind and think logically. I had always been good at that and needed it now more than ever.

As I mulled over my options, I saw Elise.

She was about to take her seat and could tell something was wrong.

"You look like you've seen a ghost! What the hell did your parents say?"

As I looked at Elise, I did some calculations in my head.

Tim and Chase had been missing since Friday, and somebody had called my mother on Saturday. It was now Tuesday, meaning it was possible, maybe even likely, that the killers were already in Paris, staking out Les Deux Maggots.

My heart sunk to the bottom of my stomach, but this was no time to wallow in the moment.

It was time to man up.

"Sit down, Elise. We need to talk."

33

LEROY

Leroy Archer was destined to become old school at birth.
 It was the mid-eighties, and Leroy's father, Alvin, thought kids were behaving like punks at the time—Who knows what he'd think now.

Alvin longed for the day when kids respected authority and didn't talk back to their fathers and, more importantly, their mothers. His son would be different.

His rationale for naming his newborn Leroy was that if he gave him an old-school name, he'd grow up showing respect like "Leroys" of previous generations.

His wife, Susan, thought Michael, Jordan, or Jackson would be great names. Being in the mid-eighties, she loved Air Jordan and the King of Pop.

Alvin thought that a name truly meant something, and like in most debates in their household, he won out. Leroy Michael Archer was born on January 1st, 1985.

Susan had convinced Alvin to give Leroy the middle name Michael, which he acquiesced to. However, Susan's hope that her son would be called by his middle name never came to fruition.

Leroy's parents raised him in a tough but fair household. He was free to have fun with his friends, but his curfew was always a few hours earlier than theirs.

His father occasionally made him end a friendship if he thought the other kid was in trouble. He focused on treating Leroy right from wrong.

Leroy knew that Brooklyn in the mid-eighties was a less-than-desirable area, but he always had enough food and enjoyed what he thought was a normal childhood. His father constantly lectured him about respecting authority, your elders, and your parents.

It got old sometimes, but Leroy understood his father just wanted what was best for him.

Leroy was eleven when he decided he wanted to become a police officer.

His best friend, Jordan Tyler, who *was* named after Air Jordan, was walking home one night with Leroy when a bullet not meant for either of them, nevertheless found its way into Jordan's back.

The assailants drove away, but not before Leroy was smart enough to get their license plate. Neighbors heard the gunshots and called police. Leroy stayed by Jordan's side until they got there, telling him he was going to live through this.

Leroy wasn't even a teenager yet, but he was already a thoughtful young man. As he sat there holding Jordan, he thought the thug aspect of the projects was what was ruining their neighborhood.

How did people expect kids to study, finish high school, and go to college when there were gunshots almost nightly, and local gangs were always trying to recruit people his age?

If people could eliminate the neighborhood's criminal element, it would make his neighborhood a better place to grow up in.

As he held on to Jordan, these thoughts circled his brain, and he decided to become a police officer and protect Jordan and kids just like him.

Unfortunately, he couldn't protect Jordan on this day. The injuries were too severe, and as Leroy sat there trying to comfort his best friend, Jordan closed his eyes for the last time.

The license plate that Leroy remembered led police to arrest the perpetrators. It turned out the shooters mistook Jordan for someone who was going to testify against them for a different crime.

Realizing the danger that Leroy could be in, the officers never made him testify. They had gathered enough evidence from the raid on the house, which was predicated on Leroy taking down the license plate.

Leroy made friends with a few officers and kept in touch with them over the years.

Leroy was an easy target in high school when his classmates discovered he wanted to become a cop.

He was called an "Uncle Tom," among other things. When he tried to explain that he loved his fellow black men and wanted to create an environment where they could prosper, his explanation often fell on deaf ears.

His father was impressed, and that was what mattered most to Leroy. Alvin Archer had managed to raise an old-school son in a challenging time and place.

He would have preferred that Leroy had become a teacher or a lawyer, but Alvin had imparted his stubbornness to his son, and he knew Leroy would become an excellent police officer.

One day, at the beginning of his junior year of high school, Alvin Archer asked his son if he would consider attending college before enrolling in the police academy. Leroy said he would.

The very next day, as he was on his route as a U.S. postal worker, Alvin Archer dropped dead of a heart attack.

Leroy was crushed. He had always looked up to his father and knew how much he had sacrificed for him. After delivering the eulogy at his father's funeral, Leroy went up to the casket, said a prayer, and then promised his father then and there that he would go to college first.

※

Leroy went to Colombia on an academic scholarship and graduated with honors.

Most people expected him to attend a top-notch business or law school, but Leroy moved back to Brooklyn and enrolled in the police academy.

Upon completion, he asked to be stationed in the inner city. Leroy was well-liked, but some people thought he must have a screw loose.

He could have been going to Harvard Law, but instead, he was walking the beat in the worst part of Brooklyn.

Leroy did this for two years, and even though he knew he was doing some good for the community, he realized that he'd have to rise in the police force if he was going to make a big difference.

He asked for a change of venue to Manhattan, and even though some of his old friends thought he might be selling out, Leroy had to do this.

Around this time, his beautiful girlfriend Jade decided to leave him. They had fallen in love at Colombia, and she took a job on Wall Street when he got the job with the Brooklyn Police Department.

He had always been driven, but Jade felt it was now detrimental to their relationship.

Leroy worked sixty hours a week, and even when he was home, his caseload was always on his mind. When Jade tried to converse with him, she felt like she was talking to a zombie.

Leroy promised he'd get better, but he never did. He loved Jade with all his heart, but his life as a police officer made him what he was.

He was going to improve the inner cities of New York, and he was sorry if this made him a tough man to live with.

When Leroy decided to take the job in Manhattan, Jade knew it would only get worse. She decided to fold a losing hand. Leroy was crushed, but he decided his work embodied who he was. He loved Jade, but he was more than just the sum of their relationship.

※

Leroy quickly rose through the ranks once he got to Manhattan.

When he arrived, he was twenty-five and started as a beat cop, just as he had in Brooklyn. He was soon promoted to detective, and after two more years, he was promoted once again, this time to sergeant.

At twenty-eight, he was the youngest sergeant the NYPD had ever had. A few people joked that it must have been some affirmative action stunt, but this was always tongue-in-cheek because everyone knew Leroy Archer deserved it. He was a fantastic cop.

After spending a few years as a sergeant, he became a lieutenant, again becoming the youngest to do so.

He was thirty-one years old, and there were rumors of him running for political office in the future. Leroy did nothing to downplay these rumors.

If he wanted to make the significant changes in the inner cities he desired, he needed to rise above lieutenant.

And Leroy Archer was well on his way.

Of this, there was no doubt.

※

So, on a day like any other, as Leroy pondered his ascension in the department, Officer Billy Braden entered his office and handed him the letter that Bryce Connor had written.

"Lieutenant, I think you might want to take a look at this," Braden said.

"What do we have here?" Leroy asked. He slid on some gloves and only pinched the corner of the letter.

Braden looked down at his gloveless hands and realized his mistake. Leroy didn't say anything, and Braden appreciated that.

"I'm guessing it has to do with that body we found on 27th Ave. this morning. Some teenager gave this to an officer on 31st Ave. earlier this morning. The officer read it and immediately sent it down to us. He asked the teenager who had given it to him, and the guy said it was a white male, approximately thirty years old. The officer walked the kid around but didn't see the thirty-year-old anywhere."

"Hmmm," Leroy mused. He read the note three times. "It sure doesn't sound like the work of Anthony Solari, does it?"

"What do you mean, Lieutenant?"

"Well, when was the last time you heard about an Anthony Solari hit that took place in a back alley? And when was the last time you heard of a Solari hit involving a knife?"

"Uh, I guess never."

"That's right," Leroy said.

"But why would the guy who wrote this note say he heard one of the murderers mention Solari? What would he have to gain?"

"Well, I can't answer until we find out who gave us this note. But there's another possibility."

"What's that, Lieutenant?"

"Maybe the killer was trying to deflect the attention from themselves and toward Solari."

"What makes you think that?"

"If the man or woman who wrote the letter is telling the truth, the murderer didn't mention Solari until after he looked over and realized there were witnesses. If you were committing murder for Solari, why the hell would you shout out his name once you knew people were watching you?"

"It's a good point, but it would be exceptionally fast thinking on the killer's part," Officer Braden said.

"It certainly would. But that doesn't mean that's not how it went down," Leroy said.

He read the letter for a fourth time as Billy Braden remembered why Leroy Archer had risen so quickly. He was one smart cookie.

༺༻

LEROY PUT TWO HOMICIDE DETECTIVES IN CHARGE OF LOOKING INTO THE murder of Freddy Macon, as well as trying to find the writer of the mystery letter.

Leroy was overseeing a few higher-profile murder cases in Manhattan, and this case didn't yet fit that profile, so he'd likely be hands-off on this case to start.

The detectives working the case gave him occasional updates, but they seemed to have hit a dead end. The note, which was from a generic spiral notebook, did not contain traceable DNA, so it was hardly something they could narrow down.

When the case looked to have stalled, Leroy reiterated to the officers that they should look into people who had beefs with Anthony Solari.

Something still didn't ring true about that. If somebody walked up on you as you committed a murder, why the hell would you say the name of the guy who ordered you to make the hit?

Leroy sent the detectives on their way and got back to overseeing more time-sensitive murder cases. He didn't think about the murder of Freddy Macon again until several weeks later when Gina Sawyer barged into his office.

※

Leroy didn't work every Saturday, but it sure seemed like that lately.

One Saturday afternoon, he was looking over more paperwork—there was always paperwork these days—when he saw an attractive woman walking down the hall and being held back by an officer.

He must not have been holding her very hard because she got to Leroy's door and flung it open.

"Are you the highest-ranking officer here?" she asked.

"Lieutenant. But yes, I am."

The officer trying to constrain her was considered incompetent by his fellow officers, and Leroy had to agree.

"I'm sorry, Lieutenant. She asked who the boss was right now and then ran toward your office."

"Don't worry about it, Officer Longley. I'll talk to her. You can go now."

Officer Longley sheepishly walked out of Leroy's office. The pretty young lady sat down.

"Thank you. I'm Gina Sawyer."

She extended her hand, and Leroy shook it.

"Lieutenant Leroy Archer. How can I help you?"

"My husband is missing. He was supposed to call me after work last night, and I never heard from him. We're currently separated, but he's trying to get back together with me. There's no way he wouldn't have called last night or at least this morning. His best friend Chase is missing as well."

Great, Leroy thought. A missing husband and his best friend. Probably passed out drunk somewhere or at some girl's house they shouldn't be at. Still, she was here, so he'd let her talk.

"Okay, tell me what you know."

Gina told Leroy that she thought Tim had been acting weird lately. A little jittery. He was a tough guy and would never admit it to her, but he was looking over his shoulder occasionally and didn't seem his usual confident self. She had talked to Chase's wife, Victoria, and Chase had been even more jumpy than Tim.

"How long has he been acting this way?" Leroy asked.

"Two or three weeks, I'd guess," Gina said.

Leroy asked her to describe Tim—white, early thirties, good-looking, successful.

Leroy's brain was festering with an idea, but he couldn't quite figure out what it was. He told Gina she would have to wait until tomorrow to file a missing persons report, but his instincts told him this wasn't just a drunken night out.

He told Gina that if they had not heard from Tim or Chase by Monday, they should return to police headquarters and bring Chase's wife. He wouldn't be in the office on Sunday but would meet with them on Monday.

"Thank you for your help. Something is wrong here. I just know it."

Unfortunately, Leroy felt she was probably right.

※

Gina returned on Monday with Chase's wife, Victoria.

They still hadn't heard from their husbands, and Tim and Chase's phones went straight to voicemail. Leroy made a note to have their last dialed calls checked.

Victoria told a similar story to Gina. Chase had been acting weird for the last several weeks. He seemed even more paranoid than Tim. Victoria said Chase constantly asked her if certain people were following them, often thinking he saw the same people repeatedly.

Chase did this several times a day. Victoria knew something was very wrong.

Leroy told them to get him the names and numbers of their closest friends. He said he would check their phone records and get back to them the next day, which was Tuesday.

As they left, Leroy sat back in his chair. He had become a cop to help make the inner cities safer.

And now I'm going out of my way to help on a case of two missing, rich, white guys?

Leroy quickly chastised himself, knowing he was in the wrong.

A minute later, he calmed down and knew he'd continue on the case. It intrigued him, and he felt something more was happening beneath the surface.

※

Leroy got clearance to check the two cell phones. Tim's phone appeared to have nothing out of the ordinary. His last phone call was to his wife at about 1:30 p.m. the day he went missing.

Chase's cell phone showed that his last action was to order an Uber at nine o'clock on Friday evening. Leroy called Uber corporate and explained that he was an NYPD lieutenant. They swiftly gave him what he wanted after that.

The Uber driver, Ensign, told him that he had dropped Chase off by the docks. He was insulting and appeared nervous.

Leroy called his most trusted officer, Billy Braden. Braden had brought him the note from Bryce a few weeks earlier, but they had yet to learn these cases were related.

Leroy told him to drop everything and that he was coming with him.

※

Leroy drove them down to the docks and parked where Chase Andrews had been dropped off.

"If you were planning to hurt someone around here, where would you do it?" Leroy asked.

"Closer down toward the docks," Braden said. "There's still a chance of being seen up here. Down there, there's nobody."

Leroy agreed, and the two headed off to the water.

Most of these abandoned warehouses had doors that were unlocked. They were so heavy, however, that they would never open on their own. Leroy and Billy peeked in a couple of them, not seeing anything besides a few rats the size of a chihuahua.

There's an old urban legend that there's a rat for every person in New York City. Not down by the abandoned docks. Rats were the head honchos down here.

They came to the last set of abandoned warehouses next to the Hudson River. Leroy approached the one on the left and noticed that the latch had been shut.

"This is a little odd, isn't it? All the other door latches aren't shut except for this one," Leroy said. "Let's get this open."

Officer Braden had his doubts but helped Leroy get it open.

He thought Leroy had the best instincts of any cop he had ever known. There were many times when Braden had thought Leroy was "wrong on this one," and it turned out Leroy's intuition was correct. He had learned to stop doubting him.

They got the latch to the door open and entered the vast warehouse. Nothing jumped out, but Leroy asked Braden to walk around and see if he saw anything peculiar.

He checked old garbage cans and looked behind rusted, non-working equipment.

He was about to think Leroy was "wrong on this one" again when he saw Leroy looking at a section of the concrete ground about forty feet to the left of the front door.

Braden walked over.

"What is it?" he asked.

"It's tough to see, but I think there's some smeared blood on the ground right here."

Braden saw what Leroy was talking about but wasn't impressed.

"This could have been a forklift injury twenty years ago."

"It could be. However, blood becomes darker over time when it is embedded in concrete. This hasn't even started turning purple, much less a light brown. This is still red."

Braden couldn't argue. It did look like it was something recent.

"Call forensics," Leroy said. "Let's get them down here to look at this."

"Can they get DNA from blood dried in cement?" Braden asked.

"You'd be amazed what they can do these days."

❦

As Leroy waited for forensics to arrive, he walked out of the warehouse and looked at the Hudson. It was the most obvious place to dispose of the bodies.

But he couldn't just ask his superiors to send people to dive into the Hudson to look for two dead bodies when he wasn't even sure a murder had occurred. He needed more evidence.

❦

They waited for forensics until they removed the concrete and returned it to their lab for testing. Then, Leroy told Officer Braden it was time to return to the station. They had other cases to work on.

That would all change the following day when Leroy would receive a call from none other than Bryce Connor.

34

LOU, CHARLES, & SOLARI

When Charles was ten years old, and Lou was eight, they received some heartbreaking news: They were only fifty percent Italian.

This in and of itself wouldn't be so crushing, but for two kids who looked up to the local mafia members like they were movie stars, rock stars, and professional athletes rolled into one, it was crushing.

You see, if you were only fifty percent Italian, you couldn't join the mafia.

And for two troublesome kids growing up in the *Little Italy* section of Manhattan, that's all they wanted.

Luckily, the local mafia kingpin had taken a liking to Lou and Charles—especially Lou—so their heritage didn't prevent them from hanging out with their heroes. They just knew they would never officially join the mafia.

The kingpin's name was Anthony Solari, and he had gained control of his syndicate when five people above him in the mafia were killed on the same day in separate incidents.

People within the Solari family blamed rival mafia families, but some people always suspected Anthony Solari.

When Solari took over, he brought Lou and Charles to help with some of the small collections around town. At this point, they were seventeen and fifteen and had already dropped out of high school.

Their father had a big gambling problem and constantly owed Solari money, so even though they were only teenagers, Solari could use them for smaller tasks at no cost.

Over the intervening years, Solari began to trust the younger brother, Lou, more than almost anyone in his outfit. Charles was good for dirty work, but Solari never trusted him as he did Lou.

Solari didn't think Charles was the sharpest pencil in the box. On the other hand, Lou was very street-smart and would have been on his path to being a made man if he had been 100 percent Italian.

By the time he was twenty-one years old, Lou had committed his first murder for Mr. Solari. By the time he was thirty, the number of murders had reached double digits.

⁂

WHEN HIS FRIENDSHIP WITH SOLARI CAME TO A CRASHING HALT, LOU HAD murdered upward of twenty people. Charles was involved in a few of these, but Lou tried to leave him out whenever possible.

It was the summer of 2007 when everything changed between Lou and Anthony Solari.

Although he wasn't an official part of the mafia, Lou had become a major player.

Think Robert De Niro in *Goodfellas* or Robert Duvall in *The Godfather*. Neither was 100 percent Italian, but they were essential, nonetheless.

There were rumors that one of the three rival New York families was trying to eliminate Solari. Solari heard the rumors and decided to take action.

With Lou and Charles's help, Solari planned to take out the leader of the three rival families on the same day.

Yes, it was straight out of *The Godfather.* Sometimes, art imitates life.

For a job this big, they would need Charles's help. He was to kill mafia boss Peter Ricci first, then call Lou, who, with Solari's help, had designed the murders of the other two mafia dons. Ricci was the most powerful one, so they had to ensure he was dead first before killing the other two.

It would have been pointless to kill the other two if Ricci hadn't died. If any of the other families had planned on killing Solari, it would have gone through Ricci.

Ricci had been seeing a prostitute named Holly for some time now, and Charles had known her from around town. Solari felt that was there in and had Charles get closer to her in the weeks leading up to the proposed killings.

At Solari's suggestion, Charles told Holly he would give her $20,000 if she would schedule an "appointment" with Mr. Ricci for Thursday night at a hotel of their choice. Charles would get a room a few doors down from the one Holly had reserved for her and Ricci.

She would then text Charles the word "here" once Mr. Ricci had joined her in the hotel room. She was nervous, but Charles was certain she would go through with it. After all, $20,000 was $20,000.

When Charles got the text, he would enter the hotel room and dispose of Ricci, who would likely be in a compromising position.

The night it was to go down, Charles was sitting in the hotel room two doors down. He had two handguns equipped with silencers.

One of Solari's drivers was waiting downstairs. Charles had always planned on sparing Holly and giving her the $20,000.

On the morning the killings were set to go down, Mr. Solari informed Charles that Holly couldn't be allowed to live. Charles didn't like it, but he knew he shouldn't argue with Antony Solari.

It looked like Holly wouldn't be collecting her $20,000 after all.

Holly had told Charles that Ricci should be there by 7:00.

When Charles hadn't received a text from her by 7:15, he became a little worried. By 7:30, he was freaking out. At 7:45, he walked out of his hotel room and peeked toward her room.

The door was slightly ajar, and Charles knew something was wrong. He ever so slowly walked up to Holly's room and peered in. She was lying on the bed, dead, her head at a gruesome angle. Her neck had been broken.

Charles got out of the hotel as quickly as he could and went downstairs to the waiting car. He called his brother and told him what happened.

He said Ricci was nowhere to be seen. Lou, disgusted with his brother, had to call Solari and tell him the bad news.

Solari, although a complete psychopath who would kill his own family if he saw fit, was also an intelligent, contemplative man. He told Lou not to go through with the other two murders.

He reasoned that if he did, Ricci would know that Solari was the one who had orchestrated all of this. He was still holding out hope that Ricci hadn't received much information out of little Miss Holly before he killed her.

If Holly had said anything, Charles had become a liability, and by familial bonds, so had Lou. The more Solari thought about it, the more he realized doing away with Charles and Lou was necessary.

He had grown fond of both and didn't like what had to be done, but he couldn't let emotions affect his decision-making. This was only business.

Solari called Lou and said he wanted to meet him and his brother at ten a.m. the following morning.

Lou knew he was a dead man, and so was his brother. Lou had always prided himself on being a quick thinker, so he knew he better think of something fast.

He came up with an idea that seemed to be feasible. He called a local lawyer and asked if he could meet with him that night. The sooner, the better.

⁂

Lou knew if he waited till the ten a.m. meeting, they would never get out alive, so instead, Lou decided to beat Solari to the punch.

Solari ate breakfast every morning at eight a.m. at Amici's, and Lou planned to meet him there, where scores of witnesses would be present.

⁂

Lou walked into Amici's at 8:15 that morning and went straight to Solari's table. Solari was eating with three other people Lou knew to be 100% Italian, not 50% mutts like Lou and Charles.

"We need to talk," Lou said.

"I'm having breakfast with some friends, Lou. I told you we would meet at 10:00."

"Get rid of these guys before I raise my voice," Lou said.

Solari stared at him so intently that Lou unconsciously took a step back. However, Solari acquiesced and asked his friends to let them be.

Lou sat down and moved his chair to sit within whispering distance of Solari.

"This couldn't have waited till ten?" Solari asked.

"We wouldn't have made it out of that meeting alive."

Solari's smile told Lou everything he needed to know. "What do you want Lou?"

Lou took out a piece of paper from his pocket. He handed it to Solari, who started reading it.

"Law Offices of Joe Damon.

If I should die of anything other than old age, I order you to send a copy of the statement below to Peter Ricci, Mo Mancini, and Salvatore De Luca. Their addresses are attached below.

"My name is Lou Sessions. I worked for Anthony Solari. On August 15th, 2007, he planned on killing Peter Ricci, Mo Mancini, and Salvatore De Luca. Something went wrong with the murder of Mr. Ricci, and the other two were called off. I'm sure you've suspected it, but I'm telling you it's the truth. If you are receiving this, that means Mr. Solari has killed me, and I hope you seek retribution. Not for my sake, obviously, but because he tried to kill you three. I have no doubts he will try again.

Lou Sessions"

Lou Sessions and attorney Joe Damon had signed the bottom of the letter. Solari looked up and smiled again, but this time, it was more like the smile of a proud father.

"You always were the smart one, Lou! This is pretty ingenious if I do say so myself."

He leaned in even closer.

"I don't want to see you ever again. I will let you and your brother live, but if I ever hear that you tell anyone else of this, I will torture you, your brother, and any family member I can get my hands on. Is that clear?"

Lou knew that he wasn't kidding. "I understand."

"I don't want you in this part of town. Ever again. Now get the fuck out of here," Solari said.

Lou walked out of Amici's, a man without a job, but, against all odds, he had avoided death.

Solari sat back, laughed, and then spoke quietly to himself.

"Smart little devil. You're safe for now, Lou. But I may catch up with you and your brother in the future."

In the years that followed, Lou and Charles started their own business, although it wasn't one you would see advertised in the yellow pages.

People would call the Sessions brothers if someone weren't paying a debt. They were basically bullies for hire.

It would usually just consist of roughing people up. The proverbial breaking of people's kneecaps happened on rare occasions.

The Sessions wanted more, and with the help of their "mole" in the police department, they started to get involved in the drug business.

Yes, they were terrible people, but they hadn't murdered anyone since they stopped working with Solari.

Freddy Macon was different, though. They were offered $50,000. For Lou, this was just too big a payday to pass up.

When they got Freddy Macon in their truck, that should have been the end of it. They would drive him down to the abandoned docks, find out where the money was, and then dispose of Freddy.

It was supposed to go down like it did with Tim and Chase.

Unfortunately, at a stop light, Macon overpowered Charles and pushed his way out of the truck. He didn't get far, though. Charles caught up with him when he ran into the back alley behind O'Rourke's. This was why a professional hit had disintegrated into a back alley stabbing.

When they walked out and saw that three young men had witnessed them murder someone, Lou put his quick thinking to use.

He decided to yell out, "Mr. Solari just wants what is his," for the benefit of the three men.

Mr. Solari had nothing to do with Freddy Macon's murder. Lou just thought it was an excellent way to needle his old boss. Hopefully, it would also deflect the investigation from getting to Charles and him and cause Solari some undue headaches.

The police hadn't contacted Lou, so it seemed to be working so far.

❦

ONE OF THE MORE INNOVATIVE IDEAS I'VE EVER HAD, LOU THOUGHT.

It was that type of thinking that saved his life from Anthony Solari, helped throw off the investigation into Freddy Macon's murder, and led him to Tim and Chase.

Lou was so busy thinking about his own ingenuity that someone almost ran into him on the sidewalk.

He brushed off the near miss and continued walking.

Lou rounded a corner and took a left onto Saint German Place. He walked about a hundred feet down the street and looked up to see a green awning.

He was standing directly in front of Les Deux Magots.

35
BRYCE

PARIS

"If I had known it was going to come to this, I would have been honest with you from the beginning," I said to Elise as I held onto her hands.

We were still on the train, just outside of Paris.

Her hands loosened her grip on mine when I uttered, "Would have been honest with you."

What the hell are you talking about?" she yelled.

I PROCEEDED TO TELL ELISE EVERYTHING.

I described the murders in New York, my letter to the NYPD, and my rationale for not turning myself in. I also told her what Tim and Chase had done with the escorts and how I knew they'd never go to the police.

I'd almost told her earlier but didn't want to scare her needlessly.

I finished by telling her about the call with my father. How Tim and Chase were missing, and my fear that the murderers could already be in Paris.

She looked up at me. I had no idea what she was going to say.

"So all you know for certain is that your friends are missing? They hardly seem like saints. Maybe they are off doing juvenile things together."

"I wish I could believe that, Elise. It's been five days. Neither one has shown up for work or been in contact with their wives. This is more than just doing juvenile things together."

Elise's shoulders sagged.

The reality was starting to hit home. This wasn't some drunken weekend for Tim and Chase.

"So what do we do?" she asked.

"We get a hotel for tonight. It's too dangerous for either of us to go home. And obviously, you can't go to work tomorrow."

"I already took the last two days off."

"Elise, do you not understand how serious this is? We saw them stab a man to death. My guess is they have already killed Tim and Chase. And now they may be in Paris, and their only information is that I write at Les Deux Magots. Of course, you can't go there!"

I yelled the last part just a bit too loud. I looked around the train, and although it was nearly empty around us, I needed to keep it down.

I glanced at Elise, who was starting to show signs that this was getting to her. I pulled her closer.

"Things will never be the same," she half whispered/half whimpered.

I pulled her out of the hug and had her look in my eyes.

"Do you trust me?" I asked.

"Yes, I do."

"Good, because I am going to get us out of this. I promise."

She looked like she believed I would.

That made one of us.

WHEN THE TRAIN ARRIVED IN PARIS, WE FLAGGED DOWN A CAB. I TOLD the driver we wanted a cheap, quiet hotel far from the 6th arrondissement.

He nodded like he understood and took us to an out-of-the-way hotel. I paid cash for the room and gave a fake name. Maybe I was being a bit cautious, but I figured it was better to be safe.

The hotel said they wanted an ID and a credit card, but I told them I had lost both and offered to pay the deposit in cash. They seemed okay with that. The Ritz, this was not.

I took Elise to the room. She was not enjoying this at all—who could blame her—and looked like she just wanted to sleep, which was fine with me.

I needed time to think.

WHEN ELISE FELL ASLEEP, I STARTED TO GO THROUGH ALL OF MY OPTIONS:

1) We could go about our daily life just praying that Tim and Chase's disappearances weren't related to what we saw. I ruled this out instantly. I didn't want to spend my life looking over my shoulder, and more importantly, I didn't want to put Elise in harm's way. She wasn't in New York with us and

had nothing to do with this. More than anything else, Elise had to be safe. That was my number one priority.

2) I could contact the local Paris police and tell them what I had seen in New York. I could describe the two killers and hope for the best. The Paris police would have no jurisdiction on that crime, though, and would have no grounds to hold them. I didn't like the second option either.

Which left me with the final option.

3) I could face this head-on. I could call the NYPD, tell them what I saw, and inform them I'm flying back to testify. I'm sure they could have police waiting for me when I arrived at the airport in New York. This means I would probably have to testify in a trial against the mafia.

The worst part is that I would be leaving Elise. The mere thought of that hurt my soul more than you could imagine. But the idea of Elise coming face to face with the killers was even more unimaginable. I shuttered at the thought.

My mind was made up. I had to go back and face up to what I had seen. I didn't know if Elise would forgive me or if I'd ever see her again, but she would be safe, and that mattered most. I opened my laptop and looked at the earliest flights leaving Paris for JFK.

I STEPPED OUT ON THE BALCONY SO ELISE COULDN'T HEAR ME IF SHE woke up.

I used her phone to call the NYPD. I told them I had information on a murder in Manhattan of a guy named Freddy. I gave them the location, the date, and said he was killed by stabbing.

I was transferred three times until a new voice came on the line.

"I'm transferring you to Lieutenant Leroy Archer."

36

LEROY

As Leroy Archer sat in his office reviewing all the known evidence in the Tim Sawyer/Chase Andrews disappearance, he received a knock at the door.

"Transferring a call into you, Lieutenant. The guy says he witnessed a murder. Sure knows a lot of details. I don't think it's some crackpot."

"Thanks, Officer Miles. Put him through."

The officer left, and Leroy picked up the phone a few seconds later.

"Lieutenant Leroy Archer."

The voice that followed was noticeably nervous, but Leroy also sensed a resoluteness.

"Hi, my name is Bryce Connor, and I think you might be looking for me."

"I was just told you witnessed a murder, not that you committed one. Why would we be looking for you?"

"Because I wrote you guys a letter describing the murder."

Leroy sat up higher in his chair. *The stabbing in the alley!* He had to be careful not to scare off the caller on the other end.

"I read the letter, Bryce. And I understood your rationale for not coming to the police, even if I don't condone it. Can I ask why you are coming forward now?"

"Because Tim Sawyer and Chase Andrews were with me when I saw the murder."

Leroy couldn't believe his ears. That was not what he had expected at all. He paused for a few seconds to take it in.

"I assume you know who they are," Bryce continued.

"Yes, Bryce, I do."

"Are they dead?" Bryce asked. Leroy sensed that it was a struggle to get out.

Leroy knew better than to provide specific details about the investigation, but he also thought he should be as honest as possible with Bryce. If he smelled something was off, he might disappear again.

"If I were a betting man," Leroy said, immediately regretting his choice of words. He continued solemnly, "My guess is that they are no longer alive."

Bryce's voice lowered, "Mine too. They'd never be gone this long."

"I agree with you, Bryce," Leroy said. He kept using Bryce's name, hoping he would see him as an ally, which he was. "Can you tell me again exactly what you saw?"

Bryce told Leroy about the whole night, starting with his flight to JFK and ending with him giving the letter to the teenage kid the following morning. He left nothing out.

"And what happened after you gave the letter to the little kid?" Leroy asked.

"I took a cab to the airport and flew to Paris."

Leroy was taken by surprise once again. "Paris? Are you still there?"

"I am. And I'm afraid the killers are as well."

"Why do you think that?" Leroy asked.

Bryce explained that he had been on a quick jaunt away from Paris with a young lady he was dating.

He told Leroy about his father letting him know that Tim and Chase were missing and about the peculiar call his mother had received.

Bryce was pretty sure that was the killer's calling, and it was four days ago. They could easily be in Paris by now, so he decided to get a hotel with Elise and not venture near their houses or Les Deux Magots.

"I'm calling from the hotel now," Bryce concluded by saying.

"And I'm assuming you want to fly back to the U.S.?"

Bryce paused for several seconds, considering his options one last time. "I can't really say I want to, but I will for the sake of Elise. So the answer is yes."

Leroy sensed that Bryce felt he could trust him.

"I have a few stipulations, though," Bryce said.

"I'm listening," Leroy said.

Bryce wanted Leroy to send a Paris police officer or two to look after Elise once he left for the airport.

He said they were safe for the night at the nondescript hotel. Bryce also said he'd like the NYPD waiting for him when he landed at JFK.

"I'll have some of NYPD's finest waiting for you when you land. And I'll call the Paris police right now."

"Okay. I'll call you early tomorrow morning, and when the Paris police arrive, I'll head to the airport."

"Do you want to tell me the name of the hotel right now?"

"I'm a little gun-shy at the moment. I'll tell you in the morning."

"I understand. Be safe, Bryce."

"I will."

They decided to leave it at that.

Leroy went to get some coffee—eight a.m. Paris time was two a.m. in New York. It looked like he wasn't getting much sleep tonight.

※

Leroy called a meeting of the six officers who worked directly underneath him. Leroy explained it wasn't optional, and they all showed up: Officer Billy Braden, Officer Chris Efert, Officer Bob Hollins, Detective Mike Muncie, Detective Archie Guest, and Old Man Wilson. Old Man Wilson was Officer Eddie Wilson, but since he had been with the NYPD the longest of their group, he had inherited the moniker of "Old Man Wilson" despite only being forty-seven years old.

"Thanks everyone for attending," Leroy began. "Many, if not all, of you know about the case of the two missing men, Tim Sawyer and Chase Andrews. A few of you have also been told about a letter we were given by someone who had witnessed a murder on 27th Avenue. Well, it turns out that these cases are related."

Leroy explained Bryce's phone call, his friendship with Tim and Chase, and what they had witnessed that night. He also explained Bryce's fear that the killers were in Paris and how he had decided to fly back to the U.S. He would arrive at JFK at eight a.m. the following day.

"Muncie and Efert, I want you to wait outside his arrival gate. You'll have to talk to the TSA, but it should be easy. Call me if you have any problems. Guest and Braden, I need you to get a sketch artist lined up for tomorrow morning and be ready to distribute it to the usual places. Time is of the essence since we need to find out who these guys are before they return to the U.S. if they are flying in from Paris. Hollins and Old Man ... " Leroy paused, knowing he didn't like the nickname. "Hollins and Wilson, you will stay here with me. Although I have my doubts, this case may involve Anthony Solari, and if it does, it will get a lot of media attention. I'll need your help dealing with all the media whores."

Everyone smiled at this. If there's one thing that all the police officers in the room could agree on, it was that the media, as a whole, were a total pain in the ass.

Even Old Man Wilson managed a laugh. It was merely perfunctory, though. He had just received some terrible news and needed to make a phone call.

37

OLD MAN WILSON

Eddie Wilson, also known as "Old Man Wilson," had been a cop for nineteen years. And a clean one for thirteen of them.

※

HE JOINED THE DEPARTMENT AS A BABY-FACED KID IN HIS LATE TWENTIES. He wanted to do good for his community, and he had done just that for over a decade.

There was always a mysterious undercurrent with Wilson, and most people thought he was a bit odd, but he seemed to do everything by the book. Despite not being very popular, he was considered a good enough cop. That all changed.

※

WILSON WOULD PROBABLY SAY IT STARTED SIX YEARS AGO WITH A DRUG bust.

Truth be told, it started months earlier when Wilson's long-time wife, Janet, filed for divorce. Eddie Wilson had worked his ass off for over thirteen years, putting in overtime every time he could; weekends, holidays, you name it.

All so he and Janet could live a comfortable life. And now she was divorcing him? *Screw that!*

Wilson became a very unpleasant man. Cops who worked with him noticed. His wife refused to see him outside of the courtroom.

The divorce dragged on for months, the legal fees mounted, and Wilson's savings depleted rapidly. With this hanging over his head, he made a fateful decision that changed his life forever.

His former partner, Pedro Ramos, and he were called to a crime scene six years ago. When they showed up, there were two Hispanic drug dealers shot dead in the front seat of their car.

The faces were recognizable to Ramos and Wilson. These were known drug dealers and all-around bad people that the general public would not miss at all.

Ramos looked in the back seat for drugs and told Wilson to check in the trunk.

"Pop the trunk," Wilson said.

Wilson walked around to the trunk, and Ramos continued combing the inside of the car. As Wilson lifted the trunk, he looked down at 10-12 large bricks of $100 bills. If he had to guess, he would say each brick was worth $10,000.

"Anything back there?" Ramos asked.

Looking back, Wilson wishes he could blame it on the expensive divorce he was going through or the pittance he received that the NYPD called a salary, but he knew better. He was a greedy asshole with no morals.

There was no way around it. The divorce had only brought out his inner bad guy. It was always there.

He took two of the bricks and hid them quickly in the sides of his police vest. Any more would have been obvious.

As it was, he'd have to be careful not to have anyone rub up against him. Wilson knew that Ramos was as straight-edged as they came, and there was no way he'd agree to take any money.

"I asked if there was anything back there," Ramos yelled again.

Wilson pushed the bricks flusher against his side. "Get back here, Pedro. You won't believe this."

Ramos left the back seat and walked to the trunk. Looking down, he said, "Holy Shit! We better call in the big guns."

❦

ONCE HE BECAME A DIRTY COP, EDDIE WILSON NEVER TURNED BACK. HE would steal money when given the chance, but that wasn't often enough. Drugs were different.

There were many opportunities to take a little dope here and there, and Wilson took full advantage every chance he could.

Drug dealing was a nasty profession, and Wilson didn't want to be a part of it. It's not like a cop could be out there on the street peddling dope, anyway.

He talked to one of his low-level informants, whom he swore to secrecy. That informant put him in touch with a man named Lou Sessions.

The informant mentioned that Lou Sessions had recently started a business for himself and had the connections to make this happen.

Eddie Wilson didn't want to spend much time interviewing potential business partners, so he met with Lou and liked him well enough to start a business with him.

※

Lou Sessions and Eddie Wilson forged a profitable partnership for several years. Early on, Lou learned all he could about his new business partner.

Within a few days, he knew that Wilson was a cop. Lou was happy with this new information.

First, he knew people wouldn't complain about the drugs Lou was selling. They were taken during a drug bust, for Christ's sake. Second, Wilson would be easy to blackmail if it ever came to that. He was a cop stealing drugs, after all.

Lou never told Wilson he knew where he got the drugs, but he didn't need to. Wilson knew these guys had done their homework, and so had he. Lou and Charles Sessions used to work with Anthony Solari, and that's how they had the contacts to make this happen.

※

After four profitable years, Wilson suddenly went to Lou and told him he wanted out—just like that. He explained to Lou that he had amassed enough money, and it was no longer worth the risk.

"I know what you do for a living," Lou said.

Eddie Wilson shrugged as if this was no big surprise. "Yeah, I figured after almost five years, you probably did. Then you can understand why I want out. The protocol is changing, and too many officers are being called to each crime scene. I just can't do it anymore. You can be assured that I will never mention you or your brother. If I did, I'd go to jail for life, and a cop doesn't last too long in jail. I'm going to quit the force soon and go live on an island."

Lou stared Wilson down. "No, that's not going to work."

"You don't call the shots!" Wilson yelled.

"Actually, I do. How many years are you in?"

"Eighteen years."

"That's about what I thought. No one quits two years before his pension. That would arouse suspicion, don't you think?"

"Possibly," Wilson admitted.

"So if you want to leave the drug business, I will let you. We don't need your drug seizures anymore, to be honest. However, we will need an occasional tip as to what the Manhattan police force is up to. You will get that information for me. If you don't, I will leave the country, but not before sending something to the NYPD about their favorite officer, Eddie Wilson, and you will spend the rest of your life in jail. After two years of occasionally providing information to us, you can retire without suspicion and head to that tropical island."

Wilson bowed his head. There wasn't much of a choice. "I'll give you two years. Not a day longer. After that, I'm out of here and off to the Caribbean. Okay?"

"It's a deal," Lou said.

※

Lou used Wilson sparingly in the intervening year and a half.

He became known to Lou and Charles as "the mole." Lou had to ensure the NYPD wasn't on to him a handful of times. Wilson had told him that he had nothing to worry about each time. It had been pretty easy work, and Wilson was counting the time down until he could retire.

Wilson was exactly six months away from retirement when Lou had called him asking about information on the guy killed in the alley. *What the fuck,* Wilson had thought.

He had never agreed to help Lou get away with murder. And yet, he knew he would. He couldn't risk spending the rest of his life in jail. Officers didn't do too well in jail, no matter how much they tried to separate them from the general jail populace.

※

That's why, when the meeting with Leroy Archer ended, Eddie Wilson excused himself for a lunch break and went home and grabbed the untraceable phone he used on rare occasions.

Wilson called Lou, who he knew was in Paris, and told him that Bryce Connor would be flying out of Charles De Gaulle and into JFK at eight a.m. the following morning.

Lou listened to Wilson, saying "I see" a few times and "Good work" as he hung up the phone.

Wilson bowed his head and wondered if he had just caused Bryce Connor's death.

38

THE KILLERS

After learning valuable information about Les Deux Magots from Bryce's parents, Lou booked the two flights to Paris.

When they arrived in Paris, they found a hotel in the 6th arrondissement, about a half mile from Les Deux Magots.

By the time they checked in, it was late Sunday night so they decided they would go to the cafe the next day.

Lou did have one stop that night. He went to a local kitchen appliance store and bought the biggest knife he could find.

They obviously couldn't bring their guns on the flight, so this would have to do. He looked down at the twelve-inch blade. Yeah, this would do just fine.

When Lou returned to the hotel, he told Charles they needed the element of surprise to kill Bryce. They couldn't just casually approach Les Deux Magots since he had seen their faces. They needed to scope out the cafe. When Bryce showed up, they would watch him from afar and eventually follow him home. Then, they would have the element of surprise they so desperately needed.

THE FOLLOWING DAY, THEY WOKE UP AND TRIED TO DRESS LIKE REGULAR, everyday Parisians. Lou wore a beret and sunglasses, and Charles wore a Paris St. Germain football hat with the requisite sunglasses. Lou had told Charles, "Hide your face as much as you can."

They walked to Les Deux Magots and got an inside table at a cafe across the street. With their disguises, Lou thought they were in no danger of Bryce spotting them.

They sat there for thirty minutes and observed everyone walking in and out. There was no sign of Bryce.

Lou told Charles to wait there and headed across the street. Although this contradicted what he had told Charles the night before, Lou figured this was worth the risk.

Lou planned to take a quick peek inside, and if he didn't see Bryce, he'd approach a waitress to ask for information. Scanning the cafe as subtly as he could, he didn't see anybody resembling Bryce.

After researching Bryce and finding some pictures online, Lou was sure he'd recognize him, but there was no sign of him at Les Deux Magots. He went up to the nearest waitress. Her nametag said, Dolores.

"Hi, Dolores. My name is Tommy, and I'm looking for an old friend of mine, Bryce Connor. He likes to write here."

Dolores's face lit up. She had really taken a liking to Bryce and thought that he and Elise made a great couple. *Plus, when I gave Elise the letter he left, I had a small part in them becoming a couple.*

"You know Bryce?" Dolores kicked herself for a question that had already been answered.

"I sure do. We're old friends from the States. He told me he was writing at the best cafe in France. He said they had the best waitresses, too!"

Lou was trying to charm the old waitress in front of him. It was working.

"Well, I would hope so. He's dating one of them," Dolores said.

"Would that be you, Dolores?"

Dolores appreciated the sentiment at fifty-three, even if it was in jest. "No, silly. He's dating Elise, a young, beautiful French girl."

Time to get to the point. "I'm only here a few days. Do you know when he might stop by?"

"They are on vacation right now. But Elise works on Wednesday, so I'm sure Bryce will be here. He always sits outside and writes his novel when Elise is working. They are truly a great couple."

"Thanks so much, Dolores. You've been a great help. You don't know where either of them lives, do you?"

"No, sorry, I don't."

Lou figured it was time to get out of there before arousing suspicion.

"Thanks for your help, Dolores. And please don't tell him about this. I'd rather surprise him on Wednesday."

DEBUT NOVEL

Dolores faked zipping her lips. Lou leaned down, grabbed her wrist, and kissed the back of it. Dolores blushed as Lou walked away.

※

Lou went back to the cafe across the street and told Charles they should return to the hotel so they could talk in private.

Once they were back in the privacy of their hotel room, Lou said, "Apparently, Bryce and his new girlfriend Elise are on vacation. Elise works on Wednesday, and Bryce will be there, so we will stake out the cafe and eventually follow him home. The woman I talked to will certainly remember me, so I think it's better if we lay low till Wednesday. Are you ready for some room service over the next few days?"

"Whatever you think is best, Boss," Charles responded.

※

They slept in the hotel Monday night and stayed there all day Tuesday, refusing housekeeping but ordering room service twice. They worked through all the contingencies that they might encounter.

At eight p.m., Paris time, Lou's phone rang. He knew who it was.

Charles watched Lou go talk in the corner and heard him say "I see" a few times before finally saying, "Good work."

Lou walked back over to Charles. "Plans have changed. We are going to Charles De Gaulle Airport tomorrow morning."

※

They sat there that night and discussed the difficulty of killing someone in an airport. Unfortunately, it had to happen that way.

If Bryce arrived at JFK, he'd have the NYPD waiting for him, and it would only be a matter of time until they discovered the brothers' identity. They wracked their brains.

Charles suggested waiting until Bryce went into the bathroom and then shoving him into a stall and stabbing him to death.

"Yeah, real subtle," Lou remarked.

Just when he thought there wasn't anything they could do, Lou thought of something that might work. It was a long shot but not an impossibility.

"Charles, could you go to a local drug store and buy things to put into a syringe that could kill a man?"

"Piece of cake. Clorox and some pills would do the trick. Dissolve a shitload of sleeping pills in there, and it's nighty night forever."

"Well, then, what are you waiting for?" Lou asked.

The brothers shared their usual grotesque laugh as Charles headed to the store.

※

Lou went online and paid for two flights to Boston, assuming they would have to kill Bryce in the international terminal. He also figured staying away from New York for a few days might be a good idea.

He booked the flight for an hour later than Bryce's, giving them time to commit the murder and still board their plane. Assuming the police hadn't found the body and shut down the whole terminal by then.

※

When Charles returned, he dismantled the syringe and placed the pieces in different parts of his luggage. A syringe might arouse a few questions from airport security.

Charles then made his Clorox/sleeping pills concoction and put it in a tiny mouthwash bottle.

"This will kill more than gingivitis," he said.

Lou laughed heartily and thought it was one of Charles's better one-liners. Charles wasn't known for his humor, after all.

"I think this bottle is small enough to get through security," Charles said.

"Will it kill him?"

"I dissolved over fifty pills in there. If I can plunge this whole thing into him, he's never waking up."

"Good work, Charles."

Lou sat back in his chair and thought about his plan.

They didn't want to inject him with others around, but it might be possible to do it so subtly that no one saw. Ideally, Bryce would go in a bathroom, and they could inject him with the needle from a neighboring stall.

No witnesses. The perfect crime. Prop his head up against the wall so all you see are his legs below the bathroom stall. He wouldn't be found for hours, maybe longer.

And by then, Lou and Charles would be on a flight back to the United States.

39
BRYCE

PARIS

After I got off the phone with Leroy Archer—whom I already trusted implicitly—I walked back into the hotel room and saw that Elise was awake.

"Too much stress. I couldn't sleep," she said.

There was no time to beat around the bush, so I told her what I had decided to do.

"I'm flying back to the U.S. tomorrow morning."

"Just like that? You weren't even going to discuss it with me?"

"Elise, there's nothing I would rather do than stay here with you. I love you! But if I stay, you are at risk. I don't want to spend our days in Paris looking over our shoulders. That's no way to live."

"Then let me come with you."

"I'm going to be testifying against the mafia. At least, I think so. I'm not sure the U.S. would be any safer than here."

"But you are still going back there."

"It's to keep you safe. I've talked to someone in the New York Police Department, and he is contacting Paris police. They will keep you safe until they know the killers are in custody or headed back to the U.S. If I remain here, I'm a target, which makes you a target, and I can't live with that."

"So, is this it for us?" Elise asked, on the verge of tears.

"Absolutely not," I said. "I'll be back in Paris as soon as possible, and it will be like nothing ever changed."

"You don't really believe that, do you? Everything has changed."

"I knew you'd hate my decision. In time, I think you'll understand it."

"This is bullshit."

"You're right," I said. "But keeping you safe is what's most important to me."

❧

I woke up the next morning at 4:30 a.m.

It was by far the toughest morning of my life. I'd had hangovers where my whole head was throbbing, but it was nothing compared to the knots in my stomach that morning. For all I knew, I was saying my final goodbye to Elise.

And if I ever saw her again, who knows in what capacity that would be.

Elise was right. *Everything had changed!*

We hugged, and we cried, but I still wouldn't budge.

If Elise and I had gone to Paris together and something had happened to her, I'd never have been able to forgive myself.

This was far from ideal, but Elise would remain alive.

I called Leroy Archer in New York and gave him the name of our hotel, and the room number. Less than twenty minutes later, a Paris policeman arrived at our room.

I made one request. Keep Elise at the hotel for at least one more day. Maybe then she could return to work or her place, but not until we knew more.

They both agreed. Elise begrudgingly.

❧

Elise and I said our final goodbyes.

"I love you," I said.

"I love and hate you right now," she said.

We hugged a final time.

"Don't get killed," she said.

And with that, I walked downstairs, flagged a cab, and headed toward Charles De Gaulle Airport.

40
BRYCE

CHARLES DE GAULLE AIPORT

I arrived at the airport at 6:30 a.m. with only the bag I had taken on our vacation to Normandy.

My mind was on Elise.

Had I made a mistake? Should we be doing this together, one way or the other? Was I right, and this was the only way to keep her safe?

I couldn't decide.

❊

I DIDN'T SEE HOW THE MURDERERS COULD POSSIBLY KNOW I WAS AT THE airport, but I still kept my head on a swivel.

I went to check in, and every ten seconds or so, I'd turn around to see if I saw anything suspicious. The only thing people saw as suspicious was my behavior.

After I got my ticket, I carried my bag and headed toward airport security. After finishing, I headed to Gate B-19, where I found a seat, sat back, and relaxed.

Fifteen minutes later, I headed for the bathroom.

41

THE KILLERS

Lou and Charles arrived at the airport at four a.m.
They saw Bryce walk into the international terminal at 5:30 a.m. They wore berets and soccer shirts, and each had a newspaper to hide their faces.

They had ditched the sunglasses, figuring they'd stand out like sore thumbs in an airport.

They watched Bryce stand in line and get his ticket, but there was no way they could get close without being seen. They had hoped Bryce would use the restroom, but that didn't happen.

He headed toward airport security amongst a mass of people. They'd have to find a way to inject the syringe closer to the gates.

After giving Bryce ample time to get through, Lou and Charles used Lou's purchased tickets to enter the international terminal.

They looked at the gate for the eight a.m. flight to JFK and saw it was Gate B-19. They headed that way and sat about 200 feet away at a separate gate, shielding their faces with the newspapers. They looked over and saw Bryce sitting there.

Bryce had a few people near him, but no one sat directly beside him. Lou thought it would be possible to come up behind him, subtly stab him with the syringe while putting a hat over his head, pretending he had fallen asleep.

Too risky, he decided. Bryce wouldn't just be rendered unconscious immediately.

Meanwhile, Charles had pieced the pieces of his syringe back together and, careful that no one noticed him, put the deadly concoction into the syringe.

At that very moment, they saw Bryce walking toward the bathroom.

Lou leaned over and whispered, "Go end this mother fucker's life."

Charles nodded slightly at his brother and started toward Bryce, a newspaper still covering his face. Bryce entered the bathroom, and five and a half seconds later, Charles did the same.

42
BRYCE

CHARLES DE GAULLE AIRPORT

I couldn't get the thought out of my mind that I should have just said "Fuck it" and either fled with Elise or brought her with me.

I never should have left her, even if her safety was my primary motivation.

That's the side I had landed on.

As soon as I got out of the restroom, I was going to call Leroy and see if we could fly her to the U.S. and have her protected.

I just hope she'd forgive me for not taking her in the first place.

I entered one of the bathroom stalls. It was quiet, and no one was in a stall on either side of me as I sat down. My victory was short-lived, however, as someone sat in the stall next to me a few seconds later.

I heard a little rustling from the neighboring stall. It was probably nothing, but I noticed it since I was on high alert.

As I looked over, to my amazement, I saw a hand with a syringe rising from below the bathroom barrier. The person was thrusting it toward my thigh. The bathroom was so small that I didn't have anywhere to move to avoid it.

Instincts took over, and I did the only thing I could think of doing. I kicked my shoe toward the oncoming syringe, hoping to knock it to the floor before it punctured my skin.

Unfortunately, instead of knocking over the syringe as I had hoped, the syringe caught my shoe square and entered it.

Call it luck, God's will, or something else, but when the syringe entered the shoe, it quickly took a right turn upward and exited without puncturing any of my toes.

I didn't have time to thank my lucky stars.

I flipped off the shoe and pushed open my stall door. At the same time, I saw the neighboring stall's door opening.

I cocked my fist, and as soon as the door fully opened, I punched the guy in the nose with all my force. I felt my fist moving his bone to the left and immediately knew I had broken his nose.

I hit him in the face three more times in rapid succession, and he collapsed backward onto the toilet. He was unconscious.

I removed the phone and took a quick picture of the guy. I didn't have time to look at him closely as I punched him, but as I snapped the photo, I recognized him as the taller murderer from New York. The other one was likely close by, so I needed to get the fuck out of Charles De Gaulle Airport.

I took a left as I exited the bathroom, and out of the corner of my eye, I saw the stocky, more menacing killer looking directly at me. He stared at me and then looked back toward the bathroom, obviously deciding in which direction to head.

He eventually chose the latter and ran toward the bathroom. I'm sure the dozens of people near us had something to do with that.

◈

AS IN NEW YORK, I PROBABLY SHOULD HAVE GONE TO THE POLICE, BUT THE killers had just attempted to murder me in one of the most famous airports in the world. My faith in law enforcement wasn't at an all-time high.

Plus, if the killers had found me at the airport, surely they could find Elise at her apartment. The thought of the Paris police looking after her suddenly didn't make me feel so secure.

If the killers had made their way here from New York, maybe some other members of the mafia could be here as well.

Was I even positive that the man looking after Elise was a member of the Paris police?

The thought scared me to my core.

I was sick to my stomach.

I had to get back to Elise.

I slowly made my way through the airport, trying not to draw attention to the man with one shoe.

43

THE KILLERS

Lou sensed something was wrong before Bryce even walked out of the bathroom. Charles should have been in and out in thirty seconds.

When Bryce emerged, Lou's initial reaction was to go right after him, but he thought better of it.

Lou didn't have a weapon, and he'd immediately be arrested if he started beating someone up in the middle of the airport.

There's nothing he could do. Begrudgingly, he walked towards the bathroom.

Two men were helping Charles get up from the bathroom stall. He was bleeding and looked like he had a broken nose.

Lou saw the shoe in the neighboring stall with the syringe sticking out.

Lucky fucking bastard!

Lou grabbed the shoe and threw it in the garbage, ensuring the two men didn't see it. He pushed it down the trash and covered it with some other debris.

Lou returned to the stall and told the two men that he was Charles's brother. Charles nodded in the affirmative, and the two guys told Lou they had gotten a look at the other guy as he ran out.

"We can go with you to talk to the police if you want," one of the two said in broken English. Somewhere from Eastern Europe, Lou guessed.

Lou knew the one thing they couldn't do was get the police involved.

"Actually, there were a few cops outside the bathroom who already arrested the guy. They must have heard the scuffle and been waiting outside."

It was all Lou could come up with, but they seemed to buy it.

"Good. I have to catch a flight anyway," one of them said.

The two men scurried out of the bathroom.

Thirty seconds and one reset nose later, Lou and Charles walked out as well.

44
BRYCE

ON THE RUN

As soon as I exited Charles De Gaulle Airport, I wanted to call Elise. But something held me back.
How the hell did the New York killers know to find me at the airport?
I couldn't come up with a good answer.
I'd told Leroy Archer, and maybe he'd mentioned it to the Paris police.
Those were the only people who knew, besides Elise and myself.
That meant one of them might have a leak.
Was Elise safe? Was the man who showed up really with the Paris police?
I got in a taxi and headed back to Elise.
My stomach was in knots.
Please still be there, Elise!

When I arrived at the hotel, the officer from yesterday intercepted me before I could make it to her room. I took that as a good sign.

"What about your flight?" he asked with a thick French accent.

"They tried to kill me at the airport."

"Are you joking?"

"Do I look like I'm joking?"

"What happened?"

"I'll tell you after I talk to Elise. Is she in her room?"

"Yes."

I brushed the officer as I walked by him to Elise's room. It wasn't intentional—I was just so eager to see her.

I knocked on her door.

"What?" she said, obviously perturbed.

"It's me," I said.

When Elise opened the door, her face was a mixture of relief, nervousness, and anger.

"What? Why are you back?"

"They tried to kill me at the airport."

She embraced me, and I could feel her shaking.

"I'm so glad you're okay," Elise said.

"I'm so sorry I left you. It won't happen again. I promise I was trying to look out for you. But still."

"I'm just glad you're safe. They tried to kill you?"

I nodded.

"What now?" she said.

"I have to call the police officer in New York and then my parents. Then we are getting the fuck out of here, so start packing."

"What about the officer watching me?"

"He can't place us under arrest. And to be honest, I'm not feeling too safe with the police these days. I'd rather it just be you and me."

"This is crazy," Elise said.

I hugged her. "I know. Are you ready to get out of here?"

"Yes. I'm sick of this place already."

"Great. While I'm on the phone, I want you to think of somewhere we can go. No relatives or friends. I don't want to get any innocent people involved."

"I've heard Munich is beautiful this time of year."

"This is no time for jokes."

"I'm not joking. Do you think France is the safest place for us right now? I can call work and tell them I'm taking a few days off. Hopefully, this will be resolved by then. And Munich is just a Eurorail ride away."

As usual, she was right. It was hard to feel safe in Paris knowing those two lunatics were still out there—and maybe more than just those two.

"Munich it is," I said. "I need to make those calls."

"I'll get ready."

⚜

I STEPPED OUTSIDE TO MAKE THE FIRST OF THE TWO CALLS.

It was three a.m. in New York. I was supposed to call Leroy over an hour ago.

"Hello?"

"Leroy, it's Bryce."

"You didn't get on that flight, did you?"

I explained to him what happened, including the fact that I'd taken a picture of my assailant with Elise's phone.

"Holy shit," he said. "You're lucky to be alive. Let my officers come to you now. You can relocate hotels if you want."

"That's not going to happen. Not yet, anyway. My girlfriend and I are leaving Paris for now. If I decide I need help, I will contact you."

"Listen, we could send five officers to Paris ... "

I cut him off. "That's not going to happen, Leroy. If you mention it again, I'm going to hang up on you. How could they have known I would be at the airport?"

"I don't know Bryce. Maybe they somehow found out who your girlfriend was and are tracking her phone."

"Seems unlikely," I said, but with very little confidence.

"Can you send me the picture of the assailant?"

"I'll do it when we get off the phone."

"Where are you going now, Bryce? And when will I hear back from you?"

"Munich and I don't know. But don't bother sending any officers to Germany. We are going underground for a while."

"I wouldn't recommend that."

"No offense, but I don't care."

"I don't like it, but I understand. Send me that picture, and please be vigilant and contact me when you can."

"Until next time," I said and hung up the phone.

I TEXTED LEROY THE PICTURE OF THE GUY TRYING TO KILL ME.

I entered the room and told Elise about my phone call.

"Don't you also have to call your parents?"

"I'll call them from the Eurorail. I can't deal with it right now." And with that, we headed for the door, but I stopped and turned to Elise. "Are you sure you want to do this? Flee Paris with me, go to Germany, and who knows where else?"

"And you're never going to leave me again?"

"Never."

"Then I'm in. If we're going down, at least we'll be doing it together."

It was hardly reassuring.

"One more thing," I said. "And you're not going to like it."

"What?"

I told her what Leroy had said, and once she agreed, I snapped her flip phone in half and tossed it in the garbage.

The Paris police officer tried to prevent us from leaving, but he had no legs to stand on.

We went downstairs and asked the clerk to order us a taxi.

Our lives on the run had officially begun.

45

LEROY

When Leroy got off the phone with Bryce, it was 3:15 a.m. He looked at the picture he had been emailed but didn't recognize the man.

The only officers still at the station were Hollins and Old Man Wilson, and they were there only because Leroy had ordered them to stay until they heard from Bryce.

Leroy told them about the attack on Bryce's life, Bryce's refusal to allow officers to fly to Paris, and Bryce's plans to go to Munich.

"I'm exhausted and headed home," Leroy said. "Make sure you guys get ahold of officers Muncie and Efert and tell them they don't have to go to JFK in the morning," Leroy said.

Old Man Wilson responded first. "I'll let them know."

"Good. One more thing, guys."

He motioned the two officers to follow him back to his office. He turned on his computer, launched Safari, and brought up the picture that Bryce had sent. "Do either of you guys know who this is? I didn't recognize him, but I thought you might know since you guys have been around this branch longer."

This time, it was Hollins who spoke first.

"I'm pretty sure that's Charles Sessions. He and his brother Lou were affiliated with Anthony Solari many years back. Word was the two of them had a falling out with Solari."

. . .

SOLARI! A FALLING OUT! I WAS RIGHT ALL ALONG, LEROY THOUGHT.

They were using Solari as a scapegoat. It never sounded like a Solari hit. A knife in an alley? I don't think so.

"What have they been doing since then?" Leroy asked.

"Haven't heard much," Hollins said. "Rumor has it that they were hired to strong-arm people into paying their debts. Also heard rumors they got involved in the drug trade, but I've got no evidence of that."

"Anything else you can remember?" Leroy asked.

"No, that's it. Wilson, you were around back then. Do you remember them?"

Old Man Wilson paused for a long moment.

Fuck, Wilson thought! *How did Charles let him take a goddamn picture! I can't deny having ever heard of them. Everyone who worked here back then knew who they were.*

"Yeah, I remember hearing about them. It's been years. Never heard the drug rumors, though," Wilson said.

Leroy thanked Hollins and Wilson and told them they could go.

Once they left, Leroy went downstairs, where all the old files were kept. Leroy got all the paperwork he could find on Lou and Charles Sessions.

It wasn't much, but he just wanted to know who he was dealing with. Leroy packed up the files and headed home.

❧

LEROY HAD NEVER BEEN A BIG SLEEPER AND SLEPT EVEN LESS DURING stressful times. After a mere three hours of sleep, he woke up at 7:30 a.m.

At eight a.m., Leroy got some good news. The expedited request for the DNA at the warehouse had come in. The blood was Chase Andrews's. He was pretty sure that Tim Sawyer was killed there as well.

He called Officer Braden and updated him on everything that had happened. He asked Braden to meet him down by the docks once again.

❧

THE HUDSON RIVER WAS ALWAYS MORE PLACID IN THE MORNING.

Leroy figured if they were going to see anything in the water down by the warehouse, it would be in the early hours.

Of course, Tim and Chase's killers could have just driven the two dead bodies across town, but Leroy found that unlikely.

If you are going to make the effort of getting Tim and Chase down to an old, uninhabited warehouse right along the Hudson, Leroy imagined that's where you would dump the bodies.

He knew if the bodies were weighed down or cut into small pieces, this search may well be fruitless, but it still had to be done. Never leave a stone unturned.

Officer Braden arrived ten minutes after Leroy and greeted him with a handshake followed by a yawn.

"I don't want to see or hear you yawn. I'm on three hours sleep," Leroy said.

Braden covered his mouth like he wouldn't yawn again. He headed toward the warehouse where they'd found the bloodstain.

"That's not why we're here," Leroy said. "We already know it was the DNA from Chase Andrews. This is more of a body retrieval mission."

Braden nodded and followed Leroy as he walked down toward the Hudson.

"The river levels out pretty quickly," Braden said. "It's more likely the bodies floated downstream."

"You're probably right, but humor me for a bit," Leroy said.

Braden knew this was likely a fool's errand, but he also remembered the numerous times Leroy Archer had proven him wrong. He looked over and saw Leroy scanning the river, deep in thought.

"What are you thinking?" Braden asked.

"If you were going to throw the bodies in the river, where would you do it from?"

"I don't know. Closest to the water, I guess."

"Precisely. They'd never toss them in from up here. In their pictures, Tim and Charles look like pretty big guys. The murderers wouldn't have been able to throw them out more than a few feet, and they'd risk them landing in extremely shallow water."

Braden could guess where Leroy was headed with this, both literally and figuratively. "So you want to head down this path to get closer to the water?"

"You'll make a good cop yet, Braden," Leroy answered tongue firmly in cheek.

The lieutenant and officer headed down the path to the water's edge. As they got closer, something shone from the bottom of the water.

"We can't be that lucky," Braden said. "Did you make a deal with the devil to give you supercop powers?"

Leroy laughed. "Let's not get ahead of ourselves. It could be anything."

"It looks like a giant chest to me. Putting the bodies in something like that would be a much smarter idea than just dumping the bodies in the water where they'd float downstream."

"Maybe. Again, let's not jump to conclusions."

They moved as close to the water as they could.

"If they let the chest go from here, it could easily have angled down to where it is now," Leroy said.

"I agree. Should I call for some divers to come down here?"

"Yeah," Leroy said, and just then, his phone rang.

He walked away from Braden, who couldn't hear his conversation. A few minutes later, Leroy walked back over, and Officer Braden could see the panic in his face.

"They got to Bryce again!"

46

OLD MAN WILSON

By the time Hollins had ID'd Charles Sessions, there was no way Wilson could deny knowing who he was.

Hollins was only a few years younger than Wilson (*and yet he got Old Man Wilson as a fucking nickname!*), and Hollins would know that Wilson was lying.

They had been in meetings years before when they had discussed the relationship between Solari and the Sessions brothers.

So, while he had to own up to knowing who Charles was, he was going to deny having heard anything about them being involved in selling drugs—for obvious reasons.

When Wilson got home, he called Lou immediately.

"Hello?"

"Hi, Lou. I've got some bad news."

"Couldn't be much worse than what happened to us."

"That guy Bryce took a picture of Charles. Another officer already ID'd Charles to our lieutenant."

Lou paused a few seconds before answering.

"It's all circumstantial without Bryce. A picture in an airport bathroom? What the hell does that prove? If we dispose of him here, there's no way they could prosecute us when we got back."

"You're probably right," Wilson agreed.

"Of course I'm right. Any word on where Bryce Connor is? I'm assuming he fled the airport."

"He told our lieutenant he was with his girlfriend, and they were going to Munich."

"Where in Munich?"

"My lieutenant didn't say."

Lou thought long and hard. "There's only three ways to get to Munich. I doubt they are renting a car since they'd want to get out of town as soon as possible. And after this morning, I'd say it's a safe bet they would stay away from airports."

"Makes sense," Wilson said, adding nothing to the conversation.

"That leaves the Eurorail. Call us immediately if anything changes."

Lou was about to hang up when Wilson said, "How is Charles? I heard the kid beat him up pretty good."

"Don't pretend like you care, Wilson."

With that, Lou hung up, and Old Man Wilson realized how much he despised him.

He decided when all this stuff with Bryce Connor was over, he was going to quit the force. He didn't care how close he was to retirement.

Fuck my pension! It's not worth all this shit.

47

BRYCE

PARIS TO MUNICH

I was sick of airports, train stations, and taxis. It was like they remade *Planes, Trains, and Automobiles* into a horror movie.

The cab ride to the train station was uneventful, which is exactly what I was looking for at this point.

When we got to the station, Elise was about to use her credit card to pay for the Eurorail tickets when I stopped her. I said there was no need to leave a paper trail.

But we needed cash, so we went to the ATM, and we both took out $400. I'd rather have someone know that we were at the train station as opposed to knowing where we were headed.

We paid for our tickets in cash.

Our train was packed this time, and I didn't know if that was a good or bad thing.

On the plus side, the NY killers were much less likely to attack us on a crowded train. On the negative side, they could blend in more easily—if they were somehow on the train.

But how could they possibly be on the train? We bought tickets five minutes before the train departed and paid cash. They'd have no way of knowing where we were.

Still, something in the back of my mind told me to be on alert.

Elise was quiet most of the train ride. If she was feeling a little squeamish, I couldn't blame her. After all, her boyfriend had almost been killed, and she had decided to flee Paris with a guy she had been dating for weeks.

Not years. Not months. Weeks!

※

QUESTIONS STARTED TO FLOOD MY MIND.

What if I hadn't seen the syringe? What if the syringe had entered my foot when I blocked it with my shoe? What if I had been killed? How would my parents have taken my death?

I wasn't a parent, but I could only imagine what the death of a child must do to you—murdered in a faraway city, no less.

And that's when it hit me; I still hadn't called my parents. The last time I talked to them was the previous day when my father told me about Tim and Chase. Had that only been twenty-four hours ago? It felt like a month had passed.

I had to call them. I certainly wasn't looking forward to it, and I'm sure they would freak out, but it was the right thing to do. I told Elise I needed to call my parents and asked if she wanted to accompany me.

"I'm fine here," she said, looking around at everyone nearby. "They wouldn't come after me with all these people around."

"Why don't you come with me?" I pleaded.

"Go call your parents, Bryce. I'm fine."

※

I'D HAVE TO BORROW SOMEONE'S PHONE.

It wasn't ideal, but what were my options now that I had smashed Elise's phone to smithereens? I walked to the neighboring car, which was the scenic car.

It seemed a better place to ask someone for their phone than just walking up to a random person sitting down. The scenic car was more social.

I saw a young Asian woman sitting alone. Her phone was in her hand. I sat down opposite her.

"How are you doing?" I asked.

"I'm fine, thanks. And you?" She sounded American.

"Actually, I have a favor to ask. I'm meeting my parents in Munich and I lost my cell phone. I saw you had one on you."

"You want to borrow my phone?"

"Yeah. I'll give you twenty euros. I'll be calling the U.S., so it might be expensive. You can keep the whole twenty. It won't be near that much, but you can keep the difference."

"I'm American. I call my parents all the time. I get it at cheap rates. You don't have to give me twenty euros."

This girl was a godsend.

"Thank you so much. My name is Bryce."

"I'm Tomiko."

She handed me the phone. I told her I wanted some privacy and might walk down the train slightly. She said it was no problem.

I thanked her immensely and walked down the train car toward the bathroom. I needed some privacy.

❦

I locked the bathroom door and called my parents. My Mom answered the phone.

"Hello?"

"Mom, it's me."

"Bryce, where are you? You're in trouble, aren't you? Why didn't you call your father back?"

It was a series of rapid-fire questions.

"Mom, slow down. I will tell you everything, but you must give me a chance. Is Dad there?"

"Yeah, let me get him."

She was gone for a few seconds. When she came back, my father got on the line.

"Bryce, what the hell is going on?"

I told my parents almost everything that had happened. I left out the part about the prostitutes in New York (nothing to be gained there), and I merely told them that I had seen the killers at the airport.

If I told them what happened in the bathroom stall, my mother wouldn't stop crying for weeks, and my father might have a coronary. Besides those two things, I told them the whole truth.

I told them my motivations for not going to the police and how I had fallen in love with Elise. I was all over the map. I finished by telling them that I was headed to Munich and felt we were safe now. I wasn't sure I believed the last part, but they needed to hear it.

I sat there expecting a tongue-lashing from my father.

That would come later, but my dad tried to lighten the mood. "This wasn't quite the European adventure I had in mind."

My mother wasn't having it and grabbed the phone from my father.

"Bryce, the first thing you must do is go to the police when you get to Munich," she said.

"And tell them what, Mom? That I think some guys might be after me. That I saw a murder in New York and then saw perpetrators again in Paris? They don't have any jurisdiction and no right to arrest them. But like I said,

I'm sure the killers are still in Paris or headed back to the U.S. They aren't meeting us in Munich."

"How can you possibly know that? You can't just be out there like a sitting duck; you have to do something." She was half yelling and half crying. "I can't believe you saw someone get killed, and you didn't go to the cops—or tell us."

"I was trying to keep you guys out of it. And, I told you, I didn't exactly want to testify against the mafia."

"We can discuss the moral ambiguity later, but for now, we need to know that you are safe," my father said.

"We paid cash for the Eurorail tickets and got on the train just before it boarded. There's no way they could have followed us."

"That may be true, Bryce, but what is your long-term plan? You can't remain on the run. It's dangerous and downright silly."

"I told you about the lieutenant in the NYPD. I trust the guy, and I'll get back to him soon. It's just when I saw the killers at the airport, I'm not that keen to hop back on a plane to the U.S. right now."

"Just worry about staying safe for now," my father said.

"I will be. You're just going to have to trust me."

I knew this wasn't enough for my mom, but it would have to be.

"What is Elise's phone number?" she asked.

"She doesn't have one. I destroyed it."

"This gets better and better, Bryce. What about her email?"

I thought back to this morning and remembered it. "ThespianElise at gmail dot com."

"Got it."

"Mom and Dad, I promise you that I will stay safe. I'm in love with this girl, and I won't do anything to put us in harm's way. I'll talk to Leroy, and we'll find a way for me to get back to you soon."

I gave them Leroy's email as well and got off the phone. They were not happy, but there wasn't much they could do. They said how much they loved me and to, above all else, be safe. I told them I would.

※

I HUNG UP, LEFT THE BATHROOM, AND RETURNED THE PHONE TO TOMIKO. I thanked her one last time and offered her money again, but she refused to accept it.

I walked back to the next train car to find Elise fast asleep.

※

WITH ELISE ASLEEP, I STARTED LOOKING FOR SOME CHEAP HOTELS IN Munich.

I read some reviews and looked at pictures. Words that usually would turn me off, such as "dark," "out of the way," and "quiet" were now words that I welcomed.

I found one across from the train station. Hotelissimo Haberstock was only $70 a night. I considered it but then thought better of it. If we were still being followed, why increase our chances of running into them by staying at a hotel near the city's central train station?

I readjusted the settings and found a hotel called Leto Motel Munchen City. It was four miles from the train station. The reviews said the place was quiet, and the rooms were small, which sounded promising.

I checked the distance from the hotel to the closest police station. It was .3 kilometers away. As I had told my parents, I hadn't planned on going to the police, but it was still good to have one that close.

A few minutes later, Elise awoke, and I told her about the call to my parents and our potential hotel.

"I can't wait till this is over," she said.

"That makes two of us."

48
BRYCE

MUNICH

The train finally arrived in Munich at six p.m. local time. Less than twelve hours had passed since I entered the international terminal at Charles De Gaulle Airport, and it was safe to say that those were twelve hours I would never forget.

We walked off the train platform and stood in line, waiting for a taxi. It was my first time in Munich, but there would be no double-decker bus/pub crawl adventure today.

We got in a taxi driven by a man named Karl. He was probably around fifty, had salt-and-pepper hair, and wore thick glasses.

Like everyone else in Europe, or so it seemed, Karl spoke English. I told him the address of the hotel. He started the meter, and we headed out onto the streets of Munich.

※

FIVE MINUTES INTO OUR DRIVE, KARL TURNED AROUND TO FACE US. "Do you have friends who are following us to the hotel?"

I looked at Elise, but nothing needed to be said.

It looked like our Paris problem had followed us to Munich.

I looked back at the white sedan Karl pointed out. It was about eighty feet behind us, and sure enough, every time Karl sped up, so did the white sedan.

The car didn't immediately switch lanes when we did, but within a few seconds, it would be back in the lane behind us.

"Listen to me very carefully, Karl," I said. "I was attacked in Paris this morning and almost killed. I'm pretty sure that's who is following us. You know these city streets better than they do. Please do anything you can to get away from them."

Karl looked in his rearview mirror, and he looked to be sizing me up—judging whether to believe me.

"I'll do what I can," he said. "The only problem is we are approaching heavy traffic on this main road."

"Take the side streets if you have to," I said.

"They are very narrow around here, but I'll do what I can."

With that, Karl accelerated, and we started passing cars.

Just as Karl had warned, we suddenly came to a halt. The brake lights of the cars in front of us all turned red. The white sedan had closed to within about forty feet of us, and there were only two cars between us and them.

"We will be stuck in this for two kilometers, but about half a kilometer ahead is a side street I can take," Karl said.

"Okay."

We've all seen many high-speed chases on the news, and they're almost daily occurrences in Los Angeles. But you rarely see a slow-speed one.

But for the next five minutes, that is precisely what happened. Karl would cut in front of a car, honk his horn, and pull ahead of said car. Unfortunately, the white car behind us was doing the same thing. We heard "Küss mein Arsch" and "Verpiss dich!" emanating from the cars behind us.

Karl did everything he could to escape the white sedan, but it wasn't enough. In fact, they had gained on us a little bit.

It's not like calling the cops would do anything—not in this mess.

"The side street is coming up in a bit. It's quite narrow, and we may be driving fast, so I suggest you put on your seat belts."

I had unlocked our seat belts in case we needed to get out of the car quickly, but now we both fastened them.

Karl maneuvered us to the far left lane to take the upcoming left. Unfortunately, so did the white sedan.

There was only one car in between us now. I hoped that when we took the left, the car behind us would block the white sedan for a few very valuable seconds.

We could see the side street approaching on our left. I'm guessing the white sedan knew what we were up to. We were now one car away from being able to take the left.

A few seconds later, Karl took a left and accelerated immediately. The white sedan did the same and was behind us before we knew it.

The slow-speed chase had now become a high-speed chase again. The road would be considered a two-lane street, with cars able to go both ways, but it was extremely narrow.

It was cobblestone, and cars weren't meant to be going this fast. I yelled at Karl that we had to get off this street.

"We're going to crash, or he's going to rear-end us," I yelled.

I grabbed Elise's hand. I had managed to get her involved in this, and she was going to die because of me. She looked up at me and said nothing but had steely determination in her eyes.

The way she looked at me, I could just imagine her thinking, "I stayed with you for a reason; now get us out of this."

I was determined to.

"Get off this street, Karl!" I yelled.

The sedan was twenty feet behind us. Then ten.

And finally, only a few feet from our back bumper. My mind started to wander.

I should have gone to the cops in New York. I should have gone to the cops at the airport. I brought this on myself. But it was not only myself anymore.

I was going to get the girl I love killed, along with an innocent man who was going out of his way to help us.

I looked at the car behind us, and the two faces I knew well by then were recognizable. There was no forgiveness in their eyes, no mercy. They planned on killing us all.

"There's a small side street in 500 meters," Karl screamed. "I will have to take the left at high speed, so brace yourself!"

For this left to work, the car needed to be as far right as possible to give us the best angle.

As we got closer, I realized making this turn would be impossible. We were going too fast.

I sat back, grabbed Elise's hand, and quickly prayed to a God I wasn't even sure I believed in.

Karl jerked the wheel to the left as hard as he could. Although we made it into the alley, our momentum was too much, and we careened into the wall on the far right side.

I was on the right side of the car, so I took the brunt of the collision. I was a little dazed, but that's it. I looked around, and Elise and Karl seemed to be okay as well.

The white sedan had pretty much done the same thing as us and crashed into the same wall about twenty feet behind us.

The driver—not the one who had the syringe—was unscathed and immediately exited the car with a massive knife in hand. He walked toward us.

My door was lodged against the wall we had hit, and there was no way in hell that door would budge. As the guy with the knife approached our car, I had never felt more hopeless in my whole life.

As the man took the butt end of the knife to break the window above Elise, I hoisted her over my lap and set her to the right of me—anything to remain between the killer and Elise.

At the same time, Karl climbed out of the front seat and ran at our would-be killer. The man had just broken the window, and Karl thought this might be his chance.

He was wrong.

They collided, but the stocky man was too strong and pushed Karl back against the cab. As he did, he plunged the knife into Karl's flank.

Karl fell to his knees, grabbed his side, and felt the blood.

He then looked up and saw his nemesis raise the knife.

I had just gotten out of the back seat and leaped at the man with the knife. I grabbed the wrist of the hand that held the knife just as he was starting to guide the knife downwards toward Karl.

He was undeniably strong, but so was I, and I had youth on my side. The problem was he had gravity on his side, as his arms were above mine and headed downward towards Karl. I realized what I had to do.

I would get badly cut, but I might just save Karl's life.

I raised my forearm, putting it directly into the knife's path.

I jolted my arm up with fantastic force, and while the knife did slice my forearm, I also followed through and connected with his face, and it knocked the knife backward about seven or eight feet.

We heard voices coming from down the alley.

The guy who used the syringe had finally exited their car. He was wobbling and struggling to stand. The collision with the wall must have affected him greatly.

The voices were getting closer as I stared at the husky man.

He realized he didn't have time to grab the knife and come back at me before the people would see him. He also knew he might not easily defeat the younger foe across from him—me.

"Get back in the car!" he yelled. His partner did as instructed.

He looked back at me. "The next time, you won't have the advantage of seeing me coming. And I won't be carrying only a knife."

He turned around, picked up the knife, and headed to his car. I grabbed Elise from the back seat and led her and Karl into a little alcove in case he tried to run us over.

The man had to reverse, go forward, and reverse again to release the car from the wall.

He then stormed away from the crime scene.

I WENT TO KARL'S SIDE.

He had lost some blood, but he hadn't lost consciousness.

"Get out of here," he said, using all the strength he could muster. "You don't want to deal with the cops. I will."

"I'm not leaving until those voices get here," I said.

"People are coming. Go now."

The voices were getting closer.

I yelled as loud as possible, "Call this man an ambulance. Right now!"

A group of three or four people started running toward us.

I grabbed our bags and leaned down one more time to Karl. "We owe you our lives," I said.

Elise leaned down and kissed his forehead.

"I said go," he said.

I grabbed Elise's hand and led her down the opposite side of the alley, away from the people running toward Karl.

I looked back fifteen seconds later, and they had reached Karl. They didn't run after us.

I wondered if Karl told them not to.

While worried about Karl, I forgot that I had been cut. I looked down, and my whole right forearm was bleeding.

The cut was deep, but after the courage I saw from Karl, I wasn't about to complain. He was way worse off than I was.

Elise grabbed a dark shirt—for obvious reasons—from my bag and wrapped it around the wound. We then ran as we heard the sound of a faint siren getting closer. We both prayed that Karl would survive.

<hr />

WE GOT TO THE MAIN STREET AND FLAGGED DOWN YET ANOTHER CAB. WE asked him to take us to an out-of-the-way motel, preferably miles away from where we were.

He was a no-nonsense cabbie and either didn't notice my bandaged arm or didn't care.

Ten minutes later, we arrived at the hotel. Elise paid for the room in cash and told me to wait outside—I didn't need to answer questions about my arm.

We went to the room, and when I locked the door behind us, Elise broke down and started crying. Her stoicism throughout all this surprised me, so I was glad she was finally letting it all out.

Between tears, I heard her say, "When I was on the train, part of me thought this whole thing was romantic. I was so naive. It's not romantic at all. When the guy broke that window, I thought I was going to be killed. And someone was stabbed because of us. A nice man. A heroic man."

I grabbed her, and she started hitting my chest. It was more out of frustration than anger.

"What do you want me to do, Elise?"

"End this somehow! You're the writer. Rewrite this script. I don't like being chased. Find some way to get away from them for good. Or kill them. I don't care."

"I don't want to kill anyone," I yelled.

"You just want to get me killed?"

"You know that's not true."

Between sniffles, Elise pulled me closer.

"We can't keep going on like this," she said.

We both sat down, and no one said anything for a few minutes. Finally, Elise stood up.

"You're not going to like this," she said, "but I'm going to go to that store across the street to pick up some disinfectant and gauze pads. Don't try to talk me out of it; I'm going."

"If you go to the store, I'm coming with. That's not even up for debate."

"All right, let's go."

※

WE WERE BACK LESS THAN TEN MINUTES LATER, AND ELISE BANDAGED ME UP as best she could.

"I need to call the NYPD lieutenant," I said. "Too bad I don't have a phone."

Elise looked at me very seriously. "Did you ever consider that both times you told him where you were going that the killers ended up there?"

Her sentence hovered in the air.

"Holy shit," I said. "You're right."

※

ONE THING FINALLY WENT OUR WAY.

There was an old-school pay phone fifty feet from the hotel.

Elise and I walked down there—we decided while at the store that we were done leaving each other's sides.

It was early morning in New York, but I didn't care. If he answered, he answered.

"Hello?"

"Leroy, this is Bryce."

"How are you? Did you get to Munich safely?"

I told him all that had happened. He listened without once interrupting.

"I'm so sorry, Bryce."

"Thank you."

"I hate to tell you this, but there's a pretty good chance I just found the bodies of Tim and Chase."

"Where?"

"I'm down by the docks in Manhattan right now. We found some blood that ended up being Chase's DNA. There's a suspicious-looking chest in the Hudson River, right by where we found the DNA. It doesn't look good."

I ran through some of the great memories we'd all shared.

They were douchebags at times, but they were my douchebags. I bowed and said a quick prayer for the second time today.

"Thanks," I said.

Leroy changed the subject. "Have you considered letting me send some officers to Europe to protect you and bring you back? Or I could reach out to the Munich police?"

"You know what my girlfriend just said to me?"

"No, Bryce. What's that?"

"She said that both times I told you where I was going, the thugs from New York ended up there. Quite a coincidence, don't you think?"

The silence on Leroy's end lasted for almost fifteen seconds. It was the only time in my life where I actually thought I could hear a man thinking.

"Leroy?"

"Are you safe for the night?"

"Yes."

"Can you call me at eight a.m. Munich time tomorrow?"

I could tell his brain was churning.

"What do you have in mind?"

"I think I may have a plan to get you home safe."

"What does it involve?" I asked.

"Tomorrow, you're going to be spying on the guys who tried to kill you."

This just kept getting better.

49

LEROY

Leroy Archer didn't like to put a lot of stock in rumors, partly because he'd heard his fair share over the years, and the majority proved untrue.

But there was one that had been making the rounds that now had his attention.

Eddie Wilson, a.k.a. Old Man Wilson, had gone through a brutal divorce about seven years ago, and following the divorce, some of his fellow cops believed the drug busts he participated in often came back a little "light."

There were no charges ever brought—drug dealers didn't exactly like to admit to having more drugs at a crime scene—but the rumors persisted.

Leroy had never given them much credence until now. Rumors were just rumors, and Internal Affairs had never brought charges against Wilson.

But now, a few things made Leroy want to take a deeper look.

Hollins said the Sessions brothers may have been involved in the drug trade. Bryce had been attacked both times he'd talked to Leroy.

Those two things, taken by themselves, wouldn't mean very much, but taken together, they raised a major question: Could Wilson have been relaying information to the Sessions brothers?

When Leroy told his subordinates that Bryce was going to the airport, six officers were present, but when he mentioned Munich, only Officer Hollins and Officer Wilson were present.

Bryce said they paid for the train tickets with cash five minutes before they boarded. How could the Sessions brothers know to go to Germany, much less Munich?

He trusted Hollins to the core. Could Wilson be a mole in the department?

Leroy reviewed his conversation with Hollins and Wilson last night. He first asked them about the picture Bryce took.

Hollins answered first, which surprised Leroy. Having been there longer, he expected Wilson to chime in first. Hollins then mentioned the Sessions brothers possibly being involved in the drug trade, which Wilson denied having ever heard.

This could mean nothing, but it could also be convenient to forget.

Lastly, and most damning to Leroy, was the pause that Wilson took when Hollins asked him if he remembered the Sessions brothers.

He had a deer-in-the-headlights look like he didn't know how to answer. Leroy noticed it at the time but didn't have any significance to attach to it. He did now.

"They got to Bryce Connor again," Leroy said.

Officer Braden looked on quizzically. Leroy had hung up the phone several minutes ago and had looked deep in thought ever since.

"What happened?" Braden asked.

Leroy caught him up about what happened in Munich.

"Braden, how long have you been on the force?" Leroy asked.

"Twelve years. Why?"

That was long enough, Leroy thought.

"Do you know who the Sessions brothers are? Charles and Lou."

"Sure. They used to work for Anthony Solari. We talked about them from time to time at the station once they went out on their own."

"Would Officer Wilson know who they were?"

"Old Man Wilson? Of course, he would. He was around for all that."

"It's not something he could have just forgotten?"

"Not a chance. They came up enough to where you wouldn't just forget about them."

"Interesting," Leroy said.

He walked to the river's edge, looked over the Hudson River, and into New Jersey.

"What's going on, Boss?"

"Trust me, you don't want to know."

BRIAN O'SULLIVAN

※

Leroy looked at his watch and paced above the Hudson River. He had a lot on his plate right now, and waiting on other people wouldn't be one of those things.

He decided that Officer Braden could deal with the divers when they arrived. He told him to call him as soon as they excavated the chest.

He headed back to police headquarters.

※

As Leroy drove, he started to finalize the plan he had mentioned to Bryce.

He thought it was feasible but contingent on two things: one, that Eddie "Old Man" Wilson was exactly what Leroy feared and two, that he would take the bait.

Because there was a chance that Leroy was wrong about Wilson, he decided not to let anyone else know of his plan. If what he suspected did happen, he'd have more than enough evidence to go to his superiors.

He planned to pick a spot in Munich and tell Wilson that Bryce would be there tomorrow. He would tell Wilson and only Wilson. If the Sessions did show, Leroy would have found a mole in the department.

He also knew he couldn't be too obvious when giving Wilson the information. He hoped Wilson would ask him how the investigation was going, and he could make it seem like it was just a normal conversation.

Leroy arrived at the office and saw that Wilson was there. He wasn't ready to implement his plan yet, so he walked to his office and shut the door.

He opened his computer and saw that he had an email from Bryce Connor's mother. She wanted to fly to New York with her husband.

He weighed the pros and cons and emailed her back.

※

Leroy considered several sites in Munich before finally deciding on one. He didn't want to choose a bar or a restaurant where Bryce would have to get too close.

If Leroy's fears were valid, the NYPD had already put Bryce's life in jeopardy twice. That wouldn't happen again.

He also didn't want somewhere too big where Bryce couldn't monitor the entrance. For this reason, he eliminated the Hellabrunn Zoo and the Englischer Gartens, a huge public garden in the center of Munich.

He came across the BMW Museum, a museum dedicated to all the different models of BMWs dating back to their inception.

Leroy looked at the pictures, and the outside of the place looked big enough that Bryce wouldn't have to get close to Lou and Charles Sessions.

It also appeared only to have one entrance so Bryce could monitor everyone who entered.

Leroy opened his door and walked around the office, hoping Wilson would approach him. He needed this to happen organically.

DESPITE TWICE PASSING EACH OTHER IN THE HALL TWICE, WILSON HADN'T broached the investigation. Leroy feared he might have to make the first move but decided to hold out a while longer. He needed to have Wilson approach him.

Leroy got a call from Officer Braden instead. There were two dead bodies in the chest.

They were currently transporting the bodies to get autopsies done, and they'd ID the deceased. The divers estimated they'd been dead for between five and seven days.

Leroy wouldn't be waiting on pins and needles to find out their identification. He already knew who the two dead bodies were.

Leroy looked down at his hands. They were still young-looking but getting a little older every day. What was he doing? He had become a police officer to help clean up the inner city's streets.

Instead, he was investigating people so deranged that they crammed two dead people into a chest and then tossed it in the Hudson River.

As far as human beings go, these guys were total trash. This wasn't what he had signed up for.

But then he thought of Bryce. He really liked him from their few brief talks; he seemed like a solid guy just lost in a terrible situation. Bryce had almost been killed twice because of a department for which Leroy himself was responsible.

This gave Leroy the resolve he needed. He would do everything he could to get Bryce home safely. Then, and only then, would he examine himself and reassess his career.

A HALF-HOUR LATER, OFFICER BRADEN CALLED BACK AND SAID THE BODIES were down at the morgue awaiting autopsy. Leroy told Braden to keep him updated.

Leroy started gathering his stuff when he heard a knock at the door.

It was Eddie Wilson. *Bingo!*

"Hi, Lieutenant."

"What can I help you with, Officer Wilson?"

Wilson shut the door behind him. "I was just wondering if you've heard more news on the Bryce Connor case? Being on the run and all. Scary stuff."

"Yeah, it is scary stuff," Leroy agreed. This was where he had to be very subtle. Very delicate. He needed to give Wilson the info while not being obvious about it. "I got off the phone with Bryce a little while ago. There was another attempt on his life."

"I'll be damned. Is he going to be okay?"

"Yeah, he's all right, but he's totally spooked. I think he may cut off all contact with us sooner rather than later."

Wilson was trying to keep his intentions hidden as well. He tread lightly.

"I guess you can't blame him after all that has happened," he said.

Leroy nodded and let out an understanding smile. Wilson didn't think Leroy suspected a thing, so it was time to up the ante.

"So I'm guessing he didn't tell you where he's going next," Wilson said. It was a half statement, half question.

I've got him, Leroy thought to himself.

"All he told me was that he and his girlfriend were going to the BMW museum in Munich at ten a.m. tomorrow morning. I'm afraid that's the last time we may hear from him."

Bingo! Wilson thought. Time to get out of here before I arouse any suspicion.

"Well, let's hope he stays safe," he said.

"Indeed," Leroy said.

Wilson walked out the door.

It was a cat and mouse game where neither man wanted to show the cards they held.

The difference is that Wilson walked out of the office *thinking* he had won, while Leroy stayed in the office *knowing* he had.

50
BRYCE

MUNICH

I woke up a few times during the night.
   I guess that was inevitable, considering all that was going on. I got up for good at 6:30 and looked over at Elise, who was already awake.
"How'd you sleep?" I asked.
"Never better. Didn't you?"
We smiled at each other. Two people wallowing in their misfortune.

❧

WE BOTH WENT DOWNSTAIRS AT EIGHT A.M. AND FROM THE PAY PHONE, I called Leroy.
   He answered in a groggy voice. "Hello?"
   "Hi, it's Bryce. You sound a little tired."
   "Been a long couple of days," Leroy said.
   "You don't have to tell me," I said.
   "You're right. You've been through way worse than I have."
   "So what is this plan you mentioned?" I asked.
   "There's a lot to it, so let me talk first, and then you can ask questions."
   "No problem. Go ahead."
   "I believe that the people who murdered Freddy Macon in New York also killed Tim and Chase and are responsible for the attacks on you in Paris and Munich. No news there. I think they are two brothers, Lou and Charles

Sessions. They used to work for a big-time mafia boss in New York named Anthony Solari years ago but have since gone out on their own."

They might not still work for Solari? Could it be possible that I wouldn't have to testify against the mafia?

I wanted to interrupt, but I let him continue.

"Once out on their own, it looks like the Sessions brothers got work as strong-armers," Leroy continued. "That means they get hired by people to collect money, intimidate, etc. Rumors around town are that Freddy Macon stole a few hundred thousand dollars from the wrong guys. I'm guessing that's why the Sessions brothers were after him. They are also rumored to be involved in the drug trade. When you told me what your girlfriend said, I started getting suspicious about a specific officer in our department. It's very possible that I have a mole in my department and that he's been feeding information to the Sessions brothers. The evidence is circumstantial, so I won't give you his name, but my instincts are pretty good, and they tell me it's him."

I didn't know what to say, so I remained quiet.

Leroy cleared his throat and then continued. "I brought him into my office today and told him that you were going to the BMW museum in Munich today at ten a.m. He was the only one I told, so if the Sessions brothers show up, we know he's a mole. You are the only one who knows about this. I can't risk going to my superiors with circumstantial evidence, even if I believe it to be true. But if you see them today, I'll have enough to arrest the officer, and we could use him to set up a sting here in New York to arrest the Sessions brothers. So what I want you to go to the BMW museum after I get off the phone with you. You will call me if you see them, and I can start putting the rest in motion. I don't want you to go into the museum itself. Lord knows you've been through enough over the last several days. Just find a spot where you can survey the main entrance. I looked at pictures online and thought there was only one entrance. Once you see Lou and Charles Sessions, you are to leave and go directly to the airport. Under no scenario are you to get close to or try to engage them. Just verify they showed up there and then head to the airport. There is a two p.m. flight from Munich to New York. You have a seat on it. I will pick you up from the airport myself. Do you understand everything?"

I looked over at Elise, who was trying to read my reaction.

I had some questions for Leroy, but I had to make a quick change to the itinerary.

"My girlfriend will be flying back to the U.S. with me. Her name is Elise Mercier. Can you get her a ticket as well?"

"Of course."

"Now, a few questions," I said. "These two brothers are no longer in the mafia?"

"No. Technically, they were never really in it—they just worked for one of the bosses. I guess that's just semantics, though."

"Then why did they say, "This is for Solari?""

"When I received your letter, I didn't buy the whole Solari angle from the beginning. Murders committed under his name aren't usually stabbings in back alleys. One other thing about your letter raised my suspicions as well. You said he looked over and noticed you guys for a split second before saying, 'This is for Solari.' Who would say that if they knew someone was watching?"

"Impressive. I guess I know why you're the police officer."

"Lieutenant, but thanks, Bryce. If we catch ... excuse me, when we catch these guys, I imagine we will learn that he said this to divert suspicions away from them and toward Solari."

"It worked. When I googled Solari the night of the murder and found out who he was, I decided not to go to the police. If I had known it was just a couple of thugs, I would have gone to the cops and testified. And Tim and Chase would still be alive."

My eyes started to moisten, and Elise put her arm on my shoulder.

"First off, don't resort to merely calling them thugs," Leroy said. "Although they weren't part of the mafia per se, they worked under them. They've also killed at least three people, and my guess would be many more under Solari. So don't make the mistake of thinking of them as just common thugs; these are violent, remorseless killers. And that's why I don't want you close to the entrance of the BMW museum. Be as far away as you can while still being able to identify them. As far as the second part, you are not to blame for the deaths of Tim and Chase. Not in the slightest. They could have come to the police just as easily as you. Easier, in fact. They still lived in New York, after all. Their deaths are not on you. Do you understand?"

"Yeah, I do. Thanks."

"Any more questions?"

"How did you figure out who the mole was in your department? Was it only that he was one of two people being told where I was going?"

"He also paused a second too long at one point."

"What does that mean?" I was lost.

"I'll explain it to you at a later time. And honestly, your girlfriend mentioning that you had been followed is what set this whole thing in motion. She deserves a lot of the credit."

I smiled over at Elise.

"I'll tell her."

"I'm going to get off the phone now, Bryce. I suggest you head to the BMW museum immediately. Make sure you are there early. You don't want them to see you arriving. You need to be there first. And thank you very much for doing this. I think it might be our only way to verify my suspicions."

"Anything to get us out of this mess. We'll be leaving shortly."

"Good luck to you and Elise. Call me after you see them, and remember, head directly to the airport after you do. I'll see you at JFK soon enough."

"You're a good man, Leroy."

"Likewise, Bryce. Likewise."

I HUNG UP THE PHONE AND RECOUNTED THE ENTIRE CONVERSATION TO Elise, including Leroy's statement that her observation had set all of this in motion.

She smiled.

"I'll thank him in person."

We walked back to the room.

"Oh, I forgot to tell you," Elise said.

"What is it?"

"I found an English language Munich paper online. Karl, the taxi driver, is going to be okay. They said he suffered a stab wound but will recover. They didn't say much more about it."

"That's great news," I said. "Listen, we have to get ready now. We can't risk the Sessions brothers beating us there."

"I'll take a three-minute shower."

"Make it two."

51

THE GERMAN AUTHORITIES

Detective Joachim Acker was pissed off.
Who did this guy think he was? Some lowly cab driver was stonewalling his investigation. And for what?
Acker entered the Rechts der Isar Hospital and went up to Room 262 for the third time in under twenty-four hours. Karl Vogel sat there with that same grin on his face. It was like he was enjoying this shit.
"Mr. Vogel, warum sind Sie weigerte sich, uns zu helfen?"
Why are you refusing to help us?
"Ich helfe. Ich habe Ihnen eine Beschreibung des Mannes, der mich erstochen."
I am helping. I gave you a description of the guy who stabbed me.
"Aber ich möchte wissen, wer in der Kabine war. Es könnte uns Motiv zu geben und helfen, führen uns zu den Verdächtigen."
But I want to know who else was in the cab. It could give us a motive and help lead us to the suspects.
"Ich sagte Ihnen, ich sah sie nie. Sie haben in meiner Kabine , aber ich sah im Rückspiegel nicht. Dann, wenn ich versehentlich stürzte und der Kerl erstochen mich waren sie schon weg."
I told you I never saw them. They got in my cab, but I never looked in my rearview mirror. Then when I accidentally crashed and the guy stabbed me, they were already gone.
It was such a blatant lie that Detective Acker couldn't help but laugh.

"Zumindest versuchen, bilden eine bessere Geschichte."
At least try to make up a better story.
"Was ist der Punkt? Wir wissen beide, ich lüge."
What's the point? We both know I'm lying.
Acker laughed again. If Karl Vogel wasn't hindering his investigation, Acker thinks he might have actually liked this guy.
"Sie haben also nichts mehr zu sagen?"
So you have nothing more to say?
"Nein, ich will nur sagen, dass die Menschen in meiner Kabine waren gute Menschen, und ich möchte nicht, um sie einzubeziehen."
No, I'll just say that the people in my cab were good people and I don't want to involve them.
Acker realized this was going nowhere.
"Guten Tag Mr. Vogel."
Good day.
Detective Acker walked out of the hospital, and just like the other two times he had interviewed him, Karl Vogel refused to budge. He said he would help identify his assailant but would do nothing regarding his passengers.

❦

As for Mr. Vogel himself, he was going to be fine.
He'd have a nasty scar for the rest of his life, but that didn't seem to bother him. His wife had been there the first two times Acker questioned him. She seemed impressed by the courage her husband had displayed.
Vogel was in for some TLC from his wife whenever he was released from the hospital.

❦

Detective Acker would continue the investigation but knew it wouldn't likely lead anywhere.
They had accumulated several small clues but had nothing concrete to go on. For example, they knew Vogel's last pick-up was at the train station, which didn't narrow it down much.
The cab crashed, and the people fled the scene, so they never had a chance to pay by credit card, which could have been a big break. They checked for DNA in the cab, but as you can guess, thousands of DNA samples are scattered throughout a cab. It's only useful if you can look for a specific person's DNA and prove they were in the cab.
The retaining wall revealed that the other car that crashed was a white sedan, but that didn't add much to the investigation either. There were no cameras on those side streets, so they couldn't obtain a license plate number.
Acker talked to the people who approached Vogel and called the ambu-

lance. They said a man and a woman in their late twenties or early thirties ran away from Vogel. They were too far away to describe their facial features. They believed the guy had an American accent because he yelled at them to call an ambulance.

Joachim Acker walked out of the hospital. He got a call about a body they had just found in southern Munich. The Karl Vogel case would have to be put on the back burner.

Acker had a feeling it might be staying there for a long time.

52
BRYCE

THE BMW MUSEUM

The BMW Museum was located near Olympia Park, where the infamous 1972 Summer Olympics was hosted.

The building itself looked as if they stuck the very top—just the cup part—of the Stanley Cup into the ground. Locals called it the White Cauldron (*Weiß Kessel*) even though it wasn't white. The Silver Colander would have been more apt.

The entrance sat at the base of the Cauldron, and unfortunately, Elise and I couldn't just sit in a cab and observe. There was no place to see the entrance from afar.

The people taking the stairs up to the entrance were fed in from the right, so I decided we couldn't watch from the left side, where we'd be in their line of sight.

We would have to be to the right and behind the walkway. That way, we could see them, but they couldn't see us ... unless they turned around.

Unfortunately, when we went to the right side of the walkway, we saw a retaining wall that would block our view unless we stood and peered over it. No, thank you. We'd stand out like a sore thumb.

There was a lawn to the right of the walkway where some people were starting to mingle and set up little picnics.

We had our bags with us, which made us stand out a bit, so I figured if we sat on the grass and laid down some of our shirts, we could pass as having a picnic.

The problem was that we would be parallel to the people as they moved along the walkway leading to the stairs. We would be staring directly at them if they looked to their right.

I saw a spot where a small tree sat and decided we'd sit there. It wasn't much of a tree, more of a glorified bush, but it would have to do. It was the only way to partially shield ourselves from those who walked by.

Elise and I sat down and set up camp there.

We sat there for forty-five minutes, watching people go by. We both made makeshift bandanas to cover our foreheads and hair.

It was hot out, and the bandanas only made it worse, but we were trying to disguise ourselves at that point.

It was a good thing we had arrived early because, at precisely 9:42, I looked down the walkway and saw the Sessions brothers—I knew their names now—heading our way. I grabbed Elise's leg to alert her.

This was the scariest part.

They had about a hundred feet to walk till they were directly parallel to us. If they looked to their right, they would see us.

Whether they would recognize us was a different question. They also probably did not expect us to sit on the lawn, which helped us.

My heart was in my throat. Lou and Charles Sessions—who'd twice tried to kill me—were headed our way.

They started coming down the walkway. Fifty feet away. Thirty feet. Twenty feet. At about fifteen feet away, they both looked to their right but didn't recognize us.

Their eyes were darting all over the place. They came directly parallel to us, then mercifully passed us and started taking the stairs toward the entrance.

I could finally exhale. I leaned over and gave Elise a quick kiss.

I packed up our picnic gear, which were really just clothes, and we started walking in the opposite direction.

The way things had been going, I half expected to hear the Sessions charging and yelling at us from behind, but we heard nothing.

I put my arm in lock with Elise's, and we continued walking, not bothering to turn around.

If I were an armchair psychologist, I'd say it was a metaphor that we were looking forward and not behind us anymore.

53

LEROY

Leroy decided to set up camp at police headquarters, specifically his office.

Too much was going on, and he couldn't afford to lose the sixty minutes it would take him to drive back and forth from his home a few times a day. He would be sleeping and showering at headquarters until this was over.

Leroy could hear his old girlfriend Jade saying, "I told you that you couldn't just be normal. You're obsessed with your job."

She would have been right, of course.

AT TWO A.M., HE SHUT HIS DOOR AND CLOSED THE BLINDS IN HIS OFFICE. He turned the volume up on his cell phone as high as it would go.

If Bryce called, it would wake him up. He covered himself with a blanket he had brought and tried to get an hour or two of sleep. It would be at a premium over the next few days, so he needed to get it while he could.

TWO HOURS LATER, LEROY WAS AWAKENED BY THE RING OF HIS CELL PHONE. No one from New York was calling him this late. He knew it was Bryce.

"Hello?"

"Leroy, this is Bryce. The Sessions brothers showed up there. They walked right by us."

Leroy gave himself an inner fist pump. His unrivaled instincts were right again.

"Walked right by you? You were supposed to be a hundred yards away!"

"Wasn't possible. It's okay. They didn't see us."

You've done well, Bryce. Are you at the airport?"

"I am. We are about to check in."

"Great. I will be at JFK when you arrive."

"Thanks for everything, Leroy."

"You're welcome. See you soon."

Bryce's parents had arrived in New York earlier that night. Leroy was going to have a pleasant surprise for Bryce when he arrived.

※

IN THE INTERVENING HOURS UNTIL BRYCE FLEW IN, LEROY WOULD GO TO his superiors—maybe all the way to the top—to get an arrest warrant for Eddie Wilson, which would surely get approved.

They'd then arrest Wilson and hopefully convince him to help them get the Sessions brothers. If he refused, they might still be able to pull it off.

He imagined they'd find another cell phone besides Wilson's police-ordered one. It would be the one he would use to communicate with the Sessions.

If Wilson refused to cooperate, they'd have to use text instead of Wilson calling, texting something like "I can't get out of the office for a few hours, but …"

Hopefully, that would work. Still, Leroy held out hope they could turn Wilson to their side, so this wouldn't be necessary.

Yes, it was going to be a long ten hours or so. Leroy pulled the blanket back over him—time for another cat nap.

※

THE HEAD OF THE NYPD IS NOT THE CHIEF OF POLICE, BUT INSTEAD someone labeled the New York City Police Commissioner.

The commissioner is a civilian administrator—although usually a former cop—and they are not sworn officers who have to swear under oath to uphold the law. So, while he/she may not technically be a police officer, all lieutenants and chiefs answer to him.

If this was just a regular murder investigation, there was no way Leroy would go straight to the commissioner, but now that this case involved a potential mole in the department, he felt he had to.

Nothing is more detrimental to a police force than having a mole dishing out information to criminals. It could also cause a rash of convicted felons to ask for retrials or to have their convictions overturned completely.

Leroy hoped that Eddie Wilson's corruption started and ended with Lou and Charles Sessions.

The commissioner's secretary arrived at eight a.m., and Leroy called at precisely 8:01 a.m.

He knew he wouldn't be connected to the commissioner himself, but once the secretary heard the word "mole," Leroy was pretty sure he'd be called in as soon as the commissioner was available.

"Commissioner Sax's office." a female's voice said.

"Hi, this is Lieutenant Leroy Archer down at midtown Manhattan."

"What can I help you with, Lieutenant?"

"I'd like to meet with Mr. Sax as soon as possible. Preferably early this morning."

"Have you talked to the chief of department?"

The chief of department was how New York City commonly referred to their police commissioner.

"No, I haven't. I ... "

Leroy was about to continue when the secretary cut him off.

"That's standard protocol," she said.

"I understand that, but in this case, time is of the essence. I think I found a mole in my Manhattan department."

Leroy could tell this wasn't what the secretary had expected to hear.

"Please hold, Lieutenant Archer."

Leroy was on hold for about two minutes when the secretary came back on. "He will see you at nine a.m. His time is very important. Don't be late."

"I won't be. Thank you."

※

LEROY WENT DOWNSTAIRS AND USED THE POLICE HEADQUARTERS SHOWERS.

He returned to his office and dressed in one of the suits he had hanging in his office, and he grabbed his favorite power tie. After all, it wasn't every day that you met with the NYPD commissioner.

The case of Bryce and Wilson were front and center in his mind, but he'd be lying if the chance for advancement wasn't percolating somewhere in the back of that mind.

Finding a real-life mole in the department would considerably help Leroy's stock rise. He tied his tie into a Windsor knot and left his office.

※

AT SIXTY-SEVEN, NEW YORK POLICE COMMISSIONER JULIAN SAX HAD SEEN his fair share of allegations involving an alleged department mole.

He had seen people's suspicions of a mole become unfounded even more often. He hoped today's meeting would be the same.

With an overwhelmed police force and a public that was suddenly anti-police, the last thing he needed was another black eye for the department.

He looked up at the man entering his office. Leroy Archer certainly cut a nice figure.

He was tall, black, and had a nice self-assurance that didn't come off as cockiness. Mostly, he radiated an air of competency, and that's about the best thing you can say about a police officer.

Julian had often heard of Leroy. He was kind of a wonder kid when he joined the force. Youngest to do this. Youngest to do that.

Many people had tabbed Leroy as a potential politician down the road or even a candidate for police commissioner.

If Julian Sax were younger, perhaps he'd consider this man a threat, but at sixty-seven, if and when Mr. Archer ran for police commissioner, Julian would be ready to retire.

He offered Leroy a seat, curious to see how the future of the NYPD came across in person.

"Thank you for seeing me, Mr. Commissioner."

"It's my pleasure, Leroy. I've heard a lot about you."

"Hopefully, all good."

"Most of it has been."

"Thank you."

"You're welcome. But that is not what you came down here for. Let's get down to business. Why do you think you have a mole in your department?"

Leroy went through all the preliminary facets of the case. The murder of Freddy Macon, the note Bryce left, the murders of Tim and Chase, and the phone calls with Bryce.

He then told him what Elise said, the rumors about the Sessions brothers dealing drugs and the rumors that Wilson's drug busts ended up light.

"And most importantly, he paused too long," Leroy said.

Julian Sax realized he wasn't supposed to understand just yet. He nodded, confirming Leroy should continue.

"We had the picture of Charles Sessions from the airport bathroom, and when asked if he knew him, Officer Wilson paused a few seconds before answering."

"I see."

"It was a pensive pause as if he was weighing his options. However, other officers have said there is no doubt he knew the identity of Charles Sessions. There'd be no reason for him to pause before answering yes. You probably think it's weird that I'm putting so much stock in a slight pause."

"Not at all. I think a lot of the best police work is instinctual. Some of my most well-known arrests in my younger years were on small things like that. Reading an expression, a sideward glance. Things like that. If you read the situation as him hiding something, then go with your gut. So what happened next?"

"I set up a little sting to prove that what I thought about Wilson was true."

"And who was in on this sting?"

"No one, except for Bryce Connor."

"You know you can set up a sting easier with the help of your fellow officers."

"I know, Mr. Commissioner, but it was of paramount importance that no one else knew about it."

Leroy explained that he had to make sure that Wilson was the only one who knew about the BMW Museum, thus eliminating any other suspects.

"That is some excellent police work, Lieutenant."

"Thank you, sir."

"Don't call me sir. In fact, don't call me Mr. Commissioner. Never did like that. It makes me sound like I'm a king or something. I was a cop just like you for several years. Several decades, actually. You can call me Julian."

"I will, Julian. And you can call me Leroy."

"Trust me, I don't need your permission to call you that."

They both laughed, but it was short-lived. Julian Sax was by nature, a serious man, and this was a very serious situation.

Julian feared that this was one of the cases in which the mole was, in fact, real. Leroy had done his homework, and all signs pointed to the fact that he was right: Eddie Wilson was a crooked cop.

"And what is your plan after we arrest Mr. Wilson?"

Leroy laid out his entire plan to Julian Sax. Get Wilson to turn state's evidence, convince him to get the Sessions brothers back to New York, arrest them when they arrive in New York, and have Bryce ID them in a lineup.

There were other aspects to it, but he just gave Julian the meat and potatoes. He also told Julian something that he thought he'd like to hear and something that Leroy believed to be true.

"I know the last thing you want to deal with is a mole in the department," Leroy said. "I feel Mr. Wilson's case is limited to merely the Sessions brothers. Call it a hunch."

"Let's hope you're right. Anything else?"

"No, that's it. Thank you so much for your time Julian."

"You're welcome, Leroy."

With that, Leroy stood up, and they shook hands. He promised to keep Julian apprised as to what was going on. He thanked him one last time and walked out the door.

If that's truly the future of the NYPD, then I think we're in pretty good shape, Julian Sax thought.

DEBUT NOVEL

The police raided Eddie Wilson's house a few hours later. He was at home and didn't deny his guilt. He looked like a beaten man who was almost happy that it was all over.

When Wilson himself was searched, his police-assigned cell phone and a second one were found. Leroy had a good idea of what they would find on the second cell phone, including recent calls to Germany and France.

Leroy told the officers after they booked Wilson to put him in interview room two.

※

There were three interview rooms at the Midtown Manhattan branch of the NYPD. Everyone seemed to have their favorite, often for no rhyme or reason.

The first time Leroy interviewed a suspect was in interview room two, so from then on, he used it whenever he could. It seemed as good a reason as any.

He looked in at Eddie Wilson, not knowing whether to feel pity or anger toward the man. His pension was right around the corner, but instead, he was probably going to spend the rest of his life in jail.

But just when Leroy would start to feel a little pity, he'd remind himself that Wilson gave information to the Sessions brothers that could have led to Bryce's murder.

If he had just stolen the occasional drugs from a drug bust, Leroy could possibly forgive him, but putting an innocent person out to die? Leroy could never forgive that.

Leroy entered the interrogation room, unlocked Wilson's handcuffs, and then took a seat across from Wilson.

"Thanks, Lieutenant."

Leroy didn't respond. The last thing he wanted was for Wilson to think this was going to be a friendly conversation.

"Did you get a phone call?"

"Yeah, I refused, though. What's the point? You have me dead-to-rights anyway."

"Well, I'm going to allow you to make a second call that may help your cause."

Wilson changed the subject. "The BMW Museum was a setup, wasn't it?"

"That's right," Leroy said quietly. While Wilson was a selfish jerk, it still wasn't easy to be taking down a fellow cop.

"I should have known. Only telling me about it? That should have raised a red flag. And let me guess, the second call you want me to make will be to the Sessions brothers."

"Right again."

"I'll do it. But not because I think it will shorten my sentence. I know I'm fucked. I'll do it because they are the scum of the earth. I never should have gone into business with them."

"The drug business?" Leroy said. He knew Wilson wanted to talk, so he just needed to lead him in the right direction.

"Yes, the drug business. I'm sure you already know by now, but I'd steal drugs from crime scenes, and they'd sell them—50/50 split. A few years back, I wanted out. They let me out, but from then on, whenever they needed pertinent police information, I had to give it to them."

Leroy had to find out how far the corruption extended. For his sake, and especially for Julian Sax, he hoped not very far.

"And how often and for what reasons would they call you?"

"It was just for information on things they were involved in, and it didn't happen often. Probably only a few times in the last few years until the Freddy Macon murder."

Leroy let out a slight exhalation—this was good news.

"And what type of information would they ask for?"

"If a drug deal went wrong, they'd ask how the investigation was going. They'd ask if they had been mentioned. Things like that."

"I see."

"Early on, I could almost delude myself into thinking that what I was doing wasn't so bad. I was just updating them on the occasional investigation. I wasn't putting anyone in harm's way."

"Until Bryce Connor, that is."

Wilson bowed his head, whimpered softly, then tried to compose himself. "Lou and Charles had me by the balls. If I didn't help them, they'd turn me in. I told myself I was quitting the NYPD when this latest one was over. I would go to a remote island and repent for my sins. But I had to help them out this one last time. I had no choice."

"You always had a choice, Wilson. You were just a selfish prick who didn't care about anyone else. You know you almost got an innocent young lady and a cab driver killed as well? Yeah, you had a choice, all right, you just chose wrong."

Wilson rubbed his partially crying eyes.

Leroy was tired of this. "Get yourself together. I need you to make that call for me."

Wilson pulled himself together.

Leroy told him what to say. He didn't exactly want this emotional man on the phone right now, but it was still his best option. Leroy leaned into Wilson. "Do the right thing for once."

Leroy produced the phone that he had confiscated at Wilson's house. "I believe you'll be needing this."

"You're one damn good cop, Lieutenant," Wilson said.

"Thanks. Now make the call."

Wilson dialed, and Leroy could only listen to what Wilson said. "Hi Lou ...

DEBUT NOVEL

He's on a flight back to the U.S. You need to get back here ... It was good information ... He was supposed to be there ... He probably freaked out and went straight to the airport ... I've always given you good info, right? ... No, they won't be alerted if you fly in ... Because I know ... I'm a cop, remember ... He gets in later today ... No, they won't indict you right away. They are still collecting evidence ... I'd guess you have two days till they go to the courts ... Yes, I will find out where they are keeping him ... I said yes. I'll call you when I know ... Okay, bye."

And then Wilson ended the call. It was a grade-A performance.

"It's sad," Leroy said. "You were brilliant right there. It's too bad you didn't choose to put those attributes to good use. What a waste you have become. You deserve whatever you get. I hope you rot in jail."

With that, Leroy exited the room and slammed the door.

Wilson's face changed from being resigned to his fate to being pissed off at what Leroy had said.

※

LEROY WENT TO HIS OFFICE, SHUT HIS BLINDS, AND RAISED HIS HANDS IN victory. Everything was coming together. He'd pick up Bryce at the airport, take his statement, and then have the Sessions brothers arrested when they landed. It was a good thing Wilson was going to play ball. It made the whole case so much easier.

Leroy called someone at the FAA and told him who he was. He went through all the protocols to verify his identity. He asked them for a phone call when the Sessions brothers booked a flight back to New York.

Yup, it was all coming together.

※

TWENTY MINUTES LATER, LEROY GOT A KNOCK ON HIS DOOR. OFFICER Hollins walked in.

"Wilson decided to lawyer up."

"You have to be fucking kidding me. Just now?"

Hollins had never seen Leroy so pissed.

"Yeah."

Leroy headed to the interview rooms, fuming. "What's going on, Wilson? You lawyered up?"

Just then, a lawyer walked up to the interview room. He extended his hand.

"Tucker Hall, attorney at law. I'm here to see Eddie Wilson."

He was a forty-something guy with glasses and a smug look. Leroy and him entered the interview room together.

"What about all the talk about doing the right thing, Wilson?" Leroy said.

"You were the one saying that, not me," Wilson said. "And I didn't like the way you spoke to me at the end. You should have been nicer. If I'm going to rot in jail, why not fight this thing? You may come to regret what you said to me, Lieutenant."

Leroy couldn't believe he had felt pity for this man. He saw him now for what he really was.

"And the whimpering and tears? Those weren't real either?"

This time, "smug face" jumped in. "My client was under emotional duress. After all, his house had just been raided and he was led in here in front of all his coworkers. He didn't know what he was saying or admitting to. We'll be looking to get everything he said to you thrown out. After all, instead of getting a phone call, he was told to make one."

"He agreed to make it."

"Semantics, Mr. Archer. We'll argue it in front of a judge."

Leroy didn't want to talk to the attorney. He faced Wilson. "Deep down, you are a scumbag, aren't you, Wilson? You and the Sessions brothers are meant for each other. Don't say they're below you. You're all in the damn gutter."

Wilson avoided eye contact with Leroy.

Tucker Hall spoke for his client. "We'll see you in court, Mr. Archer. Now, I'd like some alone time with my client."

※

LEROY WENT BACK TO HIS OFFICE AND CALLED THE COMMISSIONER. HE GOT his secretary. Leroy said it was urgent, and Julian Sax quickly came on the line.

"Eddie Wilson decided to lawyer up."

"I heard."

"Already?"

"I'm the police commissioner, Leroy. I have eyes and ears everywhere."

"I'm calling to ask if I can still arrest the Sessions brothers when they fly into New York?"

Julian Sax pondered the question.

"It's obvious to anyone working this case that they committed these murders. Unfortunately, we don't have that much concrete evidence. Everything that happened in Europe is inadmissible—not our jurisdiction. And even though we found the bodies of Bryce's friends, we have no evidence linking them to the Sessions, do we?"

"No, we don't."

"So what we have is an ID from Bryce, someone who was approximately eight drinks deep on the night in question and was probably 50-70 feet from the killers at the time. And oh yeah, he saw them for a grand total of about five or six seconds."

"You're making it out like we have no case."

"Not at all. We absolutely have a case, but it's mostly circumstantial or happened in a different country. I'd have some cops tail the Sessions from the airport and keep a few outside their houses. They won't be a threat if we keep an eye on them. We'll put Bryce up at a hotel, and he'll be safe. It's only a matter of time before we get enough evidence or convince Wilson to return to our side."

Julian was making sense, but this wasn't enough for Leroy.

He couldn't just let the Sessions roam free, even if it was under police surveillance. He thought of a plan.

"What if we use Bryce as bait?"

"Again? I thought you liked the kid?"

Trust me, he'd be nowhere near where it went down."

Leroy told Julian his plan.

"Would that be enough to arrest them?" Leroy asked.

"Unquestionably."

54

BRYCE

BACK TO WHERE IT ALL STARTED

When we boarded the flight to New York, it was like a huge burden had been lifted.

Elise and I had reverted to the banter we had when we first met. No more talk of murderers, cops, train schedules, or the like. Elise and I just talking about our future together.

"I'm going to take you to Broadway," I said. "You can see all the big names in lights, where you will be someday."

"I guess I need to start working on an American accent besides Biloxi, Mississippi. How's this?" Elise tried to sound like a weight-lifting meathead. "I'm going to hit up the club tonight, brah, and totally pick up some hot chicks."

"I think my French is better than your 'American.'"

"You're crazy. Everyone loved my Savannah."

"Once they learned it was all an act." I laughed.

We smiled at each other.

"It's nice to have our old back and forth back," Elise said.

"I was thinking the same thing."

We tried to order champagne on the plane, but they only had wine, so we made do. We toasted to Hugo, and we raised our glasses to Karl. We decided we would send Karl something special when this was all over.

"Now you can get back to your writing," Elise said.

"I can't wait."

"You know, I was thinking. How about a non-fiction novel while you're at it."

"About what?" I asked.

"A guy who moves to Paris to write falls in love and then has to escape some deranged murderers."

"And what would we call this novel?"

"Hmmm. How about The Fleeing Parisian?"

"But aren't I the main character? It should be named after me."

"Your decisions are motivated by your love of The Fleeing Parisian, so she deserves top billing."

"I already said you're going to have top billing on Broadway. Do you need it on my book as well?"

Elise laughed. "The Fleeing Parisian has a nice ring to it too. It rhymes and everything."

I grabbed Elise and kissed her.

We were probably a little too eager for two people who still had a lot going on once we landed in New York.

But after all we'd been through, how could you blame us?

AS WE DISEMBARKED, I SEARCHED FOR LEROY ARCHER. I HAD GOOGLED HIM just to know what he looked like.

I recognized him from his pictures as he walked towards us.

"Bryce. I'm Leroy Archer."

I gave him a handshake and introduced him to Elise. She gave him a big hug.

"Thanks for all this," I said.

"I should be thanking you," he said to me. "And a special thanks to you, Elise. You got this whole thing set in motion."

We had walked about twenty feet when Leroy stopped abruptly. My suspicious mind got a little worried. Par for the course after the last several days.

"What is it?" I asked.

Just then, I saw my mother and father walking over.

How the hell did they know? I looked over at Leroy. His smile gave away who had invited them. I walked up and kissed my mother and then hugged my father. There was no rehashing what had happened. They were just thrilled to see me safe.

"Mom, Dad, I'd like to introduce you to my girlfriend, Elise," I said.

My mother and Elise hugged.

"Jeez, Bryce, she's even more beautiful than you said."

"Ahh, thank you so much," Elise said.

Leroy didn't want to break up the group hugs, but he had to get this show on the road.

"Follow me, guys. I have an SUV waiting for us, courtesy of the NYPD. I've also done the courtesy of setting us up for an early dinner," Leroy said.

We followed Leroy.

He showed his badge, and we basically just walked through customs. They took a perfunctory look at Elise's passport, but that was it.

We reached the parking lot, got in the SUV, and headed toward Manhattan.

❧

ON THE RIDE OVER, LEROY INFORMED US THAT THE NYPD WOULD BE watching the Sessions brothers, and we had nothing to worry about.

I was going to ask why they wouldn't be placed under arrest when they arrived back in the U.S., but everyone was in such a good mood I let it pass.

Leroy valeted the car and checked us into the Waldorf Astoria on 5th Street.

"Sorry, Mr. and Mrs. Connor, but only Elise and Bryce's hotel room will be on the NYPD's dime."

"Shouldn't they have two separate rooms?" my father joked. "They aren't married after all, and I don't want them living in sin."

"Oh, shut up, honey," my mother playfully said, and Elise laughed.

❧

WHEN WE ENTERED THE ROOM, IT REMINDED ME OF SOME OF THE SMALL hotels we had stayed in when we were on the run—only the exact opposite.

The square footage was probably eight times that of my cottage in Paris. There was a huge bath with jets that I hoped Elise and I would use later. I could get used to staying here.

"You can check out the room later," Leroy said. "Just set your bags down for now. We've got our dinner in forty-five minutes."

"After seeing this room, I'm guessing we're not eating at a Denny's."

"Have any of you heard of Per Se?" Leroy asked.

❧

PER SE WAS LOCATED IN THE SHOPS AT COLUMBUS CIRCLE, NEAR CENTRAL Park. It was opened by Thomas Keller, the owner of the world-famous French Laundry in Yountville.

Leroy talked to the maitre d', and we were then escorted to a private room with just the five of us.

"For obvious reasons, we don't want any other people listening to our conversations, so I got us a private room," Leroy said.

"Are all witnesses for the city treated this well?" I asked.

"Actually, no. Due to the delicate nature of the case, i.e., Mr. Wilson, you are being treated a little special."

"Who's Mr. Wilson," my father asked.

"I'll explain everything," Leroy said, asking everyone to sit.

For the next fifteen minutes, Leroy explained every nuance of the case.

He would take a quick break when we ordered or when they brought bread in.

My mother shuttered when she heard about them attacking me and the deaths of Tim and Chase, but for the most part, she was a trooper. Elise listened intently, and my father was a rock throughout. As for me, I knew almost all of it, but I couldn't believe just how much had happened since the fateful night I flew into New York.

As Leroy neared the end, he explained what he planned on doing now. "Since Officer Wilson has hunkered down with an attorney, we need to get one last piece of evidence against the Sessions. Now, don't overreact until I explain fully, but we are going to use Bryce as bait."

"Bait?" my mother said. "I hope you're joking! Hasn't he been through enough?"

"Like I said, Mrs. Connor, if you'll let me finish. We will tell the Sessions brothers through Wilson's cell phone that Bryce will be at a different hotel. Don't worry. Bryce will be nowhere near the hotel we give them, and Bryce and Elise will have an armed police officer outside their room at the Waldorf."

That settled my mother down.

Leroy continued, "We will also have officers watching the Sessions' houses, so we will know if they get within five miles of Bryce."

"When will this all go down?" Elise asked.

"I just received notification that the Sessions are on a flight to the U.S. They will arrive later tonight, at which point we will follow them home. We will plant the seed early tomorrow. We'll pretend to be Wilson and tell them the hotel that Bryce will allegedly stay at. We'll say he's only there for one night and will be taken to court the next day. They will get desperate. We will have twenty or more officers at the hotel, and once they set foot on the hotel's grounds, we will arrest them. Meanwhile, Bryce will be miles away at the Waldorf. There's a chance you'd have to testify if it goes to trial, but that could be a year or more down the road. And when they step on the hotel's grounds, the evidence will be so concrete that I'd bet they'd enter a plea, and it would never even get to trial."

For the first time, everyone looked satisfied—even my mother.

Leroy had one more thing to say. "Now that we've got that out of the way, let's enjoy our meal. How about I order a bottle or two of wine with our entrees? I'm sure you could all use a glass."

"I knew I liked you," my mother said.

The next hour and a half was fantastic. Leroy told us about his childhood and why he became a police officer.

My father rehashed the story about telling my mother he was going to marry her the first time they met. Everyone really enjoyed each other's company.

Most importantly, my parents really liked Elise. I knew they would. I mean, how could you not? But it was still nice to see it firsthand.

Elise and my mother exchanged stories the whole time. My mother loved hearing about growing up in Paris. They even went to the bathroom together. I'd never understand that about women.

When they left, leaving only the three men, my father said, "I told you French girls have the sexiest accents."

"Don't be creepy, Dad," I said.

Leroy laughed. "Your father is right, just so you know."

I smiled. "I know."

Leroy leaned over and patted me on the shoulder. "You have a great family, Bryce. I'm glad we got you home safely."

"Thanks for everything you have done, Leroy."

"I second what my son said. Thank you, Leroy."

The women returned to the table, and we continued eating. I know the food was fantastic, but I can't remember what I ate. What made it such a special meal was the stories we told, the laughs we shared, and the company we kept.

<hr />

WE FINALLY FINISHED, AND LEROY DROPPED MY PARENTS OFF AT THEIR hotel only a few blocks from the Waldorf Astoria.

Leroy got out and said goodbye. "It's been a pleasure meeting you, Mr. and Mrs. Connor. The next time I see you, the Sessions will be in custody, and this will all be over."

My mother leaned in and kissed Leroy on the cheek.

"Wow," my father joked.

We were all in such good moods.

We could never have foreseen what was to come.

55

LEROY

When Leroy left the dinner, he thought back to a New York Yankee baseball player whom he had idolized as a kid.

He collected all his cards, refusing to trade any to his friends even though he had over a hundred. On his fifth, sixth, and seventh birthdays, he asked his father for the same present: to meet his idol.

On his eighth birthday, his father saw that the player was having an autograph signing at a local business a few days later and promised to take young Leroy.

Leroy brought a poster, a glove, a bat, and a baseball card. He was hoping the star would sign all of them.

Leroy stood in line for two hours, but it was like staying up all night waiting for Christmas morning. The wait was the best part. Finally, he was second in line, and the boy in front of him finished. Leroy approached his idol.

"I just wanted to say that you are my favorite player in the Major Leagues. I've asked my dad the last four birthdays if I could meet you. My friends say Jose Canseco is better, but I tell them no way, that you're the best."

"That's great, kid, what do you want me to autograph?" the star said.

"I was wondering if you could sign them all since I waited four years to meet you."

"Turn around, kid."

Eight-year-old Leroy turned around, unsure what he was supposed to be looking for.

217

"You see all those kids?" the star asked.

"Yeah," Leroy said, thinking his idol wasn't being very nice.

"They've all been waiting just as long as you. It wouldn't be fair to them to sign four for you only."

"I just thought ... "

"It doesn't matter what you thought. Now pick one."

"The baseball card," young Leroy said sheepishly.

The star made a mark with his pen that must have passed for an autograph. It looked more like a straight line to Leroy.

"Next," the star said.

"It was nice meeting you," young Leroy said and smiled. The smile was not reciprocated.

"Next," the star said again.

Young Leroy walked away, a tear in his eye.

LEROY THOUGHT BACK ON THIS STORY BECAUSE HE HAD BEEN SIMILARLY embarrassed by many people he had tried to protect when he became a cop.

People he had done favors for, who then backstabbed him and made him feel wronged like the eight-year-old Leroy had been.

That's why Leroy was so happy that Bryce ended up being one of the good guys. That went for his girlfriend and parents as well. It made his job rewarding when he was doing a good thing for good people.

Bryce and his family qualified. It made up for all the unappreciative jerks out there.

LEROY CALLED OFFICER BRADEN AS SOON AS HE WOKE UP THE NEXT morning.

The tail on the Sessions had gone just fine, as Leroy knew it would. They had grabbed their car from long-term parking, drove it straight to a house in Queens, and parked it in a garage.

It wasn't clear if they lived together, but they were both there. If either of the Sessions brothers left the house, Leroy would be notified.

LEROY SAT AT HIS DESK—HE STILL HADN'T BEEN HOME—WRITING ON A PAD.

He was outlining what he would text the Sessions and had to ensure he got it right. With all the lines and X-outs, it looked more like hieroglyphics than English.

He had finally settled on the following:

"I can't call you today. It's really hectic, and there are meetings every ten minutes. They'd know if I was gone. They are transferring Bryce at eight p.m. tonight to the Hotel Pennsylvania, Room 530. 401 7th Ave. They will have an armed officer at his door. It's your last chance. They'll take him to the grand jury tomorrow."

Leroy reread it for a seventh time and finally pressed send on Wilson's phone. Ten minutes later he got a response. **"We're on it."**

Leroy picked up the phone and called Braden. "Start making the necessary arrangements that we talked about. It's on for some time after eight o'clock tonight at Hotel Pennsylvania. 401 7th Ave. I want everyone there by six p.m., though. I also need you to go there now with some officers I'm sending over. They are relocating all the people who are staying there. I want you to oversee it. If people ask, just tell them there's a gas leak."

"Anything else?" Braden said sarcastically.

"We're all stressed. Just do what I asked." Leroy said.

"Yes, Lieutenant."

※

Hotel Pennsylvania was a three-star hotel that wasn't all that special. However, its owner was a friend and donor to the NYPD, which had used his hotel before for drug busts, undercover stings, and other similar activities.

Leroy had done this type of thing a few times, and relocating people to different hotels was a pain in the ass. It was highly unlikely any patron would be in harm's way there tonight, but it's a risk the NYPD couldn't take.

If the Sessions started shooting at the hotel and somebody got hit, that would be on them, and they couldn't risk it.

The hotel patrons wouldn't know why they were being moved, so they would whine and bitch and be a pain in the ass about it.

Leroy was glad Braden was in charge of that part.

※

For Leroy, the toughest part of the day was not knowing.

They could evacuate the hotel and surround it with twenty officers, but they could never know for sure if the Sessions had taken the bait.

He didn't dare text back (as Wilson) asking if they planned to go there, but he sure would have liked to have known.

He was worried that the text had somehow scared them off, and they wouldn't be showing up tonight. Time would tell.

He kept in touch with Bryce throughout the day. He and Elise were to stay in their hotel room all day long. They couldn't take the chance that somehow someone saw them leaving the Waldorf, and it got back to the Sessions.

It was a thousand to one, but Leroy wasn't taking any chances.

He had appointed Officer Hollins as their detail, trusting the man implicitly. Considering the NYPD was watching the Sessions' house, having Hollins watch Bryce and Elise was as unnecessary as evacuating the hotel patrons, but both were still done.

Leroy had also contacted Wilson's attorney, "Smug Face" Tucker Hall. This whole charade could end if Wilson decided to testify. Mr. Hall informed Leroy that Mr. Wilson had not changed his mind.

Leroy looked at his watch. It was two p.m.

I might as well get some sleep while I still can, Leroy reasoned.

He pulled the blanket over him. He hadn't been home in two days.

※

Leroy slept three hours, which was a minor miracle considering everything that was going on.

He showered at the police department for the second time in as many days and put on civilian clothes. He felt like a cop doing an important job today and wished he could wear his blues, but everyone would be in their civilian clothes today.

He didn't want the Sessions brothers to be scared off by seeing twenty officers in their blues. They needed them to set foot on the hotel's property so the NYPD would all be in civilian clothes.

After finishing his work at the department, he went to the hotel. He arrived a few minutes after six p.m.

※

Over the next hour, Leroy explained all contingency plans to the gathered officers. He told them he expected it to be a pretty easy arrest, but these were violent killers, so you just never knew.

As Leroy saw it, there were two possibilities.

First, the Sessions would drive up to the valet at the front of the hotel (where police officers were dressed as valets), and all surrounding officers would rush them as soon as they got out of their car.

The second possibility was that they parked in a parking lot or garage or took a cab or Uber. In Leroy's eyes, these were much more likely scenarios.

If you were committing a crime, why would you valet your car? You wouldn't. But as with everything else, they prepared for it just in case.

If they did park in a lot like he expected, they would be arrested when they got within a hundred feet of the hotel entrance.

By law, that was where the Hotel Pennsylvania started. Once they stepped within a hundred feet, several officers would come at them with weapons drawn. If they even tried to grab a weapon, they would be shot.

Leroy looked at his watch. It was fast approaching eight p.m. It could be "go time" at any moment.

※

Leroy had Officer Braden call the people watching the Sessions' house. They had a van just down the street with a perfect view of the driveway and the house itself.

Inside the truck was all the best surveillance money could buy. Two blocks away, an undercover cop car was circling the area.

If that car followed the Sessions and somehow lost its tail or was spotted, several other undercover cop cars in the area would recommence the tail.

Braden gave Leroy a thumbs up. Everything was good from the surveillance truck. The Sessions hadn't left yet.

Leroy looked at his watch. It was 8:22.

※

Leroy nervously paced around the exterior of the hotel. It's not like he expected them to leave at eight p.m. sharp, but the wait was still testing his nerves.

He gave Bryce one last call and told him it would all be over soon. Leroy would call him as soon as the Sessions were arrested.

Leroy looked at his watch. It was 8:41.

His text to the Sessions had said that Bryce would be transferred to the hotel at eight. For all he knew, the Sessions might wait until midnight.

This could be a long night.

※

For the next hour, Leroy gave a quick little pep talk to each officer who walked by.

Be on your toes. The city appreciates your help. You're a good cop.

Still, no call from the van watching the house.

Leroy looked at his watch. It was 9:48. He was starting to worry, even though he knew this could happen at any time tonight.

※

At 9:54, Officer Braden got a call. The Sessions had left the house.

Braden motioned to Leroy and told him.

Leroy called all the officers over. "All right, everyone. They have left their house and are headed this way. I want you all to get to your assigned positions.

Everyone does their jobs, and this will end shortly and peacefully. Good luck, men."

Leroy looked out at all of New York's finest. It wasn't very often you had twenty cops dressed in civilian clothing.

For some reason, it humored Leroy.

※

THERE WAS BASICALLY A CARAVAN FOLLOWING THE TRUCK THAT LEFT THE Sessions house. There was only one car directly tailing it, but the NYPD now had four undercover cop cars within a two-block radius at all times.

From the house, the car took the Long Island Expressway and then 495 West toward Manhattan. Braden updated Leroy, who updated the officers every few minutes as the car got closer.

They took the 34th/35th Street exit, which led them to Tunnel Street. They were very close now, and Leroy yelled at everyone to prepare.

He then told them all to assume their positions.

From Tunnel Street, the van took a right on 34th Street. They were now less than a mile from the hotel. If they had taken 34th to 7th, they would have arrived.

Instead, the van pulled into an open-air parking lot on 34th Street, about a quarter mile from the hotel. Leroy had expected this, as they wouldn't want their car in the hotel's immediate vicinity.

Leroy called Braden over.

"Tell the closest tail to the van to call you as soon as they step out."

※

THEY DIDN'T GET A CALL BACK FOR A MINUTE. AND THEN THE MINUTE turned into two.

Braden looked at Leroy. "What's going on?"

"Maybe the Sessions are going over their plan one more time," Leroy said.

It didn't sound like he believed this, though.

The two minutes turned into five and then ten.

Leroy was in a tough spot.

He was becoming very suspicious, but he didn't want to alert the Sessions before they stepped onto the hotel's property. If they got spooked and decided to leave, this whole thing would be pointless.

For one of the few times as a police officer, Leroy Archer didn't know what to do.

Ten minutes turned into twenty.

His father had always told him to follow his gut if all else failed, and Leroy's gut was telling him something was wrong.

That's when he made a crucial decision.

"Braden, call one of the officers near them and hand me the phone," Leroy said.

Braden did as instructed.

"This is Lieutenant Archer. I want you to grab the officers on the tail and raid the car. That's an order."

"But, Lieutenant," Braden protested.

"Shut up, Braden," Leroy said. "The Sessions brothers aren't in that car."

"Are you crazy?" Braden said.

A minute later, the officer called back.

"You better get up here, Lieutenant."

Leroy handed the phone back to Braden and took off in a full sprint toward the Sessions' car with Braden following him.

The gathered officers looked at each other, unsure what had gone wrong.

A few ran in Leroy's direction.

※

Leroy arrived at the parking lot before Braden and saw five officers surrounding a handcuffed man. He was neither Lou Sessions nor Charles Sessions.

"He was the only one in the car," an officer said.

Leroy went to Braden, who had just arrived, out of breath.

"Call the van outside the house and tell them to raid the house right now."

"But, Lieutenant," Braden said for a second time.

"Do it!" Leroy yelled louder than he ever had, startling a few officers.

The call came back three minutes later. Braden handed the phone to Leroy.

"Lieutenant, there is no one in the house. I don't know where the fuck they went."

Leroy dropped the phone and started to feel dizzy.

His mind drifted to the movie *The Silence of the Lambs*.

At the end of the film, the officers surround a house expecting to arrest the serial killer, Buffalo Bill. However, they made a mistake, and Buffalo Bill was not there. Jodie Foster's character finds herself facing the killer alone in a different location.

"Jesus Christ," Leroy said. "Bryce ... "

56

THE KILLERS

Lou's suspicions were on high alert well before the text he received from Eddie Wilson.

The false information about the BMW Museum slightly raised Lou's suspicions. It was not that something unforeseen could not have happened; it was just the first time Wilson had provided inaccurate information.

Lou wasn't suspicious yet, but he had taken note of it.

The phone call that Wilson made didn't help things. Again, it wasn't anything obvious; it was just a feeling Lou had. It felt like he was putting on a performance.

He still wasn't sure anything was wrong, but he had now taken note of two incidents involving Wilson. That wasn't a good sign.

What sealed it for Lou was that he knew he was followed home from the airport.

They were actually quite good, having one car tail him for a while and then turning off and having another car resume the tail.

What gave it away was that one car that had taken a side street earlier ended up behind him ten minutes later.

Lou decided then that Charles would return to his house with him. It would be easier to fight this battle together.

When Lou arrived home that night, he made a mental inventory of all the cars parked on his street. The van that was there the next morning hadn't been there the night before.

Not that Lou should be giving lessons about how to tail someone. Munich was a total disaster. So was Paris. They had behaved like complete and total amateurs.

Lou wondered if maybe it was time to hang it up. They were getting sloppy, and that could get them pinched at any time.

If they were lucky enough to eliminate Bryce and get out of their current predicament, Lou would seriously consider an early retirement.

He'd join Wilson on that tropical island—if Wilson wasn't in police custody already.

Wilson's text about Bryce moving to the Hotel Pennsylvania was entirely believable, but Lou, with his recent doubts about Wilson, wasn't convinced.

It was also the first time that Wilson had ever texted Lou. Was it possible he really couldn't get out of the office? Sure. However, it was also the only way the police could converse with Lou if Wilson had been compromised.

He looked out the window of his house and saw the van was still there. If they left their house, they would undoubtedly be followed.

What to do, Lou thought. He had the origins of an idea, but it could only work if they found out where Bryce was really being shacked up.

After all, if the police had Wilson's phone, they certainly wouldn't be texting Lou where they were actually keeping Bryce. They would give him an alternative spot.

He called Paul, the man who had helped them kill Tim and Chase, and told him he needed him to come over to the house.

Lou explained the exact route he wanted him to take to get there.

※

LOU LIVED IN BAYSIDE, WHICH WAS AN UPPER-MIDDLE CLASS SECTION OF Queens. It was in the northeast section, and Lou lived in Weeks Woodlands.

His house was a two-story colonial with a two-car garage. He knew the police were watching the front of his house, and if he had a street behind the house, they would undoubtedly be watching the back as well.

This was where Lou had an advantage.

Behind him was another set of houses, and behind that was another set of homes. Behind that, you guessed it, was another set of houses.

If the police wanted to watch the back of his house, they'd be three sets of houses removed, and it would be impossible to do so. There were walkways and a path between the houses but nowhere to park a car. An officer would stand out like a sore thumb.

Lou had told Paul what street to park on and how to get to his house's back door. He told him that if he saw a cop, he should just pretend he was walking along one of the paths and that he should not, under any circumstances, continue to Lou's house.

Fortunately, Paul didn't encounter any cops and got to Lou's back door without incident. The people in the van couldn't see the back of Lou's house, and they had no idea they were now dealing with a third person.

❧

Lou sat Charles and Paul down. Lou was looking very serious, so they knew not to interrupt.

"I don't think our good friend Bryce will be at the Hotel Pennsylvania tonight. The van outside and the fact that Wilson texted us instead of calling us make me think we are being set up. So here's what I want you guys to do. It's dangerous, especially for you, Charles, but it has to be done if we are going to get out of this mess. I want you both to go out the back and take Paul's car back to Manhattan. I want you guys to drive down by the Midtown Manhattan branch of the NYPD. This is their gig, and the officers will come from that precinct. I imagine they will be sending a lot of officers to the Hotel Pennsylvania in hopes of eventually arresting us there, but I want to know where any other officers are headed. That's how we'll find out where they are hiding Bryce. It may take several fruitless trips, but you'll eventually find out where the other cops are headed. Charles, be sure to keep your head down and wear a hat and some sunglasses. If you find the location, send Paul in to scope out the place. Paul, I want you to hover around the elevator without drawing attention to yourself and see what floor the police officers are going to. Come back here when you're done. This won't go down until after eight tonight, so you don't have to rush. Got it?"

"Got it," they said in unison.

Charles and Paul left, and Lou thought, *Maybe it's not time to retire just yet. This is a plan befitting a genius. A mad, homicidal genius but a genius, nonetheless.*

❧

Charles and Paul drove into Manhattan and waited down the street from the police station. Paul was driving and knew what Lou wanted but didn't know the best way to go about it.

He couldn't just chase a cop car speeding away from the station. He'd be asking to be pulled over, and he was sure the cops would love to know who was in his passenger seat.

They sat there for an hour, but it hardly seemed like a mass exodus was leaving the station. Individual cars were leaving, but that's not what they were looking for.

Finally, six cop cars slowly pulled out of the parking lot and left together. This was more what he had been expecting.

Since there was a big group of them, they drove slowly enough so that Paul could follow a safe distance behind. He followed them to 7th Ave., where they all drove into an underground parking garage together.

Paul continued driving and passed the Hotel Pennsylvania half a block down. This didn't prove much, either. Whether they had Bryce or it was a setup, they would send cops to that hotel.

Paul and Charles returned to the police station and spent another hour of watching individual police cars speed off on their own. If Lou hadn't ordered them to do this, Paul would have been out of there. This seemed pointless.

He started daydreaming and Charles had to point out that two cop cars were leaving together.

He had been so bored he had turned the car off, so he quickly turned on the ignition and set off in the direction of the police cars.

They drove through Manhattan traffic and ended up in front of the Waldorf Astoria. They parked in front and got out.

Paul abruptly got out of the car.

"What are you doing?" Charles asked.

"Your brother said to find out what floor they are getting off on. Circle around the block until I get back."

Charles wanted to yell at him that he was the third fiddle, and he didn't get to tell Charles what to do, but it didn't seem worth it.

Paul was right, after all. If he was going to find out what floor they were headed to, he needed to get in there now.

Charles walked around to the front of the car, got in, and started circling the hotel.

<hr />

PAUL ENTERED THE HOTEL DIRECTLY BEHIND THE POLICE OFFICERS. HE tried to keep his head down and not make eye contact.

The officers headed toward the elevator, and Paul knew this was his chance. He got on the elevator with them right before the door closed.

"What floor?" one of the officers asked.

"Seven," Paul said.

In times of trouble, always go with Mickey Mantle's number.

Paul stood there and tried to act naturally. He couldn't afford to alert their suspicion and, god forbid, get arrested.

If they knew who he was, they could tie him to Lou and Charles, and then this plan would all come crashing down. Luckily, he didn't have to wait long as the officers pressed the button to the second floor.

The elevator arrived on the second floor, and the officers stepped off. Paul was able to commence breathing.

Lou was going to be proud of him.

I GUESS THE RUMORS ARE TRUE, LOU THOUGHT TO HIMSELF.

For years, he had heard the NYPD would hold potential witnesses on the second floor of the Waldorf Astoria. He'd never asked Old Man Wilson.

Lou had devised his plan while they were gone. Now that they were back, he went over it with them.

Originally, he planned to have the three of them go out the back door together, but he changed his plan for a few reasons.

First, he didn't need or want Paul with him. Second, and much more importantly, this plan would give the Sessions brothers an alibi for Bryce's murder.

Paul was to drive Lou's van, and because the windows were tinted, the cops could not see that only one person was in the car.

After Paul left, Lou and Charles would head out the back door and drive Paul's car to the Waldorf, where they now assumed Bryce was staying.

He wanted Paul to pull over a few blocks from the Hotel Pennsylvania, sit there, and not get out of Lou's truck. The cops would be watching him, but it didn't matter.

If Lou was right, they set this whole thing up to arrest Lou and Charles when they stepped foot in the Hotel Pennsylvania.

Therefore, they would not approach the truck if Paul parked it off the premises.

Lou figured they'd let him sit there an hour, possibly longer because their little sting was up once they raided the truck.

They needed them on the Hotel Pennsylvania premises, and that's why they would let the car sit there for so long.

"And the best part is that you have done nothing illegal," Lou told Paul.

By the time an hour or two had passed, Lou and Charles would have finally disposed of Bryce and driven as fast as hell back to Queens and the back entrance of the house.

When the cops finally checked the truck and found Paul, they might well raid the Sessions house, but Lou and Charles would be back home with an unassailable alibi. They had never left the house.

He explained this all to them without interruption.

Finally, Charles asked, "But how are we going to get close to the officer or officers who are sure to be watching Bryce?"

Lou laughed to himself. *We are going to use your face to get what we want, Charles.*

"I'll explain on the way," Lou said.

Charles and Paul watched as Lou went to his room and reappeared with a full police uniform, belt, and cap.

"I sure am glad we got a few of these from Wilson," he said.

DEBUT NOVEL

❧

At 9:54 p.m., Paul went from the house to the inside of the garage, got in the Sessions van, and backed out of the driveway.

Lou watched as Paul drove past the police van and down the street. He was partially afraid that the cops might raid his house immediately, thinking they were gone, so he and Charles waited ten minutes.

With no sign of the police, they went out the back door, got into Paul's car, and drove toward the Waldorf Astoria.

❧

Charles liked the plan, but he asked Lou to repeat it one more time.

"We're going to get off on the second floor, and I'm going to hold you in front of me, saying, 'I've got Charles Sessions.' I'm betting it will only be one cop. Two max. After all, they think we are headed to the other hotel. That's where they need the officers. All the officer will see is your face and a cop behind you. He'll be so shocked to see you and trust me, they've all seen a picture of you by now. He won't know what to do. He'll also see the police uniform behind you, so he's certainly not going to shoot. I'll be holding you in a way that shields my face. When we get close enough, I want you to quietly say, 'Now.' I'll already have my gun drawn, and when you drop to the ground, I'll shoot him between the eyes. He won't have time to outdraw me since my gun will be drawn and ready to shoot. I have a silencer, and I also highly doubt anyone else will be on the floor, so we don't have to worry about some hero calling 911. And at that point, we'll be alone with Bryce ... and hopefully that sweet piece of pie he had with him in Munich."

❧

With the head start that he had, Paul had already been sitting in the parking lot near Hotel Pennsylvania for twelve minutes by the time Lou and Charles pulled into their own parking lot across from the Waldorf.

Lou scanned the front and didn't see any cops patrolling.

There are no cops here because you all think we are sitting in our car in a parking lot by the Hotel Pennsylvania. That's where you are wrong, you stupid fucking pigs.

Lou told Charles to lower his hat and under no circumstance to look up at the cameras when they entered the hotel. Sure, later on, the videotape may show two people with features that resemble the Sessions brothers, but they were back home in Queens the whole time.

There was a police van outside their house that could attest to that. Also, Lou had instructed Paul to tell the police that Lou and Charles were still at their home. And when they raided the house, sure enough, the Sessions brothers would already be back.

There was a large group of drunk guys about to walk into the hotel. They were loud, and it looked like it might be a bachelor party. It was perfect.

"Let's go. We walk in behind them," Lou said.

They lowered their heads and followed behind the drunk guys and into the Waldorf. The guys crowded into the elevator.

"We got room for two more," one of the drunks said.

Without looking up, Lou said, "We'll take the next one."

Thirty seconds later, a new elevator arrived, and Lou and Charles got on it alone. They took it up to the second floor, opened the door, and got out.

OFFICER BOB HOLLINS WAS BORED.

He didn't want to have to watch Bryce and Elise. He wanted to be at Hotel Pennsylvania and see the look on the Sessions' as they were arrested.

I hope you assholes rot in hell.

Hollins had received a call from Officer Braden fifteen minutes previous, telling him that the Sessions were parked a quarter mile from the Pennsylvania Hotel.

It was now 10:45, and Hollins was expecting a call from Lieutenant Archer or Officer Braden soon, telling him it was all over.

He'd then drive Bryce and Elise down to the station and celebrate with all the other officers.

I guess I'll just have to join the celebration a few minutes late.

Hollins looked down at his phone again, half expecting to see Leroy Archer calling.

Instead, he heard the elevator stop on the second floor and the door open. It was probably just some drunk guy getting off on the wrong floor. He had heard people partying on the floor above him.

Ten-to-one odds it was one of them.

He saw an incoming call from Officer Billy Braden but figured he'd take care of the partiers first.

But when the people turned the corner, it wasn't some drunk guys he saw, but instead a police officer holding someone in front of him.

I don't have a replacement coming. It's just supposed to be me. What the hell is going on?

"I've got him," the officer said.

He spoke again. "I've got Charles Sessions. He was downstairs in the lobby headed up here to do god knows what!"

This was all wrong. The Sessions were currently outside the Hotel Pennsylvania in their car. Officer Braden had just called him and told him that. Charles Sessions couldn't be here!

Hollins looked at the guy the officer was bringing toward him, and couldn't believe his eyes. Sure enough, it was Charles Sessions, the guy Hollins had ID'd for Leroy a few nights before.

Who was this officer who wasn't showing his face, though?

Hollins lowered h is hand down to his right side where his gun was. Something was wrong here.

"Show yourself, Officer," Hollins yelled.

They were now twenty-five feet from Hollins. He couldn't just shoot Charles Sessions. There was a police officer behind him, for Christ's Sake.

But why wasn't the officer saying anything?

"Just a second," the voice behind Charles Sessions said. It wasn't a voice that Officer Hollins recognized. Who was this officer?

"Show yourself!" Hollins repeated.

He grabbed his gun with his right hand, prepared to pull it out and shoot if necessary.

Hollins heard Charles Sessions quietly say, "Now," and then Charles dropped to the floor. Hollins secured his gun and raised it as he saw that the police officer behind Charles Sessions was not, in fact, an officer.

It was Charles's brother Lou.

Hollins aimed to fire his gun, but Lou already had his weapon set on him.

The last thing Officer Hollins ever saw was Lou Sessions pulling the trigger.

57
BRYCE

THE WALDORF

There were worse things than being stuck in a posh hotel room with a girl you loved.

We used the bath with the jets twice ... before noon. We lay in bed, and I turned on in-room movies and watched a few of those. This must be what rich people do all day.

Once it got to eight o'clock, we stopped enjoying the lap of luxury and waited patiently to hear news back from Leroy.

Around 8:30 p.m., he called me and said the Sessions brothers hadn't left their house, but he wasn't worried yet. Over the next hour, there was no news.

Elise and I weren't nervous; we were just ready to get this all over with. Anxious would probably be a better word.

He called back at 9:30, and they still hadn't left the house. Leroy seemed matter-of-fact about it, so I still didn't think anything of it.

Around 10:30 p.m., Officer Hollins knocked on our door. He had done this a few times throughout the day, and I think he was as bored as we were.

He told us that the Sessions brothers were parked outside the Hotel Pennsylvania and surrounded by undercover officers.

I looked at Elise. "It's almost over, baby."

She came up and hugged me. Spending a whole day in a hotel room was starting to wear on her. "Finally," she said.

ABOUT TEN MINUTES LATER, I THOUGHT I HEARD SOMEONE ON THE HALL OF the second floor.

Leroy had told us that they would evacuate the entire Hotel Pennsylvania since that's where the Sessions would be. As for the Waldorf, they had evacuated our floor only since we had an armed police officer outside our door.

But it's not like the elevator was turned off. Someone could accidentally appear on the second floor at any time.

What worried me was that I heard Hollins shuffle his feet.

I yelled at Elise to turn off the TV as I put my ear to the door.

I heard Hollins say, "Show yourself, Officer," and heard a muffled response. Then, a few seconds later, Hollins again said, "Show yourself."

Then I heard a little *ping* and someone dropping to the floor. I looked out of the peephole and saw Officer Hollins on the floor with a hole in the middle of his forehead.

I was in shock. Somehow, against all odds, the Sessions brothers had found us.

When was this ever going to end? I couldn't think about that now. I had to focus.

We couldn't possibly leave the room. They were waiting right outside, and we'd be target practice.

How the fuck did this happen? I thought the Sessions were just surrounded at the Hotel Pennsylvania! I had a million thoughts going through my head, but I didn't have time for them—I had to think of an escape plan.

I grabbed a desk and hit it against the window as hard as possible, but the window was thick and didn't budge. I tried it again with no luck. I did it a third time, and the window didn't break, but it started to splinter.

If I put my whole weight into it, I knew I could break it, but then I'd also go out the window. I looked down, and it was probably twenty feet—maybe more.

Even if Elise and I survived the jump, we'd probably be seriously injured, and we'd still be target practice if they looked out the window. No, we had to stay and fight.

They shot at the locked door. I grabbed Elise and put her in the corner, directly to the right of where you would enter.

I looked around for a weapon and grabbed an iron. It's all I could think of. They fired a few more shots at the door, and I saw the hinges get blown off. They'd be inside within a second or two.

A hand peeked through the broken remnants of the doorknob and reached around to open the door. I ran over to Elise, raised the iron over my head, and waited to crash it into the skull of the first person to walk in.

Charles entered first, and although I had planned on hitting him in the head, I saw a gun in his hand, and that was my first worry.

I raised the iron and brought it down as hard as I could on his right arm, which held the gun. The force of the blow knocked the gun across the room. I had probably broken his forearm as I heard him scream out in pain.

As this happened, Lou's arm came through the door, and he tried to put it at a ninety-degree angle and shoot at us. I lifted the iron again and brought it down on Lou's hand just as I had to Charles.

His gun went flying across the floor as well. The two guns were now halfway across the room, close to the splintered window.

I ran over to grab one of the guns but was gang-tackled by Lou and Charles. I hit Charles with a forearm, but it only stunned him. I needed to knock one of them out, or it would be two against one, and I would lose.

I almost grabbed one of the guns, but Lou tackled me into the wall. One of the guns slid under the bed, but it was still closer to myself and the Sessions, so Elise couldn't grab it.

Lou crawled toward the other gun, which had been kicked up against the floorboard below the window.

Charles was standing between the two of us, and there was no way I could get around him to prevent Lou from getting the gun.

My life was flashing before my eyes. When Lou got the gun, he would shoot and kill Elise and me.

New York. Paris. Munich.

And now it was going to end here, back where it all began.

<hr>

WHILE MANY PEOPLE TOLD ME WHAT I DID NEXT WAS COURAGEOUS, IT WAS nothing more than trying to save Elise's life. I had a split second to do something, or she was dead. And so was I.

As Lou bent over to pick up the gun, I realized what I had to do.

I pushed my back leg into the ground to gain as much momentum as I could muster. I would need it. With all my momentum, I would propel off my back foot and tackle Charles in the chest.

The key was to push Charles so hard that he would carry his momentum into Lou. Lou was standing right next to the splintered windows that were about to break, so if I did it perfectly, I knew I had a chance to knock him out of the window.

It was now or never.

I propelled off my back foot and launched myself into Charles's chest.

It was a perfect tackle, and I struck Charles so hard that he went down almost immediately. My momentum carried me right into Lou, who had just picked up the gun.

I connected with his chest flush, and he had no time to try and shoot me. We careened into the window with so much momentum that it never had a chance.

As soon as we hit the window, we were going through it.

I stopped Lou's immediate threat with the gun, but I realized that Charles would be alone in the room with Elise.

Right before Lou and I tumbled out the window, I yelled, "Run Elise!" as loudly as possible. As we broke through the glass and hurtled toward the concrete below, my only thought was that I hoped Elise would get out.

◊❈◊

People often say that things will slow down to a crawl in desperate times.

This was definitely the case as Lou and I were launched out of the window, still attached to each other.

Everything slowed down in my mind. I was above him, so if I could remain on top, he would take the brunt of the fall, and I could use him as a cushion.

Unfortunately, he realized the same thing and tried to roll me over mid-air. I thought I had him until the last second, when I overcompensated, and my shoulder took the brunt of it as we hit the ground. I heard it shatter as it hit the pavement, and everything turned black.

◊❈◊

I don't know how long I was out, but when I woke up, I was in more pain than I had ever been in my thirty-two years on earth.

My shoulder was shattered and my hip and butt on my right side were in tremendous pain. I looked up and Lou had grabbed his gun that must have skidded away from him when we landed.

He was walking toward me.

There was nothing I could do now, and I resigned myself to my fate.

He was standing above me and had adjusted the gun, pointing it directly at my temple.

In my last moments on earth, my thoughts turned to Elise, and I hoped she had managed to escape. That was all that mattered to me now.

I closed my eyes and waited for the sound of a gun to go off ... and then I heard it.

58

ELISE

When Bryce yelled, "Run Elise," Charles was still shaken up on the floor from Bryce's tackle.
Elise knew she should have run but had to see if Bryce had survived the fall.
She ran over to the window and looked down. Bryce was on the ground, having fallen over twenty feet. It looked like he was out cold.
Was he dead? Oh God, please say it's not true.
Lou Sessions was getting up, but Bryce still wasn't moving.
"Bryce! Get up!" Elise yelled to no avail.
And then she heard a noise behind her.
Charles was getting up.
Elise quickly ran over and grabbed the gun that had fallen under the bed. She pointed it at Charles.
"Don't move, or I will shoot!" Elise yelled.
Charles laughed. Elise had no idea why he was laughing, but she held the gun—she was in charge. Charles let out another loud laugh.
Elise realized something must be wrong. She didn't know much about guns—or what she wasn't doing. She looked down, and it hit her— the safety was on.
It must have been knocked into safety during the struggle.
Elise quickly tried to turn the safety off, but Charles was already moving

toward her. He collided with her, and Elise lost control of the gun, which landed on the bed.

Charles grabbed Elise by the neck and started choking her. She tried to put up a fight but was no match for Charles's strength.

Elise could slowly feel everything starting to go dark.

She knew she'd be dead soon.

59

LEROY

"Jesus Christ ... Bryce."

As soon as he uttered these words, Leroy knew he had to reach the Waldorf as fast as humanly possible. There wasn't time to worry about how the Sessions had outfoxed him.

He would worry about that later. What was of the utmost importance right now was getting there before it was too late.

"Somebody give me the keys to a car," Leroy yelled.

Although his car was only a quarter mile away, every second counted.

One of the undercover officers threw him a set of keys and pointed to a black Ford Crown Victoria ten feet away. Leroy got in.

"Braden, call Officer Hollins right now and tell him to lock himself in the room with Bryce and Elise," Leroy yelled.

He didn't wait to hear Braden's answer. Leroy peeled out of the parking lot and was going over sixty m.p.h. within seconds.

Officer Braden called Hollins's cell phone, but the call went unanswered.

The Waldorf Astoria was more than a mile from Hotel Pennsylvania. Luckily for Leroy, it was almost eleven p.m., and the roads were as clear as they could get in Manhattan.

He didn't want to crash but could live with himself if he did. He couldn't live with himself if he got there a second too late.

✺

HE DROVE INTO THE WALDORF PARKING LOT AT FIFTY M.P.H. AND SLAMMED on the brakes right as he got parallel to the front entrance.

People looked at him as if he was crazy, but he couldn't care less.

He leaped out of the car with it still running and sprinted toward the entrance.

✺

LEROY OPENED THE WALDORF'S FRONT DOOR. HE LOOKED AT THE elevators, but none were on the ground floor. He couldn't risk waiting for one.

"Where are the stairs?" he screamed at the woman behind the front desk.

"Around the corner," she said, scared of this man in front of her.

Leroy ran around the corner, punched open the door to the stairs, and ran up the stairs, leaping three stairs at a time.

A few seconds later, Leroy opened the door to the second floor and sprinted toward Bryce's room. The first thing he saw was the body of Officer Hollins lying on the ground.

Fuck, they're all dead because of me. I'm too late.

There might still be time for Bryce and Elise, he reminded himself.

Leroy saw the splintered door to Bryce's room.

Please still be alive.

He stepped over Hollins body and shoved open the door.

✺

LEROY HAD HIS GUN DRAWN AS HE ENTERED THE ROOM. HE LOOKED UP AND saw Charles Sessions choking Elise.

When Charles made eye contact with Leroy, he lightened his grip on Elise and looked at the gun on the bed.

At that moment, Leroy would have had to shoot Charles in the top of the forehead since he held Elise in front of him.

It's a shot he would be willing to take, but there wasn't much room for error. If he were a few inches off, it would be catastrophic.

This wouldn't prove necessary, as Elise performed a brilliant move.

Elise stopped fighting and let her body go limp. She moved her head to slide through Charles's ever-loosening grip.

She fell to the floor, and Leroy now had a clear shot at Charles's chest.

Not that Leroy needed any excuse to shoot him, but Charles took a step like he was going for the gun.

He didn't complete that first step, as Leroy shot him three times in the chest, one piercing the heart.

Charles Sessions crumbled to the ground—dead before he hit it.

❧

Elise was still catching her breath but managed to say, "Window."

Leroy walked to the now nonexistent window and looked down.

He saw Lou standing above Bryce with a gun, pointing down at him.

Lou glanced up at Leroy for a split second; it was all the time Leroy needed.

Leroy fired twice, hitting him in the chest both times.

Lou staggered back and fell to his knees, but he was still alive, and the gun still dangled ominously from his wrist.

Leroy brought his gun up one more time, aimed between Lou's eyes, and pulled the trigger.

60

THE KILLERS

When Lou and Charles looked into the eyes of Leroy Archer and knew they were going to die, they both reacted the same way.

They didn't feel any remorse, didn't think to repent, and didn't acknowledge all of the carnage they had caused in their lifetimes.

It was a fitting end.

They died just as they had lived—as cowards.

61

BRYCE

COMING TO AN END

As I heard the gunshot go off, I remember being surprised that my mind would have the time to process a gunshot before I was hit.

I then heard a second shot go off, and I knew I was still alive.

I looked over at Lou Sessions, who still had his gun aimed at me. He wasn't hit, either.

I was still a sitting duck, but Lou made the catastrophic mistake of looking up toward the room we'd fallen from. I'm sure he was looking up to see if his brother was okay.

Instead, Leroy Archer appeared at the window. Lou swiveled back toward me, but by then, it was too late.

Leroy shot Lou two times, and Lou fell to his knees.

He still had the gun dangling from his wrist, but as I looked up toward Leroy, I knew this was finally going to end.

Leroy took aim and shot Lou Sessions between the eyes. He fell back and crumbled to the ground, and I knew his days of terrorizing me were over.

"Is Elise alive?" I yelled upward.

The pain in my shoulder was unbearable, but all I could think about was Elise.

"She's alive, Bryce."

I looked back up, and Elise had made her way to the window.

The tears were now inevitable.

THE NEXT HALF HOUR WAS A BLUR.

Leroy was by my side a minute later, followed by Elise.

I gave her a long embrace, and for a brief moment, I forgot about my shoulder.

I had never felt more emotional in my life. I hugged her and cried like I had never cried before.

❧

POLICE OFFICERS, AMBULANCES, AND HOTEL GUESTS STARTED TO ARRIVE ON the scene.

I was getting dizzy as the adrenaline wore off, and the pain in my shoulder worsened.

Elise turned to Leroy. "I think Bryce should go to the hospital."

At that very moment, I saw my parents approaching.

They were staying a mere two blocks from the Waldorf, and they must have seen all the commotion.

That must have been a brutal walk over, as they feared what might have happened to me.

The crying began anew.

A minute later, they put me in an ambulance as Elise, Leroy, and my parents looked on.

The EMT kept repeating, "You're going to be okay."

As I looked up at the four people in front of me, I knew he was right.

62
BRYCE

EPILOGUE

The commissioner's office commended Leroy for his "quick thinking" and "courage under duress."

Commissioner Julian Sax said that "his decision to raid the car at Hotel Pennsylvania showed his impeccable instincts" and "his decision to drive directly to the Waldorf Astoria undoubtedly saved Bryce and Elise's lives."

In their private meeting, Leroy lamented to Julian Sax that he should have put police near the back of the Sessions house, but Sax disagreed.

"You can't just drop a bunch of police officers between rows of houses. You did everything an excellent cop could do. And then you did way more than that."

Julian also told Leroy that he had a bright future in law enforcement, alluding to a future beyond being a lieutenant.

That sounded good to Leroy.

All of the accolades that Leroy was getting felt great, but his proudest moment came in a conversation with his mother.

She told him how proud his father would have been of him.

Leroy thought back to his childhood and the great times he had with his father, and a big smile crept across his face.

DEBUT NOVEL

❦

My parents stayed for several extra days, ensuring I would be okay before they flew back to California.

I think the doctor was happy to see them go. Every time he stepped into my hospital room, my parents bombarded him with a game of twenty questions.

In the end, I think my parents were more disappointed to be leaving Elise than me.

With me bedridden for those first few days, they spent a lot of time together. Elise also really enjoyed their company.

My parents finally flew back to California with promises from Elise and me to visit soon.

When they returned to San Francisco, they received cards and flowers from all their friends and family who had heard what had happened.

They even got a call from Uncle Jake, who somehow managed to sound magnanimous in his praise of me.

❦

Karl, the cab driver, spent eight days in the hospital, but his prognosis was excellent.

Elise and I even had a Skype session with him in our relative hospital beds.

"Now that my wife knows just how courageous I am, she can't keep her hands off me," Karl said.

His wife, who was with us for the Skype session, didn't deny it.

❦

As for me, I was in the hospital for a total of six days with a broken shoulder, several broken ribs, and a bruised hip. Like Karl, my prognosis was excellent.

The NYPD offered to put us up in a hotel once I got out.

"And we don't want to stay at the Waldorf this time," Elise joked.

Leroy was very busy dealing with the detectives and tying up all the loose ends of the investigation, but he was able to come by for a few visits.

We promised to keep in touch, and I had no doubt we would.

He was one of the good ones.

❦

I highly recommend having a beautiful girl at your beck and call for nearly a week.

I might have even milked my injury a few times to get more "attention" from Elise.

If asked, I'll deny it.

❦

IT HAS NOW BEEN THREE MONTHS SINCE THIS LIFE-CHANGING EXPERIENCE.

Elise and I live in a shoebox-sized apartment in Manhattan, but we love it.

While I decided not to write a novel about the experience, I agreed to write a series of articles for the *New Yorker*. The story had received a lot of national attention, and I had several offers to write about it. The advance they gave me helped pay our astronomical rent.

Elise has already booked a few off-Broadway shows. She's going to make it huge, I have no doubt.

In the meantime, she's taken a job serving at a cafe near Central Park. I write there all the time.

It's my new Les Deux Magots.

❦

MY DEBUT NOVEL, WHICH I WORKED ON IN PARIS, IS ALMOST FINISHED, and quite a few publishers are already showing interest. My story and the upcoming New Yorker articles have led to a lot of interest in me in the literary world.

After all I went through, I'll welcome any help I can get.

"Have you come up with a book title yet?" Elise asked me.

I couldn't seem to come up with a title that satisfied me.

"I'm thinking about just calling it Debut Novel."

"Well, that's freaking stupid," Elise said.

And we laughed.

❦

TODAY, ELISE AND I ARE HAVING A LITTLE PICNIC IN CENTRAL PARK.

We are eating P, B, and J sandwiches and talking about our futures. We agree that if/when we get married, it will be at Hugo's restaurant overlooking Omaha Beach.

"And we can honeymoon in Munich," she says.

We can't stop laughing.

Book deals. Marriage. Honeymoon.

All that stuff seems so far away.

For now, I just want to enjoy the sun shining down on us and the company of the beautiful girl across from me.

That's enough for me.

THE END

ALSO BY BRIAN O'SULLIVAN

Thanks so much for reading DEBUT NOVEL!

I wrote this thirteen years ago, and I've only now come around to publishing it.

It may not be perfect, but it's me in my early phases of writing, warts and all. I hope you enjoyed it, and I'd be honored if you left a review :)

If you haven't read any of my other other novels, I'd suggest starting with **THE PHOTO ALBUM, THE BARTENDER,** or **REVENGE AT SEA,** my first Quint novel.

Thanks so much for your support!

It means everything for a self-published author like myself.

Cheers,

Brian O'Sullivan

Printed in Great Britain
by Amazon